The Blackwater Sailing Club

The Blackwater Sailing Club

E.K. Wicher

A pressure cooker of paranoia and sexual tension, a vice-commodore intent on running guns to separatist-terrorists, several murders, and an aging dam near to bursting.

So you want to join the Blackwater Sailing Club?

Written by E.K. Wicher
Edited by Anita Dolman
Cover by Giles Morrell

Reference is made in this work to Michael Collins, a historical figure. All other characters in this work are fictitious and any resemblance to real persons, living or dead, is purely coincidental. For those readers who feel they might recognize certain geography and locations in this story, please forgive my distortions and exaggerations.

ISBN: 978-1-7774547-1-5

EKWicherbooks
1400 rue Archambault
Sainte-Adèle
Quebec J8B 2X6
Canada

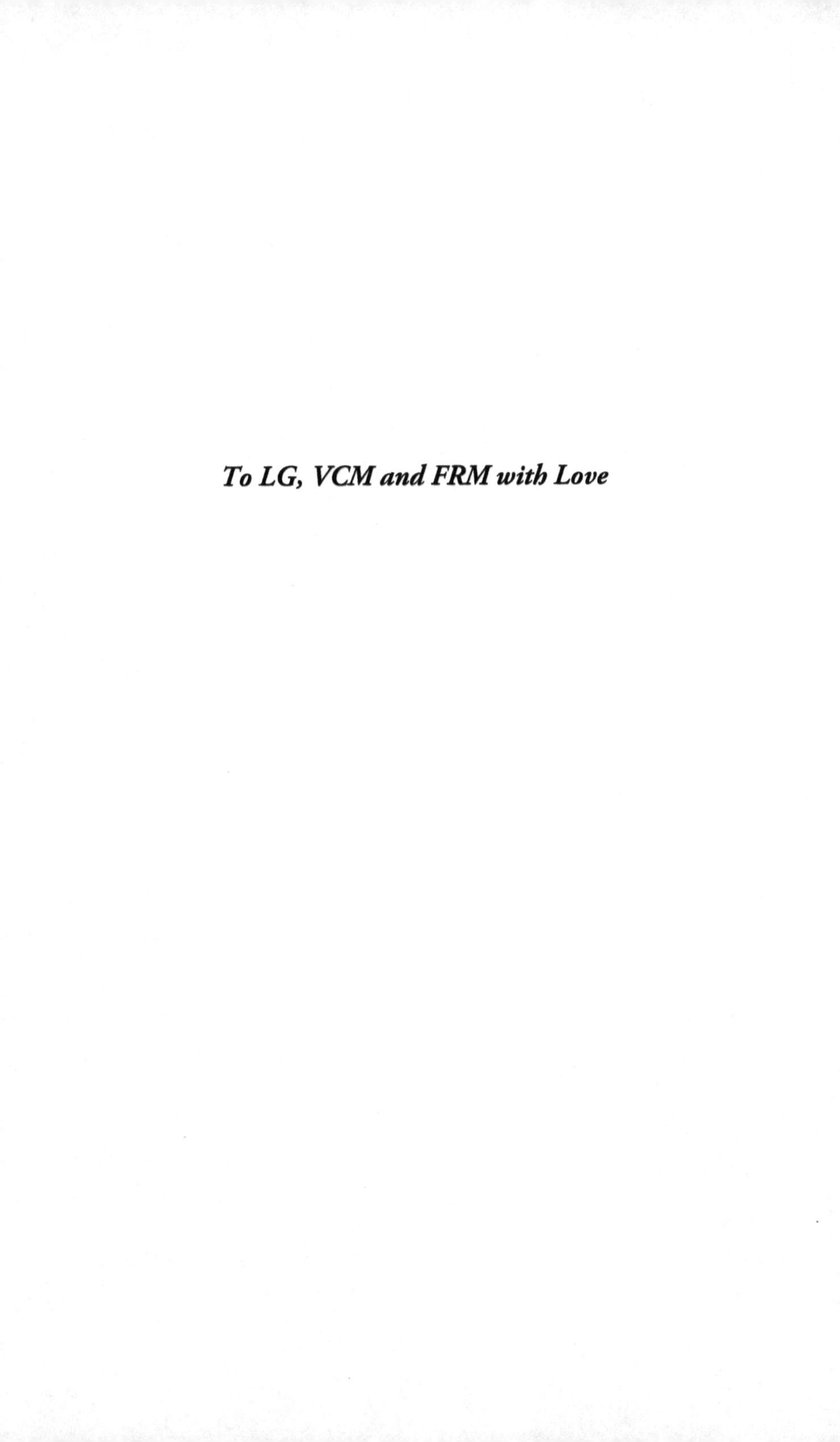

To LG, VCM and FRM with Love

Foreword

They dammed the Noire River in the Province of Quebec in 1927. Like many others in eastern Canada, it was built to last.

The same year, Michael Collins was ambushed on a country road in County Cork, Ireland, and shot dead. This story carries the rumour of his assassination across the Atlantic to the Irish community of the Noire Valley, bringing with it the seeds of violence and rebellion.

The newly-filled reservoir behind the dam attracted cottagers along its shores, and was ideal for water sports. The Blackwater Sailing Club, founded in 1962, proved a delight for generations of vacationers. But, a hundred years after construction, the dam was fast deteriorating.

In this fiction, Quebec is no longer part of Canada. It has realized its republican dreams, but has lost territory as America becomes greater still.

Part I
The Drowning (1927)

Chapter 1

I T IS A long time ago now, but the events of that year are still clear in my mind, as I write this for you.

It was June of 1927 when Sean Pardle first appeared at our farm, riding a log hauler driven by a Frenchie going back up to the camp: Uncle Sean, Pa's baby brother. You should have seen Pa's face. He was really glad to see Sean. It must have been twelve years, more; anyways, my lifetime ago. Pa was gabbling with delight as he introduced us, hugging me but never letting go of his brother's elbow. He wanted to show off the land straight away, our very own property that ran all the way down to the river and along to Rourke's Road. It was good bottom land along the Noire River, Province of Quebec, Canada, and the hunting was all you could wish for. Too bad it would not last.

They unloaded Uncle Sean's tin trunk and a long, wooden case. It was near six feet long and looked like a coffin. When they hefted it, the driver ventured a clumsy joke: "*La Belle Mère?* Your mother-in-law?" I could imagine the body inside.

"Tools to set me up in business," Uncle Sean replied with a black look. The driver shut up after that.

The men carried the box into the barn, and the driver took off up the road.

"Nosey git," said Uncle Sean.

Then we all went into the house, the brothers swinging the tin trunk between them.

"This calls for a celebration," said Pa. "Margret, fetch two stout, and a ginger beer for yourself."

"No," said Uncle Sean. "Wait a tick till I open the trunk."

He fiddled with the lock and lifted the lid. There, wrapped in an old pullover, was a bottle.

"Not Old Corkie?" said Pa. "Jesus, Sean, you've carried that a ways."

The level in the Old Corkie lowered fast, as I sat nursing my ginger beer, still as a mouse and all ears. They were talking about back in Ballygish, where they had grown up, about how Uncle Sean and Pa had taken down T.J. O'Neill, a bully drunk who could lift a heifer above his head. And the time they had nearly drowned taking that wee cockle out on an ebb tide, but didn't. How they had snuck up to watch Maeve McGinch and her friends swimming in Body's pool. That was when Pa caught my eye and jerked his head in his way that could say good morning to the Father, bad cess to the collector, or "Margret, did you finish the drying up?"

From the kitchen, I heard Pa explain to Uncle Sean about the dam, how it was nigh on finished. It was the talk of all the villages between Belltown and Newbridge, and Uncle Sean had already got an earful when he was waiting for a ride up from Gilmour's Mill.

Our farm was below the line, the one on the map everyone pored over. Pa said that meant our fields would be drowned and we would have to move. The line was in the papers and posted on the notice board beside the general store. It divided the valley into above-the-line people and below-the-line people. The former wore expressions of tight sympathy, which slipped into twitches of relief when they looked away. Below-the-line people received notices by special delivery.

Pa showed the offer to Uncle Sean. He had known that Dominion Hydro would expropriate his farm. The agent for the company said it was a good price, based on how other farmland was selling.

"Everyone gets the same per acre, so I suppose that's fair enough," said Pa. Uncle Sean sat at the other end of the table, his face still, expressionless. He could do that; freeze like a rock, staring at nothing.

"Well, it's your farm," he said, finally.

The men were like that, measuring their self-worth in acres and fence lines. After their initial disbelief, they worked off their rage on the stiff clay of the fields, while the women went into a frenzy of baking.

Chapter 2

W E WERE ALL on the porch after a bite of lunch, Uncle Sean on the rocker, and Pa having to take the stump he used to split kindling wood. I was balancing on the rail.

"So, Maggie. How old are you, then? Thirteen, or I'm no judge. You have the look of yer Gran."

I liked that, since I was only eleven, and Mrs. McGuire from two farms over still called me her Russian doll. She said it was because I looked like Mama. Who was Polish from a village over Ontario way, and died. And then, Mrs. McGuire would go all red, and say "you poor thing."

"You have Irish eyes, for sure," said Uncle Sean. I thought that was great.

Uncle Sean had his cheerful face on, the same as Pa had after mass and his Sunday bottle of stout. My uncle had thinner features than Pa, although with the same grey eyes. He had black hair, and plenty of it, unlike Pa, with his bald spot. Uncle Sean was also shorter than Pa and, when he shook my hand, his skin felt smooth. It was clear he hadn't scythed a field in a while, or pitched stooks onto a wagon lately, but he looked fit.

"Sean can run a mile like the wind," said Pa. "He would give you a race, Margret," said Pa.

"Ah now, I'm more of a walker these days. Walked all over France," replied Uncle Sean. "Why don't you show me around the farm, Maggie? I'm sure you know all the secret spots which your Dad forgot to show me."

He gave a big wink to Pa.

"Yes, why don't you two go off?" said Pa.

So, after clearing away lunch, the two of us headed north from the farm. We turned left on Rourke's Road, which led down to the river by Jack's Rush. From the bank we watched the logs as they slipped one by one down the smooth tongue of water between the near bank and a little, rocky island. A single, stunted pine tree clung to the island. I always thought that must be a desperately lonely place to grow.

I explained to Uncle Sean we called it Banana Island. When he asked why, I told him I didn't know. It had always been Banana Island. I said maybe the tree had bananas in summer, and we had a laugh. Uncle Sean asked if that was where we went skinny-dipping, peeling off our clothes like a banana.

"You've been skinny-dipping, have you not, Maggie?"

Well, I wasn't about to say.

We were quiet for a bit as we followed the path along the bank. The logs as they bobbed past us, hurrying down to the Eaton Chute. That's where the river pours over a ledge and drops into the long reach that leads all the way to Gilmour's Mill. Pa always said I'm to keep well clear of the Chute.

Uncle Sean wanted to go right out to the point overlooking the Chute, to see the water roiling away.

"It looks like a famous place for a picnic," he said. "What with the falls and all."

But I said we should get back. It was nearly time for tea. So, we headed back up the pasture, away from the river, alongside the rocky hill Pa said was "nowt but a wee mole hill." But to me it was my mountain. It marked the end of our land, going south. The top was bare rock that poked above the white pines growing on the slopes.

Uncle Sean agreed it was a veritable mountain.

"You could have a rare scramble up there," he said.

We turned our backs to the mountain and started walking by

the hedge at the top of Pa's best pasture. After a short distance, we came to a small area fenced off from the field.

"What's in there?" asked Uncle Sean, peering over the fence.

I told him this was where Pa buried his old shepherds, and my black cat Tommy, that Pa said had been killed by a fisher weasel. Pa put a white flagstone over each grave, and carved the animal's name into it with his stone chisel. He was an artist with the stone chisel, was Pa. He said the devil might come for his own, but wouldn't be able to get under the heavy stone.

I told Sean that Mama lies sleeping in the big graveyard at Belltown. Pa had done a special stone for her. Pa said Father O'Connor had complemented him special.

"Oh, aye," he said, walking on. "And who is this, now?"

We were passing the gate leading onto the road up to New-bridge, when we saw a man walking towards us. It was Mr. Rourke from the next farm.

"Good day to you, Margret," said Mr. Rourke. We don't see many strangers, and he looked suspiciously at Uncle Sean. I explained this was my Uncle Sean over from Ireland, county Kerry. And Mr. Rourke, who was from the North, said it looked like rain, and that he must be getting along now.

"Now, there's a grumpy old bugger," said Uncle Sean, after we had walked on.

✧　✧　✧

"BACK JUST IN time," said Pa, bringing his baking out of the oven. "There's butter and jam on the table."

"Young Margret led me a right dance," said Uncle Sean. "We must have walked an Irish mile at least. That's twice as long as an English mile, Maggie, which means you really have to stretch to keep the yards the same."

That was Uncle Sean for you, telling stories, making me

laugh.

"We met one of your neighbours. O'Rourke, wasn't he, Maggie?"

"It was Mr. Rourke, Pa," I said. "Walking down to the station."

"Not a very welcoming fella," said Uncle Sean. "Who else you got around here? The country seems full of Irish."

"There's more up towards Newbridge, and a fair share of prods. Plenty of *Canadiens*, although they mostly stay on the other side of the river. There's Joseph Collins, of course. He farms just up from Rourke's."

"Collins, eh? No relation to the Big Man back home? The one who got himself shot?"

"Maybe," said Pa. "Cousin to Michael himself, I think. Joseph wore a black armband three Sundays in a row after we read the news."

Even I had heard that someone had shot the Irish leader.

"Bastards ambushed him, murdered," I overheard Pa say to Mr. Rourke. It had been the talk of the valley.

Chapter 3

I T WAS A rare occasion when Pa fired his guns. He had two; a shot gun to scare the pigeons from the fields, and an old rifle for deer and wolves.

"Wolves, Margret," he said. "We wouldn't want wolves eating you. And I could make you a nice warm muff from a wolf pelt." But Pa never shot a wolf, although on a cold winter night you could hear them howling way back in the hills. And besides, he didn't use the rifle anymore because of the accident.

It was last fall, and I saw it happen from the open window. Pa was walking down the field beside the house, holding his rifle in one hand, when it went off.

"Jesus!" Pa shouted, and a bad word. The shot echoed all the way up the valley.

The next day, Mr. Rourke from the next farm came around especially to give Pa a piece of his mind. It seemed the bullet had whistled over Mr. Rourke's head as he was moving his cows into the byre. That was when Pa hung the rifle high up above the mantle. He hadn't taken it down in months.

Uncle Sean had been with us maybe a week. It was just after breakfast, and he was at the kitchen table looking up at Pa's rifle.

"Hey, may I borrow that antique?" he said. "I could give it a good cleaning, and maybe try to get us some game."

"Well, I suppose so. Just keep away from the farms up the valley, Sean," said Pa.

Uncle Sean stood and lifted down the rifle. "Ammunition?"

Pa fumbled at the back of the drawer in the big kitchen

dresser.

"Here," he said. "That should keep you going for a while." He passed a small cardboard box to Uncle Sean.

"Well, now. I'll be off then." Uncle Sean winked at me and went out. Through the window I saw him head across the field towards the woods at the back of our mountain. We heard cracks all afternoon.

"I was setting up the sights," he told us later, when he came back for his tea.

After that, Uncle Sean was out with the rifle first thing most mornings. As I walked up to the road to catch my ride to school, I would hear a bang—always just the one, but enough to set the crows off cawing and circling the trees up by the road. Later, I might be in the kitchen when he slipped in the backdoor, saying "Rabbit for supper," or "Guess we'll find out how beaver tastes."

At the beginning of October, he got a deer, a five-point buck.

"You're a crack shot, Sean," said Pa, punching Uncle Sean on the shoulder. They hung the buck on a hook in the barn, dripping blood from its nose. I didn't go in there for two weeks.

Then we had a Sunday roast.

"You should try this, Maggie," said Uncle Sean.

I had a bite. It wasn't bad, but I couldn't help thinking it tasted a bit skunky.

"Now, that's venison," Pa murmured appreciatively.

But the strange thing was that Uncle Sean wouldn't eat a bite.

"It just doesn't settle in me stomach," he said. "Pass the potatoes, Maggie."

Pa was giving away meat up and down the valley for days after.

✧　✧　✧

I WAS CURIOUS about Uncle Sean's hunting, because he always went out alone.

"Is it because I'm a girl?" I said the third time of asking to go with him.

"Ach, no, Maggie," he replied. "A hunter has to be alone, except for the hunted. It's a bond. Three's a crowd."

Then, one Saturday morning, I was mucking about as usual with Gerry McGuire from the farm up the road. We were at the machine gun nest. At least, that's what Gerry called the corner of the field where bushes had grown around a circle of rocks. You could crawl in and watch across the field towards the river.

"That's where Fritz will come from," said Gerry, aiming his stick, and that's when we saw Uncle Sean where Gerry was pointing, flat on the ground in the long grass beside the river. We wouldn't have seen him at all if Gerry hadn't been looking for imaginary Germans. He was just laying there, beside a tuft of grass, his cap over his face. He seemed to be sleeping, Pa's gun pushed out in front of him.

"Lie still!" Gerry told me. He had flattened himself on the ground, under a thorn bush. "He's waiting for the Germans. And when one of them moves, it's 'Bye bye, Fritz.'"

I wondered how long we would have to wait for the Germans.

"Shsh!" whispered Gerry. "It could be hours."

After ten minutes, we got bored. We crawled back out of the nest and walked towards the farm. Halfway home, we heard the bang. The crows took off again, calling us names.

That evening, there wasn't much conversation at tea. Soon after we'd finished our plates, Uncle Sean got up without a word, and went out.

Pa caught me staring after Uncle Sean.

"Don't you worry," he confided. "He'll be right as rain by tomorrow. But, he saw things during the war he can't forget. And there's been unpleasant business over in Ireland. Now, he is over here for a rest."

And, most of the time, Uncle Sean seemed a cheerful man. He would tell jokes that made me laugh, and stories about places I could never hope to see; about rare times in France, and the singing sand hills back in County Kerry. But, once in a while, his face would harden and he would stare past you with empty eyes, as if a curtain of rain blurred his vision. No, that couldn't be a tear, I would think; it was just a soft morning.

And, a few days later, we were all sitting around the fire in the evening, with the dark shut out by thick curtains. It was snug, Uncle Sean and Pa had glasses in their hands, and Uncle Sean was saying again how beautiful it was in France, but that the hunting in Ireland was better, if you took his meaning. Pa suddenly hit the table with his palm, making me jump.

"That's enough, Sean," he said. "Margret doesn't need to hear your politics. France was all mud and shit, not wine and Mademoiselles. And, as for the old country, she can keep her bogs and her Black and Tans and all that nonsense."

Uncle Sean said loudly that Ireland was the Free State now, and all the better for the traitor Collins being dead. He said Dev would set things to rights. But Pa said De Valera would ruin the country, and there was no call for that here in Canada. Uncle Sean said a word that I didn't understand. So, I went upstairs to read Just William in bed. I had had enough of grown-ups.

Chapter 4

THE SLOW RISE of the water was narrowing the strip of farming land along the valley, washing over the old field boundaries. It pressed people closer, rubbing together old prejudices. Pa always says space is the wonder of Canada for those who have escaped a tight country.

Pa had scouted out a new property west of Belltown, in Glen Happy. I liked the name, and we would move there by the end of the summer. But, for several weeks we would live rough—camping, if you like, out of the Orange Hall on Freely Road with two other families. I was excited and looking forward to the move. It was high summer, so we lived mostly out-of-doors anyway. Besides, I knew one of the families. It was Gerry McGuire's dad who had fixed things for us all with the Orangemen. The McGuires were nice, even if they were prods.

Now that construction on the Noire dam was completed, the novelty of soon-to-be-drowned communities up the valley to its north drew voyeurs from the city. Most days, there was traffic on the road, and cars stopped at our farm to ask directions to the dam. Once, a reporter and a photographer came from one of the city newspapers. Pa was courteous. He answered the reporter's questions with a resigned gentleness, although I heard his accent grow stronger as he described his "be-oo-tiful" bottom lands, the fields soon to drown.

Pa said he wasn't against progress and, yes, his family would be staying on in the region. The reporter even asked me if I minded moving away.

"No," I replied. "It will be great camping at the Orange Hall." I had my picture taken, swinging on the gate.

When the story came out the following week, Pa read it to me, sitting at the kitchen table. Electricity would power the future, it seemed, and the expropriation of land was for the public good. I don't think Pa was convinced that Dominion Hydro had the right to drown him off his land. Not here in Canada.

"Well, we have to move, Margret." said Pa, after he had finished reading. "But I'm sure you'll like Glen Happy and soon make new friends. I'll not be farming though. I'll find other work."

✧ ✧ ✧

SOMETIMES THERE WERE different visitors to the farm—men who came and talked to Uncle Sean. Pa found reasons to be away when that happened, usually a trip into Belltown for feed, or up the valley to take hay to a neighbour, though there was really no need, because the season had been good. He had business, he would say, with the Dominion Hydro agent, or needed to consult the map again on the new property.

"See no evil, speak no evil," was one of Pa's favourite expressions.

I once overheard the men talking with Uncle Sean. They had met in the barn, right under the hayloft where I had business myself with the new cat and her kittens. I could see through the cracks in the floorboards when they came in. I kept really still, holding my breath. Some of the men were only a few years older than me, others about Uncle Sean's age, but not as old as Pa. I recognized Lackie Donnell from the Church dance at Newbridge. Just because I beat him twice at the beetle game didn't mean he could dance with me. Anyway, he had spots and wasn't even eighteen. Stephen Meaghan was there, but then he would always be there when there was mischief to be made. There were two older fellas I'd seen riding the waggons up to the camps. They had the *Canadien* look, and I guessed they'd come over on Rourke's ferry from the eastern shore.

I couldn't make out much of the talk, but there were laughs when one of the Frenchies shouted *"maudits anglais"* and Uncle Sean clapped him on the back. When they came out of the barn, I saw a big man with a red beard punch Uncle Sean on the shoulder. I heard him say, "You are a right Fenian bastard, are you not, Sean?" Then they both laughed and walked up the lane to the road. Later, I tried calling Gerry a "Fenian bastard." He said I was a "feckin' ejit," so we were quits.

Pa came back when it was turning to dusk, and after all the men had left. After tea, when no one said much, Uncle Sean showing me a card trick. Pa said the trick was "nowt but leggydemain."

✧   ✧   ✧

NEXT MORNING, I came down to breakfast early, and found Uncle Sean had beaten me to it. He had put a cloth over the kitchen table and was pulling something through the barrel of a gun. Not Pa's wee rifle: this gun looked bigger and heavier altogether. I must have made a noise, because Uncle Sean looked up.

"Why, a Good Morning to you, Maggie," he said. Then I saw he had three other guns on the table, lined up like they were all at attention. He finished pulling the string right through the barrel of the one he was holding, and out popped what looked like a tiny brush. He picked up a rag.

"Pass me that oil can. There's a dear," he said. "We have to keep these beauties clean or they don't shoot straight."

He cradled another one of the guns and worked the bolt in and out.

"Jesus, Sean, don't be doing that in front of the girl!"

Pa had come down, and he looked none too happy.

Uncle Sean shrugged. "Maggie, will you just put the kettle on?" he said.

✧   ✧   ✧

LATER, I HEARD the two of them shouting in the barn. Then there was a pause, and Pa came stamping into the house. His faced looked as black as the time he'd caught Gerry and me up in the hayloft. We were just making tunnels in the hay not, as Pa had said, "some bloody love nest."

"Don't fuss yourself, Maggie. It's just brother stuff," he said. "Now, you stay in the house, and finish peeling those potatoes. We have a wee job to do, Sean and I."

Anyway, a few minutes later, I saw Uncle Sean emerge with a bridle on the dray-horse. He had hooked on the old sled we used when the snow came, and he had loaded the long box which he had arrived with. It was the one that looked like a coffin.

Pa went outside and spoke quietly to Uncle Sean. The potatoes could wait: I was at the door, listening. You could hear Pa's idea of a whisper from across the yard.

"You know where to cache it? You'll be wanting a hand, I suppose?"

"Aye," replied Uncle Sean.

Pa and Uncle Sean led the horse through the gate and up the lane to the top field. I went upstairs to watch them from the gable window in our attic. They crossed the field towards my mountain and disappeared into the trees at its base.

I guessed where they were going. There is an old mine near the top of the mountain. Gerry and I had found it years ago. It wasn't much of a mine—just a short drive, along a seam of shiny mica. Gerry said it would make us rich as the King. When we asked Pa about the mine, he said it had been dug a few years back when everyone was crazy for easy money. He called it Gilmour's mine and said it had never made a cent. The mine ended a few yards in, in a small, round space that was dry enough, and that Gerry thought would make a great hideout.

After a few minutes, I saw Pa and Uncle Sean trudging back across the field, the horse pulling an empty sled. I guessed the long box would stay in the hideout for a while.

"Sean will be leaving," Pa said at tea that evening.

I looked over to Uncle Sean.

"Aye, Maggie. Your Uncle Sean is soon off on his travels again."

Chapter 5

ONE MORNING, IT must have been early July soon after the summer holidays had started, a truck pulled up on the road just by our farm. The sign on the truck said Dominion Hydro, and four men got down from the cab. One carried a telescope on a tripod. He put it down in the middle of our lane, while at the far end of the field another man stood holding a long pole.

The man with the telescope didn't seem pleased. He wanted the pole held upright and still, not waving around. Eventually, he raised an arm, and the man with the pole put it over his shoulder, and walked over to join him. The two other men followed the pole guy to bang in orange pegs. Soon there was a line of pegs across the middle of our top field. The pegs jumped the lane, then marched on through Rourke's best pasture, where he kept his two dairy cows.

That evening after supper, I crept out to meet Gerry in the lane. He carried the big hammer from his Da's work shed and a flashlight. We went across the field, wiggling the stakes till they came out one by one. Then we went down nearer the river. I held the rough wood while Gerry banged in the pegs.

Pa was angry the next morning when he saw what we had done.

"Do you think that would ever stop them, girl?" he said. But he wasn't really mad, and he left the pegs where they were.

✧　✧　✧

THE NEXT DAY being Saturday, Pa was driving the rig into town to talk to the agent about the compensation. He hadn't wanted Uncle Sean or me to come with him.

"I'll need you tomorrow, Sean," he said before going. "We will head up to the new place to run some fence wire. It's a two-man job."

Uncle Sean was standing close behind me as we watched Pa disappear up the lane.

Then he said, "Now then Maggie, you wanted to try shooting. Seeing your dad's gone off, I say we head down to the woods and set you up for some target practice. We might as well take a picnic. You can work up quite an appetite shooting."

I turned around so fast, I collided with a chair and scraped my shin.

"Seriously? You're not kidding me?"

"No, it's time you learned a thing or two," said Uncle Sean.

Which was just great. After showing me how to make sure it wasn't loaded, Uncle Sean let me carry Pa's long rifle. We walked down to the river path and along to the trees at the base of our mountain. I asked him where the other guns were.

"Back in the box, Maggie. They are much too heavy for the likes of you."

At the edge of the woods, he found a low bank and put down a blanket on the grass.

"Stay here, you, till I pin up the target."

He walked away, taking big strides and counting out loud.

"Thirty yards to that tree," he said when he came back. "If you miss, you'll hit the mountain behind. You can't miss that!"

He showed me how to pull back the bolt and load the bullet.

"It's a bolt-action," he said. "You pull the bolt back to cock it, and then all you do is point and squeeze the trigger. Lie down on the blanket and rest the stock on top of the bank. Look along the sights, breathe in, let it out, and when you're almost out of breath, fire. There is not much recoil on a wee gun like this."

My heart was sure beating fast, and even when I let out my breath, I could still hear it pumping away. I squeezed the trigger gently, like Uncle Sean had said, and there was a loud crack. I felt my shoulder knocked back, but it didn't hurt at all like Gerry had told me.

"Great," said Uncle Sean. "Try again."

I pulled really hard on the bolt, but couldn't bring it all the way back. I guess your fingers get stronger with practice. Uncle Sean pulled it back for me again and slipped in the bullet. I fired.

After five shots he said, "Let's see if you would make a hunter." So we walked over to look at the target on the tree.

"Three in the ring! You're a natural, Maggie."

I was pretty pleased. I gave him a hug, and we went back to the blanket.

"Hey why don't we shoot something better?" said Uncle Sean. He pulled over the basket we had carried down and took out three bottles of Pa's stout. "We can set these up on that stump over there, but it's a waste not to drink them first. Have you never tasted beer before, Maggie?"

Now, I had sipped from Pa's glass just before washing it up, so I said yes, of course.

"It's not Guinness, but it goes down easily enough after the first taste," he said. He took a bottle and levered off the cap. "Here, try this."

So I did and it did.

He had drained his beer quickly, and waited for me to finish. Mine was fizzy from being jogged about, and the foam got up my nose, so that I spluttered.

"Wait. Let me." Uncle Sean leaned over and wiped my face

with his handkerchief.

"Better now?"

I nodded.

"Might as well crack the last one," said Uncle Sean. He took a big swig from the bottle and passed it to me. I shook my head.

Then he took the empty bottles, set them on a stump and came back. I fired five more shots but never hit the bottle. Uncle Sean was laughing and trying to help me aim properly. He leaned over me, took the gun and stood it against a tree.

"Enough of that, now," he said. "Let's lie here for a while."

Which was fine by me, because I felt sleepy after the beer. It was kind of warm snuggled on the blanket on the soft leaves, and I must have fallen asleep, because when I woke up Uncle Sean was standing, looking down at me. He had his thin face on, the face Pa said was Uncle Sean remembering the war.

"You best get off back to the house, Maggie," he said finally. "Your Dad will be home soon and be wanting his tea."

Chapter 6

THE CROWS WERE crying again. I suppose that woke me, because, thinking back, I hadn't heard a shot. It was light outside, so I guessed I had slept late. I was used to Pa waking me at half six most school days, and half an hour earlier on weekends, when I had more chores.

"Rouse yerself, Margret," he would shout up the stairs. "The chicks won't feed themselves."

This was a Saturday. I knew I was already behind. I got up and went down to the kitchen. There, the stove was black and cold, which was odd, since Pa always stoked it first thing. Pa had left me a sort of breakfast on the kitchen table: a bowl with oats and a slice of bread. There was a note under the milk jug.

"Margret," he had written. "I had to go down to the falls early. I think Sean may have had an accident. Get yourself some breakfast. Pa."

By the time I had got the stove lit, gone out to the well with the jugs and pumped enough water for a wash, put the big kettle to boil, and fed the chickens, I heard Pa's footsteps outside the house. His tread was usually slow, measured. But now I thought he must almost be running. He burst through the back door.

"Ah, Margret, there you are. Uncle Sean has had a fall, and I think he's gone in the river. He's probably swum out downstream. But run along to McGuire's. Tell him there's a man in the river. Ask if he and his men can meet me down by the pool below the falls. He'll know what to bring. Hurry now. I'll meet you down there."

I flew out the door and up the lane. By the time I got to McGuire's, I was out of breath and my hair was where the west wind met the east. It's true; there is no managing my hair. That my mother was Polish and my dad Irish would explain it.

Mrs. McGuire opened the kitchen door when I knocked.

"You look like a scarecrow, Maggie," said Mrs. McGuire. "Whatever is the matter?"

I caught my breath.

"Pa says Uncle Sean's gone in the river, Mrs. McGuire!"

"Poor child," said Mrs. McGuire, after she had listened to my story. "Now, you stay here and have a bite to eat while I tell McGuire to get the cart hitched." She went outside.

"McGuire! McGuire!" I heard her shouting as she disappeared around the corner of the house.

Two men came out from behind the barn to see what the noise was about. They were timber cruisers who lodged at the McGuire's farm during the summer and shared a cabin beside the barn. Their work for the forest company was to mark trees for felling the following winter. Their names were Jean and Gaétan. In their spare time, they helped with odd jobs around the farm.

Mrs. McGuire came back with her husband.

"Now, Maggie. What's all this about?" Mr. McGuire asked me, and I had to explain again.

"Right, then." He turned towards the two men. "I'll get the horse, and you two pull the cart out of the barn."

I watched the men wrestle with the harness. Jean fetched pikes and a coil of rope from the barn, and threw them into the back of the cart. The pikes were poles with sharp points used for rolling logs.

Mrs. McGuire said I should stay with her, that a drowning was not a fit sight for a young girl. Then she turned bright red and started to fuss. I said I was told to get straight back home. I put my coat back on and, accepting a bag of cookies from Mrs. McGuire, ran outside and climbed up into the cart with Gaetan. Jean sat in front beside Mr. McGuire.

The horse was trotting along the road at a fine pace. We passed my mountain, and two minutes later, Mr. McGuire pulled to a halt where the road came down close to the river, just below Eaton Chute.

"There's Pa!" I pointed to the distant figure standing at the point overlooking the pool below the falls, the place we called High Rock. He was quite far away, but he saw us arrive and waved. We got down from the cart, the men grabbed the equipment, and we started walking along the rough trail that skirted the water. It led through young pine trees to a viewpoint with a bench. Visitors could sit there and look along the break of the falls, and down into the swirling waters below. It's a famous place for picnics.

Mr. McGuire clambered up the path in front of us, panting with the effort to where Pa was standing. Pa pointed to a gun that lay on a patch of cushion moss near the cliff edge.

"It was just lying there. Fired, of course. I heard the shot, must be two hours ago."

I kind of hung back behind Jean and Gaetan, and I don't think Pa knew I was there.

"He'll have gone over, then," said Mr. McGuire, peering over the cliff edge at the river below. I knew High Rock. Gerry had made me stand at the edge one hot day last summer, and said I just had to jump. From the rock, it was twenty feet down into the black water. Gerry said it was so deep that if you hold your nose and go straight down, you never touch the bottom. I didn't want to, but Gerry said he wouldn't look, so I took off my dress and jumped. Well, I had to, really. I plunged into the water and then rose slowly to the surface. The water got up my nose like when you laugh drinking a soda. Gerry flung himself off, too, and splashed down beside me. I saw him go down and down in a cloud of bubbles. That was last summer.

Now, the wind was blowing from the southwest and there was a swirl of dirty white scum in the bay, along with floating logs and other rubbish. You couldn't see below the surface at all.

"Gaetan, Jean. Get down there and feel with the poles," said Mr. McGuire. "Most of what goes in here gets spun around the bay. We'll find him here for sure." The two men scrambled down the bank beside High Rock and started prodding the floating logs, pushing them out to sweep away the scum to see beneath the water. Gaétan ran out on the floating logs, balancing with his pole, just like an acrobat in the circus, jumping from one to another.

"No sign of him down here, Chief," he called up.

McGuire looked out over the bay, scanning the far shore.

"We'll work our way around," he said to Pa. "You had better look after your wee girl.'

And that was when Pa noticed me. I came forward to the cliff edge, hoping to see Uncle Sean swimming in the pool below, but there was nothing but scum.

"Ach, careful Margret! Mind the edge," said Pa. "You shouldn't be here."

Then turning to Mr. McGuire, he said, "I'll take her back, Jim, and then call the mill. Maybe they can send one of their pusher boats up here to help search."

Pa and I watched Mr. McGuire and his men retrace their steps along the edge of the bay, and pick their way along the rocks on the far side. Pa picked up the rifle.

"Margret, did you hear Sean going out hunting again this morning?"

"No, Pa. Just the crows," I said.

"All right," he said. "Let's go home."

Turning to follow Pa, I scuffed my shoe on a rock. A patch

of moss fell away. You could see where it should go. That's the thing with cushion moss—you could peel it from its rock and it would come away in clumps. Then you had to fit it back together like a jigsaw. The moss had been loose, and it slipped easily over the smooth surface. Where the moss had been, I saw a red smear on the rock, red as the blood dripping from the hanging buck. Then I followed Pa along the path that followed the river around the outside of my mountain towards the farm.

When we reached the middle of the paddock by our house, Pa turned and looked towards the dark pines at the far edge of his twenty acres field. There, at the bottom of my mountain, was a line of boulders Pa had pushed to the edge of the paddock. Beside them was the white fence with hawthorns where we buried things. Two black birds were circling—ravens this time, not crows, by the size of them. I heard Pa swear beneath his breath, his face as wet as mine.

"Bloody birds," he said. "They see everything, and they never forget. Sorry, Margret."

"Don't be sorry, Pa. We can come back one day and visit our mountain. It's way above the markers."

"Sure, Margret. But you'll have to swim. Your mountain is going to be an island."

✧   ✧   ✧

JEAN FOUND UNCLE Sean eventually, caught under a willow tree way downriver. He and Gaetan pulled him out of the river. Two constables came from Belltown to collect the body.

That Wednesday, Pa brought Uncle Sean from the undertakers, after the coroner had given his verdict. I saw the body lying in his coffin on the big table in the front parlor. He looked asleep, with his hair slicked down like it was still wet, and his face thin and unsmiling.

"Death by misadventure," Pa told me. "Sean tripped and fell after his gun went off, banging his head on the rocks on the way down."

I said nothing about the cushion moss.

That evening, Mr. McGuire came over with a bottle, and the Rourkes and a few from other families up the valley. Few came to the wake, since Uncle Sean had not been here long. Those that came offered their condolences to Pa and me. The man with the big red beard came, the one I had seen in the barn with Uncle Sean.

"A loss to the cause," I heard him say to Pa. "Would you know where a certain box may be …?"

"I would not," Pa replied. "Help yourself to a beer." Red Beard sat down on a chair beside Mr. Rourke.

After what seemed hours of sitting around the coffin, talking about the weather, the dam, whatever the hell McKenzie King thought he was up to; saying anything but drowning in the river far from your own country, and dying. Eventually, the beer ran out, and conservation with it. People started to leave.

"Thank you for coming," said Pa at the door. "We'll be burying Sean in Belltown graveyard next Saturday at three."

I spent two days avoiding the front room so as not to see the coffin. Pa was in the barn much of the time. I heard the tapping of his hammer and chisels.

"A stone for Sean," he told me. "It only right he should have a stone."

On Saturday morning, the hearse came from Belltown to collect Uncle Sean. Pa and I followed slowly, riding in the trap. We buried him far from Mama: on the side near the road, and three rows down. Pa said Uncle Sean hadn't thought to reserve a plot.

A week later, Pa finished carving the words on the gravestone, and took it to leave with the warden at Belltown cemetery.

When he returned, he was angry.

"Father O'Connor saw the inscription and said it was improper, that I couldn't say that on a gravestone. Not proper! He said to change it, or just put a plain cross on Sean's grave. 'All right', says I. 'We'll put up a cross.'"

"As for the stone, let's lay it in our own cemetery. Sean won't mind if he's not underneath."

✧   ✧   ✧

OVER THE WEEKS since we buried Uncle Sean, I watched the waters overflow the banks of the river, and creep slowly up the sides of the valley. You couldn't actually see the water rising, but yesterday it was halfway up our lower field, and had swallowed the pegs that Gerry and I had moved. It crept up the sloping fields, encircling the rocky outliers of the surrounding hills. It filled the side valleys to form bays; created islands. It was time for us to leave.

Mr. McGuire and the Rourkes came to help, and I watched the pile of furnishings grow on the grass under the big maple, before they carted it away to store in Mr. McGuire's barn until our new place was ready. Then, the men took the house apart, plank by plank and post by post, till all that they left was the square of the stone foundation.

Later, I helped drive our cows up the hill to Mr. McGuire's top field, which was on higher ground, well above the line. It was a long, tiring day, but before tea at the McGuires, Pa and I went back down for a last look at the old house. One corner of the foundation was already being lapped at by small wavelets. I wondered whether it would just wash away like a sandcastle.

"Margret," Pa said to me. "Remember, this will be our land beneath the water. No one can take that away from us, now."

Chapter 7

S O, GRANDDAUGHTER, THAT'S nearly all I remember about 1927, the year Uncle Sean and our farm drowned. There's not much more to tell.

When they finished the Noire Dam and stopped the flow of the river, the water backed half of the way to Newbridge, creating a reservoir fifteen miles long. The shoreline along the valley sides was more or less where the engineers had said it would be. Our farmhouse had completely disappeared.

Getting near Christmas that year, Dominion Hydro finished installing the generating equipment. To mark the occasion, the chairman of the company held a switch-throwing ceremony in the generator hall. Important folks came up from the city, and sat beside the Mayor and councillors from Belltown. Everyone who had worked on the dam came back with their wives and families. The company had invited all the families who lived below the line. Pa took me, but few others came.

To close the dam bypass tunnels, the chairman pressed a switch on the control board. We could hear the rumble of the flow slowly ease and finally stop. Simultaneously, the new turbines began to spin, the hum growing in volume until we had to shout to be heard. At the front of the hall, the company had erected a large dial to display the mounting voltage. When the needle on the dial reached a red line, a bell rang, and the chairman threw a second switch to light the Christmas tree. There were hundreds of fairy light; the crowd applauded, the chairman bowed, and there were gifts under the tree for the children. Mine was a bronze plaque with the inscription "Dominion Hydro Noire Dam 1927."

Before they flooded the valley, the company men took photographs of the farms, the houses and barns. They'll be yellowing in an archive somewhere, together with the deeds of transfer to Dominion Hydro showing the old field boundaries. Archived maps still trace the submerged road and the old railway line that ran near our farm, although both are only marked by faint dashes. Pa said that the land expropriated by Dominion Hydro was the best farmland in the valley, but there is no argument now: the voices of the farming families forced to move are still, and only ghost fields lie beneath the water.

Our working valley turned to the pleasures of cottage country; for summer visitors to enjoy rural life a short drive from the city. They say access to a wide expanse of water is essential during these hot summers.

Part II

The Blackwater Sailing Club (2027)

Chapter 8

IT WAS A dismally misty morning, a half-melt with the temperature hovering about zero, when American tanks crossed the Canadian border at Lacolle, fifty kilometers south of Montreal. They charged through the pay station, using the fast-track lane for vehicles with transponders, and roared up Autoroute 15 towards Montreal. Their timing coincided with that of the early risers among campers completing their northward migration after wintering in Florida. Together, they formed a mixed column of armoured vehicles and returning sun-seekers. The traffic stayed well-spaced to avoid the worst of the spray thrown up from the tracks of the military vehicles. It moved, for once, below the posted limit.

It was not until the commander of the American force, Captain Beauchamp Krause, reached the entrance ramp to the bridge across the St. Lawrence River into the City of Montreal, that he stopped his M2 tank, slewing its forty tons of uranium-hardened metal to block both northbound lanes. He swiveled the turret to point its main weapon south, at the trailing line of vehicles.

Meanwhile, a second tank crossed the median, scattering a line of orange and black bollards from the construction zone, to block the southbound side of the highway. Approaching the tailback from the blockage, drivers jockeyed to exit onto the slip roads looking for alternative routes. After twenty minutes, the highway was deserted. No further traffic emerged from the mist.

Captain Krause was under strict orders not to test the bridge with the weight of his tanks and, anyway, he had reached his objective. After forty-five minutes, the south shore of the St. Lawrence was now the de facto political border between the new Republic of Quebec and Greater America. He looked at the time—it was only twelve minutes past eight—and thought that his platoon might just have set a record for the fastest tank sprint in history. He sipped the tall, milky coffee a drone had just delivered. All had gone as planned, although Krause felt the weather could have been more accommodating: the flag on his communications aerial was hanging limp in the dank weather.

Tweets from Washington insisted that the 'adjustment' was simply a matter of ensuring security along the northern border of Greater America, an action that should in no way affect friendly relations between the two republics. The south shore of the St. Lawrence Seaway now marked the administrative border, a shift north of some fifty kilometres.

The White House countered protests from Quebec by pointing to the Border Adjustment Force. Its continued presence—at no expense to Quebec, the President noted—ensured the new republic's security. American men and women—dedicated peace keepers—would help guard Quebec's fledgling republic from the monarchists, and the threat of reunionist agitators from 'Upper Canada'.

"No, don't thank me," insisted the President, during a press conference with Madame Josée-Mathilde Papineau, his Quebec counterpart. The official transcripts omitted Papineau's muttered retort.

And so, in the time it took Captain Krause to order and drink his coffee, *la Montérégie*—that southern part of the Republic of Quebec bordering the states of New York, Vermont, and New Hampshire—became the USBAZ, the US Border Adjustment Zone.

Despite assurances that life would remain as normal, changes in the USBAZ began to be noticed immediately. On road signs, kilometres reverted to miles; speed limits from fifty kilometres per hour to thirty miles per hour. On the weather forecast, *Météomedia* now reported temperatures in degrees Fahrenheit.

Even more noticeable to locals was the influx of workers from the south. At first, pickers and field labourers arrived to help the harvest on *la Montérégie's* ailing farms. These were welcomed: housed in temporary barracks, they seemed quiet and respectful when sighted in the *supermarché*. But, far from returning south at the end of the growing season, the workers stayed over the coming winter. The influx grew ever larger in volume over the next few years. Monolingual notices appeared in Spanish.

"Bienvenidos a la zona, una nueva vida para todos!" Welcome to a new life in the USBAZ!

The strategy behind Border Adjustment became clear: transport refugees from Mexico and Central America crossing into the southern United States north to the USBAZ. To accommodate the influx, the USBAZ authority controlled rents, and took right of first refusal for any housing sale. Market values declined precipitately. Long-time residents sold at a loss, and soon, a growing number of angry Quebecois were crossing from the USBAZ to Montreal and the north shore of the St. Lawrence. It was a domino effect: not a cleansing, more a voluntary transhumance. Campsites filled with RVs, and spare rooms in family homes became crowded with unwelcome relatives. To avert a crisis, the government in Quebec City directed regions outside the metropole to billet those displaced. Using emergency powers, it organized the largest redistribution of displaced people to the less populated west and north since the early days of colonization.

✧ ✧ ✧

PAUL LOESS KNEW he'd been living in far too much house for a single man, but the notice had been the last straw. He sympathized with the refugees, but to have the family imposed on him—and to have no say in the matter—well, that grated.

Paul had struggled to understand the details of the letter, delivered by hand to his doorstep. The legal terms, all in French, were obscure. But the overall meaning was plain enough: Péladeau, family of five, relocating from Longueil to Pontiac, and Paul's address.

The Péladeau family's vast camper van now sat squeezed beside his ancient Subaru in the entry. Nicole and Marc seemed pleasant at first. The family occupied the ground floor, leaving Paul one bedroom and a little studio at the back of the house. They agreed to share the kitchen and left Paul the use of one bathroom. Their three children were respectful and shy, initially, but that soon wore off with familiarity and their belief that Paul couldn't quite understand their French. He wished he couldn't, frankly. Still, it was having to put down his cat—young Leanne Péladeau had allergies—that he finally accepted the offer of compensation from the *Bureau d'hébergement*, and moved.

Paul had heard of a community for people needing to downsize radically, and, by luck, had become friendly with a resident there who agreed to sponsor him. The crucial interview was this morning. He had left plenty of time to drive his old SUV on the road north from Hull to the Blackwater Sailing Club, following the directions given him over the phone. He turned off the main road onto *chemin* Glen Rourke, and let his car coast down a gentle incline. At the bottom, he bumped across a disused railway crossing and stopped.

Paul got out. In front of him was a dilapidated chain-link fence, buckled by the snow load of many winters and overhung with vines. Large trees crowded in from all sides, and the air was still and oppressive. A narrow gravel lane led off to his left. It looked little used and poorly maintained. According to Paul's directions, this should be *chemin* Blackwater, and the club was only a few hundred metres down the lane. He decided not to risk the deep potholes: he would walk. He returned to his car, and parked on the verge beside a gate in the fence.

Behind the fence was a clearing in the trees. A sign hanging on the gate informed Paul that the "parking" was for the use of Blackwater members only. Peering through the wire mesh, he could see rusting boat trailers jammed beneath the scabby poplars that screened the lot. Discarded trailers, their tires blistered and deflated, lay tumbled together like a mass extinction.

One trailer still carried a boat. The mast had been unstepped and lay across wooden supports at bow and stern. A grey tarpaulin draped the boat. It fell to the ground on each side, and was loosely tied with cord. Beneath the flap of the tarp, Paul glimpsed the base of a thick keel. It was a decent-sized cabin boat, big enough for a single man. This was what they had promised him, what he was paying for.

Suddenly he was in a hurry. He trotted down *chemin* Blackwater, the lane that led from the parking compound to the Blackwater Sailing Club. Unknown to Paul, before the reservoir filled this lane had been the main road running up the valley to Newbridge. It had been busy with farm traffic and, later, with motorists on day trips up from Ottawa. Encroaching vegetation had since reduced the lane's width to that of a single vehicle.

The slope increased, and Paul saw that runoff from heavy rain had eroded ruts deep into the roadbed. Crowding in from the left was a hedge of dark, dripping cedars, hinting at guarded privacy. A few steps further, and the ground fell away, giving Paul his first view of the Noire Reservoir and Blackwater Bay. In the middle of the bay, some hundred metres from shore, rose the pine-clad island that was the club's private domain.

The lane ended at the reservoir where a concrete ramp for launching boats sloped down into the water. A battered road sign for *cul de sac* warned the unwary. A bit late for that advice, thought Paul. Beside the ramp was the entrance to the club.

A boardwalk supported on floating pontoons connected the Blackwater Sailing Club to the mainland. To reach the boardwalk, visitors passed through a security gate. This was a solid, steel construction set into a wall of wood that flared out like a giant fan, its top creamed with razor wire. "Private—Members Only" announced a sign above the gate. A red pin-light blinked on the surveillance camera bolted to the gate frame. Paul wondered if he should wave.

While waiting for some acknowledgement of his presence— the place seemed deserted—he scanned the notice board beside the gate. Signs reminded members of things prohibited on the island: motorized vehicles, loud music, dogs and visitors were not allowed unless approved by the Board. Bilingual posters from environmental authorities warned swimmers of the danger of parasites in the water, and another against invasive species. The signs had faded in the sun and weather. Only one seemed recent—a political message proclaiming "Free West Quebec— Pontiac for Canada." In smaller print, Paul read that the poster was authorized and distributed by "The Committee."

"Alright, then," thought Paul, who had never heard of it.

✧   ✧   ✧

A VETTING BY the board of the Blackwater Sailing Club was the last hurdle to admission for prospective members. After cohabiting with the Péladeau family for some months, Paul had become desperate to move, and was relieved when he finally got a call from Harvey Kinnear, the club secretary, proposing an interview. Paul had been on the waiting list for a long time because the club limited membership to thirty residents. This meant waiting till someone moved away, died, or committed some unforgivable sailing crime. Paul's sponsor—the Commodore of the club, no less—had coached Paul on what to say, and what not to say. One had to have a firm grasp of the rule book.

After a few minutes, the pin-light on the camera turn to green and the lock mechanism of the gate clicked. A disembodied voice crackled from a loudspeaker beside the security camera.

"Paul Loess? Come across on the catwalk. I'll meet you on the other side."

The lock clicked, and Paul pushed open the heavy gate. He began walking towards the island along the uneven planks of the walkway. The gate slammed shut behind him, announcing his arrival.

"Shut the bloody thing quietly in future," came a disembodied voice from deep within the cabin of a boat moored near the club entrance.

The walkway was built of sections of wooden dock, twelve feet long by four feet wide, bolted together. Each dipped slightly beneath Paul's weight as he advanced, throwing him off-balance: *catwalk* was perhaps an appropriate name, he thought. Tethered by heavy chains to the gatehouse at the shore, and to a large pine tree on the island, the catwalk curved like a bow before him, straining to resist the slight current. He passed a succession of short, lateral docks, extending like fingers at right angles to the catwalk.

The yachts tied up to these docks were of modest length: Paul judged the biggest was no longer than twenty-five feet. A few of the boats at the landward end of the catwalk looked as though they seldom left their moorings. The rigging was slack and the paint dull. Owners had rigged sails for shade or to catch rainwater. Beside one boat, Paul noticed aquatic plants—water hyacinths—jostling against the hull, corralled by a line of floats.

A tiny house straddling the twin hulls of the sole catamaran. Smoke was curling from the stovepipe.

Other boats looked clean—not in racing fettle, perhaps, but certainly capable of casting off and making sail. One sailor, whom Paul vaguely recognized, raised a coffee mug in salute, before bending to fiddle with an outboard motor. To his right, moored along the shore of the island, were floating docks. These seemed to him to be more prestigious: the boats here sleeker and rigged for racing.

The planking on the catwalk ended just before the island, and Paul found himself separated from shore by a narrow channel. On the far side of the channel, partially blocking his view of the island, was what looked like a tall wooden gate made of thick boards. Paul realized that it was a drawbridge. He stood at the end of the catwalk, looking down into the dark water, and wondered whether to jump.

"Ahoy, there!" called a voice, making Paul start. A short man, red in the face, emerged from beneath the trees on the island. He bustled down the path to the shore and disappeared from view behind the drawbridge.

"I'm Harvey Kinnear," called a muffled voice. "Stand back while I lower this thing."

Pau saw the drawbridge tilt towards him. It dropped the last few inches with a thud.

"You can come aboard, now," said Harvey, and Paul walked across to set foot on the island. They shook hands.

"Welcome to Blackwater. It's this way."

He led Paul up the path that he had already glimpsed. It wound through old pines, rising gently towards the island's summit. Steep, wooden steps climbed the final few metres, above a slab of exposed bedrock, to bring them to the door of the clubhouse. Paul's expectations of a rustic hut set amongst the trees were quickly dispelled as he looked up at the looming geometrical structure made of wood, metal, and glass.

Harvey saw Paul pause, gazing up at the clubhouse.

"Hah, yes," he said. "Some people thought the architecture too modern when it was first built fifty years ago, too *avant garde*. It has mellowed since then, but it still surprises first-timers."

The clubhouse stood on piles driven deep into the rocky summit of the island, and the building soared to a turret commanding the approaches from up- and down-river.

"The view from the crow's nest is magnificent," said Harvey, seeing Paul gazing up at the turret. He held open the door for Paul and waved him through. "Go straight ahead and up the stairs. They should be ready for you. I'll follow in a minute."

Paul mounted the stairs between dark-stained, wooden walls hung with pictures of past regattas and youthful members solemnly holding cups aloft. Pennants from rival clubs dangled from the ceiling. At the top of the stairs, he faced a wall. To his right and left were doors: one open, one closed. Over the open door hung a shingle with the word "Mess" burned into the wood, Paul presumed with a poker. He glimpsed a large, windowed room with wooden benches and tables.

The door to his left was firmly closed. A sign said "Board Meeting—Knock, damn you." Good to see someone has a sense of humour, thought Paul. He braced himself and rapped on the door.

✧   ✧   ✧

PAUL COUNTED SEVEN people in the room. They were sitting on chairs scattered about a long table, and looked up as Paul entered, curious about the newcomer. At the far end, he recognized Commodore Taggart St. James. Paul had met Taggart (retired, ex-navy) the previous year. They had volunteered together: a fund-raising effort for some charity. It had been a lucky meeting for Paul, since Taggart later agreed to sponsor his membership to the club.

"Ah, Paul!" said Taggart, jumping up and coming around the table to shake his hand. "Come in. Bang on time. Sit down, sit down."

A folding chair leaned against the wall beside the door. Paul carried to the foot of the table and sat down. He looked around. The wall on his left was mostly window, heavily shaded by the branches of a pine tree. To his right, against what Paul took to be a bar, were pushed several high stools. The bar was made from an old boat, its upturned hull burnished, he supposed, by years of rubbing elbows. Examples of various kinds of knot decorated the wood paneling around the bar. Brackets screwed to the wall supported shelves lined with glasses and assorted bottles.

"You're admiring our pub," said Taggart, seeing Paul's inspection. "It connects through to the Mess. We drink both behind and before the bar."

A dutiful chuckle went round the table.

"Introductions first," continued Taggart. "On my right, here, is Mike Collins, Vice-Commodore and Master at Arms." Collins stood to shake Paul's hand. He was an imposing man, well over six feet tall. He towered over Paul.

"Michael is also chair of our 'Triple-P' Committee," said Taggart.

"Triple-P?"

"Policy and Public Relations," said Collins. "I'm responsible for cleaning the cannon. Welcome aboard, Paul."

"What's the third 'P' stand for?" asked Paul.

Collins smiled and seemed about to answer. Harvey bustling into the room distracted him.

"Sorry," muttered Harvey, coming around the table to find a chair beside the Commodore.

"Harvey, our secretary, you have met already," continued Taggart. "Next to Harvey is our esteemed Harbour Master, Garvin Bowter. He keeps an eye on the boats and docks."

Bowter glanced at Paul and gave a curt nod.

"Beside Garvin is Tom Forget, our senior sailor, and law-of-the-sea incarnate. He'll keep your straight on the rules. On my left, Philly Delario is our Madam Purser; Maude Crabbe, who looks after food, drink, and merry-making; and lastly, Benedict Countryman, our youth representative. BC for short."

Benedict did not look a day under fifty.

"And that seat," said Taggart, pointing towards a dusty armchair in the corner, "was my predecessor's. Poor chap dropped dead only last month. Hit by his boom in a gibe during a club race. I like to think he is in a better place now, polishing club silverware."

"A passed-commodore now," added Collins, winking at Paul.

"That's enough, Michael," said Taggart firmly. "To business. Paul, you will have read through our membership document. If you think of it as a condominium agreement, the terms should be familiar. As you know, it assigns you a dock, and access to hook-ups provided by the club—power, drinking water, etcetera. You have purchased our dock and boat package, and our purser assures me that the deposit has cleared the bank. Thank you."

Paul had thought the price excessive, but such opportunities were rare.

"You have free run of the island and the clubhouse Mess, of course. Now I will just run through the covenants. Waste disposal only in the morning; quiet after eight p.m. in winter and ten p.m. in summer. You contribute to painting and repairing the docks and clubhouse. Participation in club regattas and races is mandatory, saving a mechanical failure on your boat. We raise the flag every morning. I expect all residents to be present. Questions?"

Paul wondered fleetingly which flag they would run up the pole. He would find out soon enough, he supposed. He shook his head.

"No. It all seems clear."

Taggart pushed the document towards Paul and proffered a pen.

"Your signature here. Then I sign, and Harvey witnesses. There. I think that's it. Harvey, if you would be so good?"

Harvey disappeared behind the bar. He soon re-emerged carrying a tray with eight shot glasses. Each was full to near the brim.

"From the club cask. Peaty, from the Highlands," announced Taggart. "Paul, welcome to the Blackwater Sailing Club. A toast to the King! No, don't stand. We toast King Willy sitting down."

Chapter 9

PAUL EMERGED FROM the clubhouse into bright sunlight with Garvin Bowter, the Harbour Master. Paul had a slight headache; he wasn't fond of peaty whiskey, and there had been several toasts before the meeting adjourned. The Commodore had insisted they were to launch Paul's new boat, and future home, as soon as possible.

"There are no tides, of course," said Garvin, "but the water level in the reservoir goes up and down at the whim of whoever controls the dam. The water level is up today, lapping the lower third of the boat ramp. That's plenty high enough to launch."

Paul had the uncomfortable feeling that the Harbour Master would be judging him on his nautical abilities. Those were definitely a question mark. It had been years since he had sailed, and then nothing bigger than a dinghy.

Together, they walked across the catwalk to the mainland shore and up *chemin* Blackwater to the fenced enclosure that belonged to the club. Bowter un-padlocked the gate, while Paul started his vehicle and drove in. He stopped inside the enclosure, beside the shrouded boat trailer he had noticed before.

"Our past-commodore was an expert at launching boats," said Garvin. "He could back a trailer straight as a die. Pity he dropped dead. We don't get much practice now that the boats stay in the water all year. Back when the river iced over, we had to haul out by October, tarp them up for winter, and launch again in the spring. You can thank global warming for that. Nobody lived in their boats back then, of course."

"Will you be backing the boat down for me?" asked Paul.

"Huh? No. Stiff neck. You'll have to do it yourself."

Bowter dragged the covers from the bow to reveal the red hull of Paul's new home.

"There she is, a twenty-two footer. Old model, but sound design," he said.

A short ladder lay on the ground beside the trailer. Paul placed it against the boat and climbed up to peer into the small cockpit. The hatch to the cabin was closed. He wouldn't be able to lift it until he could shift the mast—it lay flat across the hatch and was firmly secured. Paul descended the ladder, feeling apprehensive. This was downsizing with a vengeance. Still, he was committed, and no government could foist a lodger on him here.

"You back the trailer straight down the lane, and then turn down the ramp into the water," said Bowter. "Last new member couldn't do it. Bloody disaster."

Back on the ground, Paul returned to his SUV. With Bowter giving him conflicting hand gestures, Paul reversed slowly to align the hitch. He got out and wound down the handle on the trailer neck, dropping the cup onto the hitching ball. It settled with a satisfying clunk. It looked solid, he thought. But he attached the chains, too, just in case.

Bowter's shouted instructions didn't make backing the heavy boat trailer down the lane to the boat ramp any easier. Correct alignment was critical for the final few feet, and it took Paul several tries before he satisfied the Harbour Master. Finally, the boat and trailer entered the water. Paul felt the rear wheels of his truck drop over the concrete lip at the bottom of the ramp.

"She draws a metre of water," called Bowter. "You'll have to back deeper."

The SUV's exhaust was bubbling below the surface of the water by the time Paul's boat broke free of the suction and started floating. The trailer was still tethered by a large strap. Paul pulled hard on the brake, got out of the cab, and climbed onto the back of the truck. He reached across the gap between the truck and the trailer to release the strap winch.

"It seems to be stuck," said Paul.

"Increase the tension," advised Bowter.

Paul pushed hard against the winch handle, freeing the latch.

"Now unclip the strap from the boat and push her off."

Paul had already reached across to unclip. He was pushing hard. The boat stubbornly refused to float free of the trailer.

"I'd say she's hung up," said Bowter. "Looks like you will have to get your feet wet. I'll walk along the catwalk to catch her."

Paul waded into the water and wedged himself between the trailer post and the bow of the boat for greater purchase. He was beginning to feel that he might have managed all of this more easily without the Harbour Master's help.

Taking a deep breath, Paul heaved the boat free. It glided towards the catwalk, where Bowter waited.

"She seems to float, at least," said Bowter, catching the boat. His tone suggested slight disappointment.

Paul waded ashore and up the launching ramp.

"Make sure you lock the gate when you drive the trailer back to the compound," Bowter called across the water. "Come straight back—I'll tow her round to your dock. The boat launch here is on the west side of the catwalk, but the moorings are on the other side. Bloody nuisance, really."

Under the Harbour Master's disdainful gaze, and despite using the lowest gear, Paul spun his rear wheels on loose gravel as he pulled the dripping trailer from the water. He drove slowly back up the hill. The return journey was much easier, but he swore to himself that he wouldn't volunteer to reverse any other boats down the wretchedly narrow lane. Once parked in the enclosure, he unhitched the trailer and pushed it under the trees to join its colleagues in the graveyard.

Paul removed his few possessions from the vehicle: two roller suitcases and a backpack stuffed with a sleeping bag. He cursed himself for forgetting to unload while down at the ramp. He shrugged on his backpack, and dragged the suitcases over the gravel to the gate. He re-attached the padlock, and went down the lane to the club entrance—a trip which was becoming increasingly familiar—to find the gate shut.

Paul could see Bowter out in the bay, at the helm of an aluminium skiff. Its stern sat low in the water, under the weight of an overlarge outboard. Bowter was manoeuvring the skiff awkwardly towards the catwalk, just ahead of Paul's new boat.

The gate to the club suddenly opened. Paul recognized Maude Crabbe from the Board meeting.

"We keep the gate shut," she said. "They try to slip in, you know."

Paul followed Maude along the catwalk, wondering who "they" might be. Coming abreast of his new boat, he noticed faded lettering on the bow. He could just make out the boat's name: the *Spindrift*. Well, that wasn't too bad. He clambered aboard and edged forward along the side of the cabin.

"Catch this," called Garvin, throwing Paul a tow rope. "Maudie can push you off."

Paul crouched on the bow of the *Spindrift*, holding the tow rope as the Bowter opened the throttle on the skiff. The two craft moved away from the catwalk and out into the west bay.

"Damn it, couldn't he wait till I tied this off?" thought Paul. After struggling with the rope for a few seconds, he managed a makeshift hitch to a stanchion.

Bowter towed Paul in a broad curve around the island. As the boats turned, they became exposed to the north wind blowing down the reservoir. Wavelets slapped against the hull.

For the first time, Paul got a view of the side of Blackwater invisible from the western shore. A modest cliff rose sheer from the water to a small plateau, crowned by tall pines, near the island's summit. The geometric planes of the clubhouse roof were just visible from this side. Paul thought he could see a faint path leading from the clubhouse down to the water. Bowter waved towards a rocky point projecting from the island.

"Reef extends offshore," he shouted. "You want to stay clear!"

He steered them around an orange buoy marking the hazard. Now, they headed directly into the wind and the *Spindrift*'s bow twitched as the tow rope slackened then grew taut in the bucking waves. To Paul's right—well, at two o'clock; no, off the starboard bow—he could see another low promontory, on which rose a short, wooden tower painted in blue and white checks. Before it, there was a viewing platform, and a short mast from which flew wisps of coloured pennants.

"Lighthouse!" cried Garvin, his voice snatched away by the wind.

After another minute, Paul heard the skiff's outboard motor throttle back. The *Spindrift*'s motion eased as they entered the calm water in the lee of the island. They were entering the harbour, having sailed almost a full circle around the island to approach the catwalk from the side opposite the boat launch.

"You're number twelve, beside *Groaning Anne*," called the Harbour Master. "I'll let you glide in. You'd better be ready to jump onto the dock to catch your boat." Bowter untied the tow rope and tossed it to Paul.

"Meet the rest of us this evening for the barbecue. Six o'clock, and bring a bottle," he called, before shearing away.

Paul was unsure whether the "Anne" Bowter had referred to was the boat or the person pulling aside its floral cockpit cover to peer at the intruder. Paul knew that berths eleven and twelve shared a finger dock, one of the short, lateral extensions from the catwalk where boats tied up. This finger dock seemed crowded with clay statues. About two feet tall, they reminded Paul of garden gnomes. Some had been fired, and reddish; others were still the grey of the unfired clay. As the *Spindrift* drifted in, Paul had difficulty finding a foothold where he wouldn't knock any into the water.

"This is a private dock, damn it. But, if you must tie up, mind the Chinese army."

He recognized the female voice coming from within the cabin of the *Groaning Anne* as the same one that had admonished him earlier for banging the gate. The owner of the voice emerged from her boat's cabin. She held out a bronzed hand to Paul, who was standing gingerly on the dock amidst the statues.

"Hi. I'm Margret Mankie and you must be Paul Loess. It's good to have a new boy. We'll be dock buddies. The last one died, you know. Cup of tea? I have the kettle on the ring."

Paul realized he was thirsty and nodded.

"Come aboard, then," said Margret.

Except for packets of dried soup and energy bars, Paul had packed little food. For a first supper on the boat he had thought to run into the mini-mart in Belltown for fish, but now he realized that once in the club and on his boat, he was little inclined to walk back up the lane to the parking compound. He would have to extract his vehicle, then face interrogation at the gate again on his return. He assumed he would soon get the hang of it, but for now he would stay on the island.

Margret poured a mug of tea and passed it to Paul. The mug commemorated a regatta triumph of the distant past.

"Mankie?" asked Paul. "That's an unusual name."

"Oh, that's from my husband's family. They anglicized the name after they immigrated. It used to have a lot more 'z's."

"Husband?"

"We drifted apart. He wasn't much of a sailor."

Paul felt he was venturing into a sensitive area. He picked up the venerable, tannin-stained teapot to change the subject.

"My grandmother's," she said, noticing. "One of the few things I have left. Apart from my name, of course; she was a Margret as well. Just don't call me Maggie, okay?"

Paul sat hunched in the cockpit with Margret sipping tea—black, no milk or sugar offered. The woman before him was in her late fifties, perhaps a little older than himself. She cut her white hair short. It framed a face creased, he assumed, by weather and self-sufficiency. Her brows furrowed with concern for a statue: he had toppled one by accident, trying to secure the *Spindrift*.

"Why all these statues?" asked Paul.

"They're souvenirs of my former lovers: clay statues to join me when I'm buried. That's why I call them my Chinese Army."

"It must be a difficult hobby to have, living on a boat," Paul suggested, after a pause.

"I converted an old shed on the island into a workshop. Once in a while, I fire up the kiln. These guys will go in the fire soon, but I'll move them over to my side in the meantime. They do tend to take over."

"Are the faces those of actual people? They all look different."

Margret's features hardened, and she tipped the dregs of her tea overboard.

"Bastards, mostly." She said it so quietly Paul barely heard her.

She nodded towards Paul's new home on the other side of finger dock.

"She's a fast boat. Randolf certainly knew how to get the best out of her. They should have given her a good clean-out after he passed away, but you never know."

"Well, er, thanks for the tea. I should really get back to *Spindrift*. I have to unpack and settle in."

"Let me know if you need to redecorate. I have clay statues to spare." Margret laughed and turned away from Paul. She disappeared into her cabin.

Paul clambered out of the *Groaning Anne*, stepped gingerly through the statues to his own side of the dock, and onto the *Spindrift*. He untied the mast and heaved it to one side. Now, he could push back the hatch and look down into the dark interior of the cabin. Turning to descend the short companionway backwards, he was struck by the musty smell. It seemed the space that hadn't been aired for weeks.

Alone, finally, he could take stock of his new home. Immediately to his right was the galley, comprising two gas rings and a sink. An L-shaped bench, with a removable table, was to his left. Screwed to the bulkhead was a modest flatscreen above recessed shelving. A locking strip secured a row of books along a shelf. His glance revealed *Inland Sailing*, *Fifteen-Minute Meals*, and several dog-eared paperbacks, including a box set of the spy novels of John Le Carré.

A curtain divided the cabin into spaces for living and sleeping. There were two narrow bunks in the sleeping area, on each side of the hull. The mattresses on the bunks fitted snuggly to the curves of the boat. Upholstered in orange and black plaid, they were shabby and emanated a disagreeable smell. Paul prodded one of them: memory foam gone senile, he decided. He opened the storage lockers over the bunks. They were stuffed with sails, with little space left over to store clothing. Reaching under a bunk, he pulled out a portable toilet.

In sum, thought Paul, this was a cabin on par with that of an eighteenth-century sailing ship. If good enough for Captain Cook, then it should be good enough for a single man whose library had contracted to a digital tablet.

Paul turned around awkwardly in the confined space, and eased himself onto the bench in the living area. On a plasticized card taped to the table beside him he read the words WELCOME LONG-TERM RENTERS. There followed a list of instructions: he was required to place crockery and utensils in the racks provided when not in use, to secure all lockers, and to adjust the solar panels daily. (Paul had already noticed these, hanging along the south side of the boat.) Bold lettering at the bottom of the list required that boats be checked for seaworthiness prior to leaving the dock. He supposed Garvin Bowter would do the inspection. Great.

The floor of the cabin was smooth fibreglass, except where a square grate covered what he supposed was a drain. Paul bent and lifted the corner of the grate, revealing a space between the cabin floor and the keel of the boat. If there were any leaks in the hull, this is where water would accumulate. To his relief, it seemed bone dry. Reaching into the hole, he felt something wedged to one side. He lifted out a dusty bottle of red wine. The price sticker still attached suggested cheap plonk.

"Cheers, Randolf," he muttered.

"Paul Loess, are you decent?" called a voice, disturbingly close by. Paul poked his head through the hatch, to see his neighbour, Margret. She was standing on the finger dock between their two boats, wearing a terry-towel robe.

"Going for a swim," she said. "You might want to order your supper if you want it to arrive before six p.m. I use Wheelimeats, 819-WEDO-FOOD. They deliver here; most of the other companies don't."

Paul thanked her for the advice. Frankly, he hadn't thought about a meal later. He had vaguely assumed he'd have a packet of noodles. Still, perhaps he should order. A pizza might complement the dusty wine.

He made the call. The order clerk at Wheelimeats thought it

would take half an hour, insisting that Paul be at the gate to receive his pizza.

"The sailing club?" said the clerk. "It's like delivering to Fort Knox."

Chapter 10

J UST BEFORE SIX, Paul found a small group clustered at the entrance gate to the club, waiting for deliveries. Margret was already there. Two men he hadn't met turned to greet him.

"Paul Loess, is it?" one asked. "We heard you were coming. Joe Tasker and Dent Hall. We're in *Olivier's Dream*, up at the far end of the dock."

They shook hands, and a desultory conversation ensued: the American invasion; the pathetic response of the Republican government in Quebec; the need for reunion with Canada; the temperature of the water, which was high for the time of year, what with the bloody weeds everywhere.

They heard the Wheelimeats bicycle brake on the loose gravel at the bottom of the hill, then steps as the rider dismounted and walked across the bridge to rap on the gate.

"Pizza, a poutine—one special, one vegetarian, and a box of wings," called a youthful voice. Tasker bent down and opened a small hatch at the bottom of the gate.

"Push them through here," he said to the boy.

"The special is for me," said Tasker, picking up the four cardboard boxes and reading the labels. "The vegetarian is for you, Margret, and Dent is the chicken. That leaves you, Loess: pizza, medium pepperoni and mushroom."

They had all ordered and paid online, but the group looked to Paul to pull out a note sufficient for a tip. He passed it back through the slot. They heard "*Merci et bon appétit*" followed less distinctly by "fuckwits" as the electric bike retreated up *chemin*

Blackwater.

The four walked slowly back from the gate towards the island, carrying their meals. Paul paused by the *Spindrift*.

"I'll catch you up," he said to Margret.

Paul collected the bottle of wine from the cabin and hurried along the catwalk after the others. He crossed the drawbridge onto the island, and climbed the path that led up the hill beneath the trees. Close to the clubhouse, Paul noticed a clearing to one side of the path where someone had brushed a circle free of pine needles. Standing in the middle was an eight-foot post. The sun was already going down, and the post cast a long shadow.

Margret was waiting for Paul at the entrance to the clubhouse. She led him up the stairs, through the Mess and back outside onto a large deck. People were already crowded around the three long picnic tables, and Paul was relieved when Margret suggested he join her for the meal.

"Dock buddies eat together," she said, while scanning the deck for free places at the picnic tables. While they were hesitating, Maude Crabbe came over to them.

"Hey, everybody," she called, getting the diners' attention. "New resident, name of Paul Loess, taking on Randolf's *Spindrift*."

Only a few looked up. A woman carrying a laden plate was returning from the barbecue. She stopped dead when she saw Paul and Margret blocking her path. Paul saw her glance left and right seeking an escape, but the narrow space between the picnic tables impeded evasive manoeuvres. He saw her hesitate, and then continue towards them.

"Olga Wilk, in *Zdrowie*. Dock number three. Welcome," she said.

"I'm Paul. Is that Milk like the drink?"

"Pronounced "v". Wilk.

"Sorry, I—"

Olga edged past, and sat down heavily in the last place at the table. She muttered something to her neighbour that Paul couldn't catch.

A couple sitting at the second picnic table raised their glasses to the newcomer. Paul gave a small bow.

"Larry Soy and Tickles Dubois," whispered Margret. "And the beard beside them is Didier Delahaye from the catamaran. He's French. Shares the boat with Sebastian Gann. Each to his own hull, I suppose. I'd rather not sit with them …"

"Anyway," said Maude, after waiting for a few more seconds. "I'm sure you will get to know us all soon enough." She looked across to the barbecue. "Must go, I think my steak is ready."

Paul and Margret watched Maude weave between the tables towards the barbecue.

"Nice welcome. Never mind, Paul. Let's sit there," said Margret, pointing to the table furthest from the barbecue. She led Paul purposefully between the diners.

"You have finished, haven't you, Lowder? Lowder Pritcher, Paul Loess."

"Still adopting strays, eh, Margret?" said Pritcher.

"Leave it off, Lowder. And remember to wash up this time."

"What's your story, Paul?" called a new voice. "Fleeing the Republic?'"

Paul turned to see who spoke. He recognized Tom Forget from his membership interview. Old Tom was wearing a flamboyant shirt, Bermuda shorts, and black dress shoes. He was sitting beside Collins, whose size and green, camouflage shirt made for a marked contrast.

"You don't have to answer," Collins intervened before Paul could reply. "Old Tom likes to wind up newcomers. We all have our private reasons for being here."

The buzz of conversation around them grew. Paul counted

over twenty diners, presumably most of the resident members. A cluster around the barbecue at the edge of the deck jockeyed to get their food on the grills.

Paul perched on the end of a bench, facing Margret across the picnic table. They opened their boxes.

"Are you going to serve that wine, then?" asked Margret. She pulled out a couple of plastic glasses and a corkscrew from a bag she had placed on the floor.

"Of course, if you are feeling brave." Paul pulled the cork and poured for Margret to taste.

"Is this really from the bilges of *Spindrift*? It pairs nicely with the Wheelimeats."

"I'll try and get something decent for next time," said Paul.

"You'll have to wait until the club organizes the next wine run. Put your order in to Maude."

Paul finished his pizza and pushed away the empty box. He swallowed the wine that remained in his glass. He grimaced.

"I'm curious about the post I passed coming up to the club-house. It looked sinister, like a standing stone."

"Oh, that," she replied. "It's called the 'punishment pole.' Years ago, we used to haze new members. Inappropriate today, I hear. It used to have a rubber ball dangling from a rope attached to the top. We would put you against the post, hands behind your back, and people would take turns to hit the ball as hard as they could. You had to stay there until the rope wound tight around your neck, and the ball hit the pole."

Paul had a flash of a disembodied head whirling around the pole, trying to reconnect with its body.

"Sounds grim. What happened if you couldn't take it?"

"They would make you walk the plank over by big rock. There's a twenty-foot drop to the water. They took the diving board away after some idiot cracked his skull, and that was one stupid tradition abandoned."

The Commodore was passing their table on his way to throw more meat on the barbecue. He overheard Margret's comment and scowled.

"Traditions, Paul," said Taggart, "are what make this club. Best remember that."

Chapter 11

"DO YOU WANT help with that erection?"

"What?"

Joe Tasker and Dent Hall were standing at the end of the finger dock. Joe pointed to the mast, still lying along the length Paul's boat, supported on crutches fore and aft.

"Help to get it up, I mean," said Tasker.

"Three is ideal," added Hall, nudging his friend. "You try to get it in the slot, while Joe and I pull it upright. Margret can tail on the safety rope.

Paul had been wondering how to raise the *Spindrift*'s mast. That was another thing that the Harbour Master had failed to mention.

"Well, yes. Thank you. If you can help right now, that would be great."

Margret emerged from the *Groaning Anne*.

"You'd best untangle all those lines, Paul. You only want to do this once. The worst is when you get the mast up and see something is twisted."

Five minutes later, they were all set. Tasker and Paul stood in the cockpit. They lifted and heaved the mast backwards until more than half of its length projected over the stern.

"Get the damn thing slotted in, Loess." Tasker was straining under the weight.

The base of the mast hovered over the metal plate to which it attached. Paul pushed down hard. At the same time, Dent Hall cried "heave", and he and Margret pulled the top of the mast towards them. It rose to a forty-five degree angle. The boat wobbled and the tip of the mast swayed menacingly. Tasker pushed; Hall and Margret pulled, while Paul desperately tried to engage the hook at the base of the mast with the receiving slot.

"There," he said, as it slid home.

Tasker gave a grunt of relief as the others pulled the mast vertical. Paul quickly attached the forestay and tightened the shrouds. The mast was stable, held upright by a pyramid of wire cables running to its tip: fore and aft, port and starboard. The *Spindrift* looked like a real sailing boat.

"Beer, I think, Loess," said Tasker.

Margret was standing on the dock staring at the top of the mast.

"What do call the whirly thing, Joe?" she asked. "The windvane that goes on the top of the mast."

Hall, who had been poking his nose into the *Spindrift*'s cabin, suddenly emerged, triumphantly holding the spindly burgee above his head. "Found it!" he called.

"It's called a 'fuck me'," said Tasker.

Chapter 12

"I T'LL BE A good evening for it," said Margret, out of the blue.

Paul had been trying to rub an unsightly green streak from the hull of his boat, at the waterline where algae had taken hold. Margret, having moved her statues to the shed on the island, was brushing fragments of clay from the dock. He guessed "it" had something to do with her pottery, but Margret explained she meant it was time to dispose of the past-commodore, recently deceased.

"It's honoring the club tradition," she said. "It's a bore, really, because we have to cart the body from the big freezer in the club kitchen down to the point. The boys will use the wheelbarrow, I suppose."

"Well, I don't have anything else on," said Paul, hesitantly. He was having reservations about the club he had been so eager to join.

⋄ ⋄ ⋄

A FEW MINUTES after sunset, Paul and Margret joined a subdued group gathered on the point below the lighthouse. There was silence but for the gurgling outboard of the club's aluminium skiff, as it idled just offshore. Fireworks were being let off far downriver—star shells, their silent detonations illuminating a distant front.

Joe Tasker was on his knees beside the water, holding the

gunwale of the *Diogenes*, the old boat that the past-commodore had sailed for the past twenty years. Volunteers had stripped the boat of anything of value, such as cleats and cordage. They had removed the mast. In its place was a bundle, tied to the roof of the cabin.

"Is that…?" whispered Paul to Margret.

"Quiet!"

"Ready?" they heard Taggart call. He was sitting in the aluminium skiff with Mike Collins. Barely waiting for Tasker's reply, the Commodore shifted the motor into forward and opened the throttle. The skiff moved away from the point towards the middle of the river, towing the *Diogenes*.

"Mike's placed charges in the hull below the waterline," whispered Margret to Paul.

"What? Say again?"

"Shsh."

The skiff dropped anchor. The group on the point watched Taggart and Collins haul in the tow rope, pulling the *Diogenes* beside them. Collins lifted a plastic gas container and balanced it on the side of the old boat. He clambered onto the *Diogenes*, and splashed the contents over the shrouded form on the cabin roof. Done, he slid back into the skiff and pushed, letting the slow current tug the old boat away.

"Ready, on shore?" Paul heard Taggart call.

Paul saw Collins lift his arm and point towards the *Diogenes*. He held what looked to Paul like a pistol. There was a bang, and a flare arched across the intervening water and lodged in the canvas shroud. It caught light with a roar, and the flames twisted into the sky. Even fifty metres away, Paul felt the heat on his face as he watched the cremation. After a few minutes, the burning corpse lurched into a sitting position as its sinews tightened, as if making a last salute before crumbling to ash.

The witnesses at the point waited as the fire died. After a few minutes, Taggart and Collins cast loose the *Diogenes*, and returned to the point. They climbed ashore. Collins took out a smart phone.

"Wait for it," he said, and pushed a button on the phone.

Muffled explosions came from below the waterline of the old boat, now a dark shadow on the water in the deepening dusk. The *Diogenes*, carrying the charred remains of the past-commodore, foundered as it drifted downstream in the slow current, sinking lower and lower in the water. It slipped beneath the surface with a hiss as the river flooded in and extinguished its glowing embers. Moonlight danced on the expanding rings of ripples.

It was a peculiar tradition of the club's to dispose of their retired leaders Viking fashion. The ashes of several had long settled on the bed of the reservoir, and the past-commodore would soon join them.

Paul felt relieved. The Blackwater community had allowed him to witness this, one of their most intimate rites.

Chapter 13

EACH CLUB MEMBER had weekly duties. The least popular was to carry the bags of accumulated compost from the docks to the pit on the far side of the island. The bags were often overfilled, their bottoms damp with some nameless liquid, and they had a tendency to split at the last moment. Paul had just completed this chore for the third consecutive week. He hoped this display of community spirit would earn him some respect in the Mess. He turned onto the path leading up to the clubhouse and found himself following Mike Collins. Paul was about twenty metres behind, and Collins had not noticed him. The man seemed preoccupied, and Paul hung back.

Collins took the steps to the clubhouse door two at a time, but hesitated in the entry hall. Then he turned right, out of Paul's view, into the short corridor leading to the kitchen. Paul followed to recover his mug, which he had left on the draining board the evening before. He'd assumed Collins would be on a similar mission, but to his surprise, the kitchen was empty. There was no sign of him.

Puzzled by this disappearance, Paul retraced his own steps, paying more attention to his surroundings. Perhaps there was some other door or exit he hadn't noticed before? To his left, ranged along the corridor, were glass-fronted cabinets housing the many trophies and awards the club had accumulated over the years. Light came from a row of windows: there were no dark corners, and, evidently, no vice-commodore.

Paul scanned the contents of the cabinets. There were silver cups given to the winners of regattas, and innumerable plaques naming the winners of lesser club competitions. Paul read a list of names of past officers of the club engraved on a fine, silver tray: there seemed to be a Collins, in various club capacities, in each generation.

On a shelf of its own rested a highly polished rifle, its wooden stock clipped to a varnished backboard, its breech bolt removed. It was, Paul read, awarded for "Special Services to Blackwater." Names and dates inscribed on a brass plate underneath went back seventy years, almost to the birth of the club.

Paul was examining a mounted fish in the last cabinet before the kitchen. It was in a poor state of preservation, and the label had fallen off. He jumped when Mike Collins materialized silently beside him.

"A fascinating collection," Collins said quietly. "Old Tom caught that fish many moons ago. The Commodore awards it to the person voted guilty of the worst sailing blunder of the season."

"I'll try my best not to win it," said Paul.

"You've been with us some weeks now. How are you settling in?"

"Oh, no regrets. It's just all the security. It makes trips off-island very difficult."

"A necessity these days," replied Collins. "As you know yourself, the influx of migrants has put a lot of pressure on all of us. The authorities are always looking for some excuse to move us off the island. Frankly, they would rather we weren't here at all. It's a sad state of affairs."

Collins turned to stare closely at Paul, then punched him gently on the shoulder.

"Never you mind," he said, "they haven't had the final word yet."

Chapter 14

FLORETTE HENDERSON WAS the only land-sider allowed to visit the Blackwater Sailing Club regularly. She had a long-standing arrangement to collect the club mail from the post office in Belltown and deliver it to the residents, along with newspapers and various magazine subscriptions. After the club restricted island access to residential members only, and despite the enhanced security measures that entailed, she'd clung tenaciously to this role. She made herself indispensable by baking pastries for Blackwater. The Commodore was partial to the treats. Every Friday, first thing, Florette filled a large box with the leftovers of her week's baking, and then had her husband Cecil drive her to the bottom of *chemin* Glen Rourke. From there, she would walk down the lane to the club.

She was careful to always arrive at the gate at exactly the time specified by Monsieur Kinnear, whom she now saw approaching. He always had such a busy air on these early mornings. Today, his clipboard was sure to list the important tasks to achieve by noon. Opening the gate for Florette was clearly not one of them. His fussiness amused her, but she disliked his unpleasant habit of moistening his lips before speaking.

"I trust the pastries are fresh, Mrs. Henderson," said Harvey. "You've brought some of those chocolate-dipped *beignets*? They're the Commodore's favourite."

Florette followed Harvey through the gate, and along the catwalk towards the club. For the hundredth time, the obsessive-ly varnished wood of Harvey's boat caught her eye. To Florette, such meticulous attention to paint spoke volumes.

Florette felt she knew more about the residents of the island than anyone else. In the Mess, they sought after her for news of the outside world, as much as for her pastries. They were, if truth be told, somewhat stale by Saturday. She could ooze motherly concern on demand, take an interest in the various liaisons and ruptures, temporary or more permanent, resulting from close proximity and cramped accommodations. It was not a voyeuristic interest for her, of course, but genuine concern that the right individuals connect with each other.

It was, for instance, no surprise for Florette to observe a growing fondness between Margret Mankie and Paul Loess. Florette had been present, slowly tidying behind the bar, when Margret was explaining to Paul the significance of the embroidered tapestry hanging on the wall of the Mess. About five times as tall as it was wide, it showed the settlements from Belltown in the south to Newbridge in the north before they filled the Noire reservoir. Red and green thread traced the original field boundaries around the farms; the old course of the river was in blue, the roads in black. Even the mill complex—long ago dismantled—appeared at the southern extremity, its chimneys belching clouds of white wool.

"My grandmother stitched that tapestry," she overheard Margret say. "She began after moving with her father to a new place over in Happy Valley, near Belltown. It's a historical document. The names of all the farmers in the valley are spelled out in that spindly, black thread."

Margret had pointed to the southern part of the map.

"… and that was my great-grandparent's farm—the old Pardle place. Drowned now, of course."

"Pardle?" Paul had asked.

"Mankie is my married name. Pardle was my grandmother's maiden name. I guess you could say that I'm the fourth generation of Pardles in the valley."

Florette was still listening from behind the bar. Her own family, on Mother's side, had settled in the valley at much the same time as the Pardles. She'd had heard the stories: how Margret's great uncle Sean had drowned; how Margret's great-grandfather had lived on the farm with Margret's grandmother, who was a young girl at the time; and how it weren't right for a young girl to grow up with just a father. Margret's great-grandmother had been a Polish girl from Madawaska-way, who died of a fever.

"And when Margret was a teenager…Well!" Florette's mother had said with a knowing look.

Oh yes, Florette knew quite enough about Margret and her hidden depths. Take those clay statues that littered her dock. A new one appeared from time to time, and Florette was sure several had the likeness of men from the club. Monsieur Collins was there, plain as day. Margret would be lying with this new one soon enough. Then, after a few weeks, there would be another statue on the dock, and the poor fool would be taking a keen interest in varnishing the wood on his boat, or out sailing all hours.

Young Margret, who had left Belltown and gone to Montreal to study at that big Anglophone CEGEP. She stayed to go to university, studying something arty. Well, she was back here now. So what did all that gadding about get her? Older, but no wiser.

❖   ❖   ❖

BEING ROOTLESS HIMSELF, having blown all around the country with his military parents, Margret's history intrigued Paul. Her description of the people who lived in the valley before the dam fascinated him. When she had told him about her great-grandfather, it surprised him to learn that the original settlers were mostly Irish immigrants. Some, she said, even spoke Gaelic, before the strap stilled that tongue in the schoolyards. Montreal immigration officers labelled them "English", and sent them west towards rumours of new land, and a fresh start.

So, O'Rourkes, O'Briens and O'Pardles had settled the valley, plus a few McCluskeys and Hendersons, McGuires and Collinses. They had piled stones at the ends of fields, cleared land for the plough and planted potatoes. They cut back the forest to the iron-hard hills. Many of the Irish dropped the "O" from their family name after the first generation.

"To balance out the entries in the phone book," Margret told Paul.

✧   ✧   ✧

ALPHABETICAL ARRANGEMENT WAS on the mind of Florette the following Friday, as she sorted through the pile of letters on her kitchen table. That morning, she had collected the week's mail from the Blackwater Sailing Club's mailbox in Belltown. Box 366 was in the middle of the post office foyer, at eye level, in a wall of postal boxes. Florette shivered with delicious anticipation each time she turned the key in the small door, watched, she felt, by the blank faces of all the other boxes, each hiding its secrets. Seldom did she find the box empty; usually, it was crammed with mail. And, most weeks, among those letters she would find something to tickle her curiosity.

She kept the treasured key to Box 366 on a chain around her neck. Monsieur Kinnear had impressed on her that its loss would have grave consequences. Every Friday before lunch, she would walk the long mile to the post office and chat with whichever lady was behind the counter. She would buy stamps, should she have mail of her own to send, then put the bundle of club mail in her small shopping trolley and return home. Today, there hadn't seemed to be anything out of the ordinary. The largest item had been a cardboard box, which she had retrieved from the special, larger box for parcels. It contained twelve balls of wool, according to the customs declaration.

"That'll be for Old Tom's socks," thought Florette dismissively.

From the mail squeezed into the box she discarded the fliers and advertising material. That left twenty-odd letters addressed to residents of the island. Several rolled magazines—weeklies or monthlies—were regular deliveries. Florette recognized the bright cover of one that investigated the lives of celebrities in their multiple homes. She would just have a peek at that later. Nice Monsieur Hall would never notice.

The letters neatly in alphabetical order, she settled in to take a more careful look. A card from Monsieur Bowter's mother was on top. She never missed his birthday. The two brown envelopes addressed to the Blackwater Sailing Club looked official: queries from the tax authorities, no doubt. A plain envelope addressed to "Mr. Michael Collins" was next. There was no return address, and no indication of origin on the envelope. Florette marked it for special attention. She slipped a rubber band over the rest of the bundle of mail and placed it to one side.

Florette pulled out a ledger. Empowered by her responsibility, she had always felt that she should be methodical in her role as guardian of the club mail. She ran her finger down the list of residents, ticking a box for those who were receiving a letter; leaving a blank for those who weren't. After a few minutes, she had tallied the week's post. When Cecil got back from curling, he would enter the numbers into a computer spreadsheet. The graphical output—which they had designed together—revealed the pattern of correspondence for each club member, with each assigned a different colour. This delighted Florette. Her joy increased as the graphs grew with the week's new entries. It gave her a wonderful feeling to be privy to such a store of intimate knowledge. She had heard of big data, and this was her small contribution.

The Collins letter, now. She looked carefully at the envelope. It should be possible with her thinnest kitchen knife, warmed on the stove to soften the glue, to loosen the end of the envelope and extract the contents. For such purposes, she kept surgical gloves in a kitchen drawer. These she now pulled on. The knife trick seldom failed her. She carefully removed the single folded sheet and spread it on the table, only just avoiding a smear of jam left over from breakfast.

"Comrade," began the letter. "Confirm delivery of two more boxes, fifteenth of this month. Usual time and place." There was no signature, merely the letter "D."

The letter mystified Florette. This was not the usual club correspondence. She was familiar with the fussy missives from Monsieur Bowter's mother; the special offers for rubber underwear and other nautical devices; the recriminatory notes from an ex-partner of Monsieur Taggart's, whom he had dumped for a sailboat; the long accounts of hiking pilgrimages from Monsieur Kinnear's athletic sister, which Florette found interesting, herself having once attempted a short section of the *Compostela*. The monthly postcard addressed to Fraulein Wilk often caught her eye—usually of lakes and mountains, from somewhere in the Alps perhaps?—but the language defeated her.

The note from "D" sparked Florette's imagination. Monsieur Collins had always been an enigma to her. She admired him. He cut a handsome figure, and he certainly ruled Blackwater behind the scenes, but she had been unsuccessful in finding chinks in his genial exterior—his polished, soft armour. It left her frustrated and uneasy; he was one of those smooth talkers. One to watch. And now there was this suspicious letter. Was he a communist, perhaps? Comrade Collins?

Florette folded the letter and carefully put it back in the envelope. It would go with the rest of the mail bundle to the club the following morning.

Later that afternoon, Florette was preparing tea for Cecil—the reheated remains of yesterday's shawarma from that new place in the village—when the doorbell rang. Fussy, her white terrier, was yapping fit to bust as Florette went to see who might be calling at this inconvenient time. Jehovah's were always a risk. But their ring was usually more tentative, fatigued after a long, dispiriting round of the neighbourhood.

Florette opened the door to find the expected pair of young men, both wearing dark raincoats grey jackets—Jehovah's, definitely. She was preparing her answer in rapid French, which was often enough to dissuade them. Then the taller of the two men spoke. He was holding out some kind of identity badge.

"*Bonjour, Madame.* My name is Captain-Agent Réjean Pénard of the *Garde républicaine*. This is Agent Gruaut. May we come in?"

Mon Dieu, les GRs—Republican Guards. Two of them. Florette pushed the growling Fussy into the parlour with Cecil, who was sitting in the big armchair engrossed with his iPad. She shut the door.

"*Entrez, entrez, messieurs.*" She ushered the visitors into the kitchen, where the lingering smell of recent baking welcomed the officers. They stood awkwardly around the kitchen table.

Florette saw Captain Pénard glance around the room.

"*Charmantes,*" he said, admiring the collection of four souvenir plates hanging on the kitchen wall. Pénard leaned closer: one was obviously *le Château* in Quebec City, another of *le Rocher Percé* at sunset, and a third showed a street scene with a church.

"That's in Trois-Rivières, *la cathédrale.* Do you like it?"

Florette was proud of the purchase; at fifty *piastres*, it had been a real bargain at the Bring and Buy.

The Agent nodded, examining the last plate, a panorama of Niagara Falls. He seemed less than impressed.

"Patriotic views are best, *Madame*."

"Er. Please sit," said Florette. "Perhaps a coffee, *messieurs*? A pastry?"

"*Merci, Madame*," said Pénard, taking a chair at the kitchen table. Gruaut remained standing. He was gazing through a window at the Hendersons' yard: a line of washing, wood stacked against the back fence.

"*Très bon*," said Pénard, after taking a large bite. "To business, *Madame*. Agent Gruaut and I are here to advise you we are reviewing your status on the *Régistre des habitants*."

Florette's heart gave that extra jump she had grown to expect when faced with a sudden shock. She had heard of the "People's List" that the new Republic instituted soon after winning independence. The list defined the haves and have-nots, based on data drawn from genealogy websites. *Les vrais et les autres.* But that was all for other people, for foreigners, wasn't it?

"You are Two-A," continued Pénard. "You can thank your mother's family for that."

Florette's mother had been a Brouard, but her father a low-level *fonctionnaire* in the former federal government, something in transport. The Brouard surname added points, her father's profession demerits.

"*Alors*, a Two-A. But, it is so easy to slip to a Two-B or even a Three when these matters are reviewed." He paused.

"How is your husband?" Pénard nodded towards the open door to the parlour.

"He has to go to the hospital every week," whispered Florette.

"*Triste.* And very difficult for you. But, of course, a Two-A gives you priority."

Agent Gruaut nodded his agreement.

"A long waiting list," added Pénard. The local community service centre is *débordé*—overwhelmed."

Florette's hand trembled as she wiped her brow. Her chest felt tight, the kitchen suddenly hot.

"I don't understand," she began.

"*Madame*, do not upset yourself. None of this need come to pass. There is something you can do for us. It's a small thing, but important for the security of the Republic. I am sure you will want to assist."

"It is simple," continued Pénard. "The Blackwater Sailing Club employs you to collect their mail. We are interested in certain persons who belong to that club. We believe you can help us. Once a week, you collect the letters addressed to the club from the post office. And you deliver it the following day. Agent Gruaut here will assist you with part of that responsibility. You will deliver the mail to him. The next morning, he will pass it back to you, and you can deliver it as normal. You need do nothing else. It is a small thing, but quite sufficient to convince us of your loyalty to the Republic."

Pénard noticed the bundle of letters on the table.

"Gruaut will take that correspondence now. Might as well get off to a good start."

"And I believe I can say with confidence that the status review will confirm you as Two-A, *Madame* Brouard," said Pénard, standing and brushing the pastry crumbs from his uniform.

"*Bonne journée*, Madame."

" 'ave a good day," said Gruaut.

✧ ✧ ✧

AGENT GRUAUT WAS sorting through the bag of mail taken from Florette Henderson. He was sitting on the side of the bed in a motel room that was the GR's temporary quarters in Belltown.

He hadn't expected to find much incriminating in the post; communications by electronic means were already being monitored, and the GR had captured some possibly indiscreet texts containing target words highlighted by the AI program. No, the reason for diverting the club mail was not to subtract, but to add. To this end, Gruaut had prepared a stack of brown envelopes of the sort used by government agencies. The envelopes contained letters from various bodies, all in fact drafted by Captain Pénard. They included requests for supporting documentation for tax purposes; questions about the status of Blackwater as a sporting club rather than a seniors' residence, and notices of upward revisions to municipal tax evaluations. There was a demand from the environment ministry for action to re-vegetate the shores of the island, and an expression of concern about the disposal of waste. Gruaut added a sprinkling of hand-written complaints from imaginary neighbours about noisy parties at the club—his own work, of which he was particularly proud. He mixed these with the genuine mail and publicity material. Agent Gruaut prided himself on his diligence in following the orders of his superiors.

✧　✧　✧

EVICTING THE BLACKWATER Sailing Club, and securing the island for the GRs was a priority set by Commander Western Division, Serge Brevet. Harassment by mail was a technique, frequently used by the GRs to achieve their goals, in this case, the abandonment of the island by the Blackwater Sailing Club. The fake communications would gradually harden in tone over the coming weeks, increasing the stress put on the officers of the club, and make ever more unreasonable demands of the residents.

Officially, the goal was to rededicate the island as a camp for rest and recreation for rank-and-file GRs. Unofficially, Brevet wanted the island for his private use. And for private revenge.

One of Commander Brevet's official duties was ensure that the local population upheld Quebec values in this far western sector of the Republic, a large area that included the Noire Reservoir and Noire Valley. His other responsibilities included security, corruption and political crime: a broad and interpretable remit.

Brevet was a local man, originally in the construction trades. He had, over the years, built up a network among local businessmen, and officials in the local municipalities. He had several usefully placed cousins, including Guy LaMolle, superintendent at the hydroelectric dam on the Noire, a few miles north of town. He had been promoted when PowerBec took over from Dominion Hydro; Brevet had seen to it.

Family and business connections had led Serge Brevet into politics. He had been active in organizing demonstrations and had developed a reputation as an agent provocateur during the struggle for independence. After the triumph in the referendum and the subsequent secession, the new government rewarded its loyal supporters with key positions in the organs of state. Brevet's loyalty and experience made him seem an excellent fit as a senior officer in the *Garde républicaine.*

Several times over the years, Brevet had applied for membership to the Blackwater Sailing Club. To his frustration, the Board rejected his candidature on each occasion. In Brevet's view, this was gross discrimination: they objected to his political views—he was a proud republican—and he spoke heavily accented English. The board members were all Anglos, notoriously hidebound in their notions of a larger Canada, and—to

Brevet's bafflement—prejudiced against power boats on the reservoir. Now, for Brevet, it was pay-back time.

Brevet like inventing ways to make life uncomfortable at Blackwater. He had convinced the regular traffic police to harass club members with speeding tickets and similar infractions should they venture off-island. Brevet had an Inspector Laborde of the Hull Centro detachment on speed dial for this purpose. And, a word from Brevet to his cousin at the dam and he could have the water levels in the reservoir dropped several feet, creating havoc for the boats moored at the club.

But it was more than just a personal vendetta, he told himself. He was convinced the club was infected with seditious ideas about rejoining Canada. His agents reported that certain members were active separatists. That was why surveillance—Brevet had men watching the club—was justified. Brevet had been at pains to explain this to his superior in Quebec City, when queried about the expense.

Chapter 15

THE CLUB HELD sailing races every other Sunday, beginning in mid-May and continuing throughout the summer and fall. From early on each race day, urgent preparations disrupted regular life on the water. Both the Commodore and Harbour Master insisted that as many boats as possible be in condition to race. Some might cry off racing on account of age or technical failure, but the club demanded a certain state of readiness. Margret Mankie disliked this bi-weekly event, as it meant unloading all the pottery onto the dock and corralling her floating garden into a safer mooring. This weekend, she had successfully argued that Paul needed an experienced crew, as it was his first race. The *Groaning Anne* would stay at the dock.

For Paul, this first race was a chance for him to build a reputation, or fail miserably. He was happy to have an experienced crew.

Paul unhooked his array of solar panels and stowed them in the cabin. The sky was overcast land a faint drizzle was falling. Paul hoped his battery held sufficient charge for him to run the *Spindrift's* electric motor long enough to clear his dock without embarrassment. He pulled the old genoa sail from its locker and pushed it through the front hatch to Margret, who attached the clew, clipped the sail onto the forestay, and ran the sheets back into the cockpit. They removed the mainsail cover and ties. They were ready.

"You had best get along to the skippers meeting," Margret reminded him. "Taggart doesn't appreciate latecomers." As if to reinforce this, they heard the loud burp of an air horn which seemed to convey the Commodore's impatience.

Paul hurried along the catwalk to join the semi-circle of sailors gathered on the island side of the drawbridge. Their focus was Commodore St. James in all his finery, a navy blue jacket and cap adorned with gold braid. Taggart stood before an easel set up in the shelter of a large pine tree, sketching the course for the day on a chalkboard. His audience was roughly split between those keen to race despite the wet and those who hoped the wind would die completely, and for Taggart to cancel the race.

The course was familiar to all in the audience except Paul. The fleet would beat hard upriver against a brisk, northwesterly wind to a distant mark, and then make the long run back to the club. Hall, who was standing next to Paul, confided that he expected it to take two to three hours.

"Do we round the windward mark to port or starboard?" asked someone.

"Starboard, of course," replied Taggart. "And give the mark plenty of room or you'll run on the rocks."

"Garvin is at the point to start you, so don't be late," he added, concluding his brief speech. He looked at his chronometer.

"Fifteen minutes to the start. Go!"

The group dispersed quickly. Paul ran back to find Margret ready to cast off. From further along the line of boats, he heard outboard motors cough, as skippers yanked urgently at starter ropes.

He glanced up to see Collins at the helm of the *Ring of Kerry*, a sleek twenty-two-footer, as it reversed into the bay in a tight curve, paused, then gathered forward speed.

"Mike never bothers to go to the skippers meeting," said Margret, seeing Paul's look. "He likes to be first to the start line."

Others followed in quick succession, following Collins. Paul climbed aboard the *Spindrift*, took the tiller, and pressed reverse on the small, electric outboard. His boat slid silently backwards into the bay, and Margret swung on at the last second. So far, so good.

Pennants streamed from the start mast at the point, a sign that a strong breeze was blowing from the north-west. But here in the island's lee, it was calm. Margret raised the mainsail as they approached the line where Paul expected to catch the wind, a sudden transition from glassy water to ruffled surface. The boats in front heeled in succession as their sails caught the gusts bullying around the end of the island. Each turned head to wind to run up their foresails, before bearing off along the start line.

Paul felt the wind catch his mainsail. He pushed the tiller to bring the boat into the wind for Margret to haul up the flapping genoa. He tightened the control sheets. Abreast of the point, Paul saw a buoy in the middle of the reservoir, marking the far end of the start line. He steered to follow the others towards the far shore. Behind him, a gun from the point signalled five minutes to the start.

"Watch the bloody flags," Margret shouted. "Garvin always gets it wrong. Go by the flags, not by the gun."

Paul nodded. He was steering to avoid other vessels tacking in front of him, then racing back along the start line. According to the rulebook, he had the right of way, but he wasn't about to argue. Taggart, his face contorted in fierce concentration, surged past.

"One minute!" shouted Margret.

Paul found himself on starboard tack, coming back across the reservoir, heading straight for the point. He would need to turn upwind when the gun went off, but other boats boxed him in. "Give me a break, you bastards!" he shouted, his cry carried vainly downwind. But no gap appeared. He imagined the jagged reef rising up beneath him; somewhere below, in the turbid water, rocks were reaching for his keel. Damn, Damn, Damn!

Suddenly, there was room. Paul wrenched the tiller over, bringing the *Spindrift* near the wind. The boom swung wildly.

"For Pete's sake, say when you're going to do that!" cried Margret.

The flag came down more or less in unison with the gun.

"Go, go, go!"

The boats accelerated across the start line: Collins in the *Ring of Kerry* took the lead, with Taggart in the *Cornishman* a bow behind, Margret was pulling in the jib sheet and Paul let the boat edge towards close-hauled—as near to the wind as possible without the foresail flapping. His heart pounding, Paul looked around to see where others were. To his surprise, he found that the *Spindrift* had made a respectable start, and were in front of several boats.

"Good job! But watch out for the weeds!" shouted Margret.

Taggart, to windward, showed no sign of letting Paul tack away from the weed bed that was approaching rapidly on the port bow. They were close enough for Paul to see the army of long, green blades, combed into alignment by the wind. A gap opened, and Paul turned abruptly behind the lead boats, just in time to avoid the weeds.

The *Spindrift* cut away, building speed on the port tack.

"Starboard! You stupid bugger!" Paul heard the shout.

He glanced right to see the *Olivier's Dream* charging towards them on a collision course. Margret reached out to push the tiller forward, and they ducked under the stern mere feet away. Tasker waved to acknowledge Paul ceding the right of way.

"Shit," muttered Paul.

Then the *Spindrift* was clear and heading across the river, as the rest of the fleet continued in pursuit of Collins and the Commodore.

"I think you can breathe again," said Margret, amused. "Those starts can get pretty wild."

They were sailing in a good wind across the reservoir towards the eastern shore. It looked as though they would follow a zigzag course, tacking back and forth, beating all the way to the windward mark, which was a small island, five kilometres distant as the crow flies. Sailing, the distance would be closer to seven. The width of the reservoir water was about half a kilometre from shore to shore, narrower where pinched at alternating intervals by rocky points. On every zigzag, the *Spindrift* would have to cross the course of the main fleet, with Paul uncertain whether the other racers would observe the rules and give way. Given his experience at the start, he rather doubted it.

His boat was in the groove, making five knots. It was nothing spectacular, but it was a good pace. Paul looked at his crew. Margret, holding the jib sheet and leaning back into the wind, was gazing at the sails ahead of them. She had a faint smile on her face.

"We might catch Taggart before the island, at this rate," she said.

Paul tried to concentrate on sailing. "Be in the moment," he said to himself. But he couldn't stop thinking about the drowned landscape unrolling beneath the keel. The forested hills bordering the reservoir had once been the backdrop to broad riverside meadows over which he was sailing. A hundred years of accumulated silt smothered once-green pastures; fathoms of dark water covered the blackened stumps of trees and the tumbled stone foundations of demolished farmsteads.

A capricious gust banished Paul's morbid reflections.

"What side should we stay on, Margret?" he asked anxiously. Paul was trying to judge whether to keep close to the west side of the water, away from the hills that were crowding in from the east.

"Stay west," advised his crew. "But watch for the flat water in the middle of the river. That's where Rourke had a barn, on a knoll by the old riverbank. Now it's a gravel bank, shallow enough for us to ground."

Paul tried to visualize the map in the Mess that showed the valley before the reservoir, tried to find landmarks, but to no avail. He could not match the current picture-postcard water, its forested banks dotted by cottage properties, to the hardscrabble farms that had disappeared beneath the rising water.

Half an hour later, the wind dropped, and the *Spindrift* slowed to enter a patch of water unruffled by the breeze.

"You can just see the mark now," said Margret.

Paul, holding both tiller and sheet in one hand, stood to have a better view. He leaned against the boom to feel if there was any pressure on the sail. Nothing. The wind had died completely. He searched the river ahead. One boat—he supposed it was still Collins in the lead—was turning to cross on a port tack behind a small, rocky island, just visible above the chop. Two others were in close pursuit. So, that was the windward mark the Commodore had said to keep clear of while rounding.

"Stop fretting," chided Margret. "The wind will pick up once we get near the shore, where the air funnels close to the bank. You can see they're already getting a puff up ahead."

Sure enough, the lead boats were already turning south, loosing their sheets for the big sails to fill from behind, as they began their run back downriver. It was, Paul thought, a fine sight.

The *Spindrift* crawled slowly towards the darker water where there was certainly wind. It was only a question of minutes, although it seemed much longer before the sails tautened and Paul's boat gathered speed enough for him to consider a tack towards the mark.

"Hold it, hold it," advised Margret. "Don't go too soon or you'll end up on the rocks."

Stomach tight with anxiety, Paul waited. Then, judging that he had a safe margin, he tacked onto port, on a course that would round the island, a good fifty metres beyond where the rocks pierced the surface.

"A good, conservative rounding. You can cut it closer next time. Don't follow Taggart, though. He actually touched in *Cornishman* during the last race." Margret was smiling.

With the wind now behind them, they could ease off all the tension. Paul let the mainsail sheet run out until the boom was almost at right angles to the boat. The big genoa billowed on the opposite side. Paul gave the tiller a light nudge to align the boat directly before the wind. He felt her surge.

They were running fast now, wing on wing. A glance forward and behind confirmed to Paul that they were in the middle of the fleet, the boats following them strung out like a stream of white butterflies.

"Relax, Loess. It's up to fate now," called Margret, who had climbed forward to stand before the mast. "If the gods want you to win, they'll send a gust downriver and it'll carry you up to the lead boats in no time. If not, just enjoy the run. You sailed well."

Paul could see Collins, in the leading boat, disappear behind a point far ahead. Collins no longer appeared to be heading directly downwind, but steered towards the western shore on a broad reach. It seemed an unlikely move by the leader. Surely, thought Paul, the better strategy would be to continue on his current course. The *Cornishman*'s captain seemed to agree and remained in full sight five minutes ahead.

"Making a delivery," commented Margret. "Mike does that during some races. He says it's an extra handicap, to allow others to catch up. Truth be told, he goes into shore to drop a package out of the view of our friends watching the club. Don't bother asking him about it—you won't get a straight answer—but once you've proved yourself, he might let you in on the secret. Give yourself a little time. There's much about Blackwater you don't know yet."

Twenty minutes later, they were through the narrows and entering the broader water just upstream from the club. This was the last stretch to the finish line. The gods seemed to have favoured the Commodore, who looked set to take the flag. Collins, now third behind the *Spindrift*, was charging towards the line on a starboard tack, but he had left it too late to catch Paul and Margret.

✧　✧　✧

"BLOODY BRILLIANT, LOESS," called Collins as his boat glided past the *Spindrift* towards the dock. "You said you hadn't sailed in years! Get yourself up to the clubhouse to celebrate! You too, Margret."

Paul was pleased with himself. Not having sailed in years had been an understatement; he had been in his teens the last time he had skippered a boat in a race.

"There will be war stories without end, especially if Old Tom is there," she grumbled. An afternoon drinking in the Mess in the company of Collins, Taggart *et al.* was not Margret's idea of a peaceful Sunday afternoon.

"I need the support, Margret." Paul insisted. "And since you are crew, you can't cry off."

✧　✧　✧

A WHILE LATER, conversation in the Mess was petering out. They had dissected the race beat by beat, and the post-mortem had established that Joe could have challenged if he hadn't cocked up the narrows again, and that Taggart should have his handicap reassessed, because his series of wins was getting monotonous.

After a couple of drinks, Paul was feeling a pleasant buzz. He was listening to Old Tom's war stories. The man had seen a thing or two; that was for sure. Suddenly, he heard Margret's voice raised. Her mood had not improved with whisky, and she was giving Collins a tongue lashing. It dawned on Paul that he was the subject of their exchange.

"It's about time, Mike," she spoke vehemently. "You have to decide! He's either in or he's out. I can't keep this up—he's my bloody neighbour, for Christ's sake!"

Collins was sitting on a bar stool. But even with the disadvantage, his height forced him to bow his head to talk to Margret. He seemed unsure how to react. Margret's face was flushed and determined.

"Well, Margret, if you're sure. It's your evaluation. Let's show him, then." With that, he stood and came back from the bar to join the group sitting in the Mess.

"Loess, a minute of your time," he said. "No, stay here, Tom. Paul and I won't be long."

Taking Paul's elbow, Collins led him away from the group. They descended the stairs and turned left into the corridor leading to the kitchen. Collins stopped beside the last of the trophy cabinets which Paul had examined before. He reached beside it to find a latch. The cabinet swung smoothly out from the wall on its hinges to reveal an opening the size of a door. Paul saw before him the entrance to a tunnel, hewn out of solid rock.

"Flick on that switch," said Collins.

Projecting from the wall at his right hand, Paul felt the knob of a light switch. He pressed it, illuminating a line of bare bulbs suspended from a cable running along the roof of the tunnel. He could see a rough floor sloping downwards into the mountain.

"They built the clubhouse over an old mine," said Collins. "Not much of a mine; more of an exploratory drive. But it gives us an extra room, now it's cleared of debris. We call it 'the wine cellar.' Follow me."

Paul stumbled down the slope after Collins. After twenty feet, the tunnel levelled out. Collins switched on another brighter light, and Paul found himself in a space the size of a large room. The walls and roof were bedrock, and the floor covered with sand. Wooden crates were stacked against the far wall. To one side was a folding table. Collins called him over.

"Help with this crate, Loess. Lift it onto the table."

Collins had selected an old box that stood to one side of the main stack. It was about five feet long. It looked more like a coffin than anything, thought Paul. The numbers and letters stencilled on the side gave no clue to the contents.

Collins unscrewed the butterfly nuts at the four corners of the crate.

"Now, this is what they found when they built this clubhouse, it must be twenty years ago now," he said, levering off the lid.

Inside were five rifles wrapped in oiled paper. By the depth of the box, Paul guessed there must be three layers, making fifteen in total.

"Three-oh-three calibre, standard World War I issue. They may be well over a hundred years old. But they're as good as new; never been fired, except for one we tested."

Collins pulled out the nearest gun and unwrapped it. He slid the bolt action in and out.

"We had trouble finding ammunition, but there are twenty rounds apiece over in that munitions box." He pointed to a smaller square box lying against the wall.

"What we are about here, Loess, is action."

Paul's satisfaction from his good showing in the race drained away. He felt queasy.

"Sorry, Mike. Feeling ill. Need some air." He hurried back to the mouth of the tunnel, turned along the corridor leading to the main door of the clubhouse, and ran outside. He sat down heavily on the clubhouse steps, breathing deeply. Margret came and sat on one side of Paul, Collins on the other.

"It's covered in the agreement you signed, Paul," said Collins. "You should reread the paragraph on the Committee for a Free West Quebec. You asked what the last 'P' in my 'Triple-P' Committee stands for. The full title, as approved by the Board, is 'Policy, Public Relations and Paramilitary Liaison'. It's a bit of a handle: we just call it the 'Committee'. Didn't you realize we were separatists here at the club?"

"Shut up, Mike," said Margret. "Loess needs a moment. Don't you, Paul?"

Chapter 16

THE PATH THAT wound around the island was too short to benefit joggers. That left swimming as the best way to exercise. Many residents found a regular swim vital for de-stressing. They could leave aside their worries and tune into the natural tranquillity of Blackwater. Most swam alone, although on afternoons when the mood of the residents had mellowed under the influence of fine weather, small groups would depart from the swim dock and head north, on the first leg of circum-navigating the island.

After the shock of the previous day, Paul had not slept well. He had woken early and lain in his bunk replaying the scene in the 'wine cellar'. Despite his efforts to repress his thoughts, the guns crawled back into his semi-consciousness. A smiling Collins kept passing him a rifle, which lay heavy on his chest.

"Try again," said Collins in his dream. "Pull back the bolt."

Paul needed to calm himself. He was bound to meet Margret soon, and possibly Collins. A swim should do it. He decided to attempt the full circuit of the island for the first time. Margret's record number of circuits over the course of a season had impressed him. At that rate, she would have got halfway to Montreal by now if she'd held a steady course.

Paul's swim trunks had survived his downsizing as an essential item. After changing in his boat's cabin, he walked along the dock in the still morning, descended the metal ladder into the water, and pushed off.

Head underwater, he opened his eyes to look down into the

dark, green void. Flickering shafts of pale sunlight lanced through the water. There was no sign of the bottom. Paul pulled himself forward in a slow breaststroke, allowing the water to slip closely along his limbs. He prided himself on being a fair swimmer, although, sadly, he'd grown unfit.

Some one hundred or so metres from the swim dock, a boom of massive logs chained together closed off the western entrance to Blackwater Bay. Originally placed to keep floating logs from getting trapped in the bay, it now deterred any "foreign" boats from intruding on private club waters. Swimmers paused at the boom after the first stage of their swim around the island.

Paul reached the boom and held on. Wavelets slurped across the slimed surface of the wood. After regaining his breath, he eased himself between two of the boom timbers. Now the swim got serious. He put his head down and pushed onward in a steady crawl.

To his right rose low cliffs; he glimpsed the sheer rock descending into the murk. A small fish darted away, and Paul wondered if a pike was lurking nearby. He turned onto his back, taking shallow breaths, and looked up at the blue sky. His thoughts drifted with the wisps of fine-weather clouds.

Then, he remembered Margret's geography lesson: the underwater farm, dead and drowned deep below him; the old road no longer walked, the enclosure where Margret's grandad had buried the pets. Paul flipped over and swam strongly towards the orange buoy that marked the reef at the northeastern corner of the island.

Suddenly, he felt the coil of a slimy something grip his ankle, and he kicked strongly to get clear. He knew this weed patch only too well from his first race. Water lilies. Could it be true that unwary swimmers had drowned, flailing helplessly in such weeds? Reaching deeper water, he turned onto the long stretch to the lighthouse point. Paul began to tire. Again, a blade of weed caressed his calf. He felt a surge of panic, a dread of hands reaching up from the murk. He quickly subdued the notion. Surely the water wasn't over ten feet deep here just off the point, just above the drowned falls? He could almost touch bottom. Almost: but not quite.

After two hundred metres, as he turned his head to breathe, he saw he had passed the lighthouse. He trod water to get his bearings. Now, at the eastern mouth of Blackwater Bay, Paul could see the end of the catwalk and the row of moored boats. He swam the last leg into the bay via breaststroke, arriving into calm water. Five more minutes brought him to the ladder. Mike Collins was waiting with a towel.

"Took your sweet time, Loess. We swim for exercise, not for floating on your back, cloud-gazing."

"First time all the way around," he replied, his feeling of accomplishment dashed.

They strolled back along the catwalk to their own dock. Paul, in bare feet, was concerned to avoid splinters from the uneven boards.

"Don't worry, Loess. Your crawl is half decent. You must work on the breathing though."

Paul was surprised by Collins. The man was being pleasant.

"Mind you, swimming ability was not the only reason we offered you a berth here at Blackwater." Collins had walked with Paul to the *Spindrift*. Now he turned back along the catwalk.

"We'll talk again later," he said, in parting.

Paul had indeed been wondering why the Board had invited him to join the club. He supposed they had considered him sound; his political views were there for all to read on the internet. Reposting *Free Pontiac Now!* on his Facebook page had seemed harmless at the time. His short-lived blog, *West Quebec within Canada*, perhaps less so. *Vive le Pontiac libre* had definitely been poking the fire. He had discontinued his postings after a while. He'd been aggrieved by the *ad hominem* tirades, which he'd guessed came from government trolls.

Paul had no problem with constitutional monarchy—who could possibly object to King Willy? Populist presidents were a disaster. Take the United States, take France, take Brazil. The shock of the final Quebec referendum results and the subsequent events had confirmed his view; Josée-Mathilde Papineau—*Madame la Présidente*—was undoubtedly an autocrat. This was hardly surprising, given her background as a headmistress.

Now he lived among people vowing to separate West Quebec—specifically, the county of Pontiac—from the Republic. After Mike Collins' pointed comment, Paul had read the clause in his rental agreement. Sure enough, he found that he had endorsed "all activities directed by the Committee in furtherance of the establishment of a Pontiac Free State in West Quebec." A footnote stated that the "Committee" had been established by vote of the Board of the Blackwater Sailing Club, appointing Michael Collins as chair. Paul resorted to the internet. After a brief search on-line, he found the committee's manifesto. It was short: secede from the Republic, and build an economy based on trade with the rest of Canada and the world.

Of course, Paul was sympathetic. It was the arsenal in the wine cellar that made him nervous. That, and the unsettling charm of Mike Collins.

Chapter 17

AGENT GRUAUT HAD the night shift. He was in a cottage hidden in the trees overlooking Blackwater Bay and the club. From the front window he had a view of the clubhouse, most of the boat docks, and the catwalk leading to the island. The evening activities at the club had seemed boringly normal: a few late swims, then early to bed. After ten p.m., the island across the bay appeared dead to the world. Gruaut streamed a long movie on his phone, before trying to find a comfortable position on the bunk.

After midnight, the wind rose, and Gruaut heard the first spatter of drops against the roof of the cabin. He finally fell into a fitful sleep at about four a.m., only to wake three short hours later hearing the muffled sounds of activity. He opened the cottage door and peered outside. Through the screen of trees, he thought he saw movement on *chemin* Blackwater near the club entrance.

His superior insisted he report anything unusual to head-quarters immediately. Gruaut looked at the time. Captain Pénard would be arriving at his office in the *Portalette*. He punched a number on his phone.

"*Bonjour. Ici Pénard.*"

"*Désolé, Capitain.* There is unusual activity at the club this morning."

"It's early, Gruaut, and I haven't had my coffee. So, what is it?"

Pénard had done his share of shifts watching the Blackwater

Sailing Club. He knew the idiots started their morning routines early. There was the back and forth of the boat dwellers visiting the "heads"—he had picked up some nautical terms—or going to take showers in the clubhouse. Rain usually meant less activity, making the shifts in the cabin seem never-ending. One started to imagine things.

"I count five new boats in Blackwater Bay, *Capitain. Attendez!* There's another one backing down the *chemin.*"

Through the screen of cedars, Gruaut glimpsed a boat trailer move past, towards the boat ramp.

"Get some photographs, Gruaut. Send them to me as soon as you can."

The phone went blank as his superior cut the link. Gruaut thought briefly of breakfast—the cold remains of a take-away were in his overnight bag. He heard the muffled roar of a diesel engine and decided against eating. The engine sounded close by—down by the boat ramp.

Gruaut was wearing green fatigues, and rummaged in his kit bag for an old, black tuque. It was better camouflage than his GR baseball cap with its silver emblem. He needed some disruptive pattern on his face, and in a kitchen cupboard at the rear of the cabin he found what he was looking for. He smeared a broad, brown stripe of peanut butter on each cheek.

Gruaut opened the side door to the cabin. Rain was pouring from the roof. Scurrying across the patch of rough grass, he made it to the shelter of the trees. Now, he was directly above the lane, screened by the dripping cedars. Moving silently, he made his way along the slope towards the entrance to the club. He found good cover a mere twenty-five metres from the boat ramp. He lay down, prone, on the damp ground.

The gate to the Blackwater Sailing Club was propped wide open. That in itself made this morning unusual. There were several figures on the ramp. All wore large, waterproof hats or hoods that obscured their faces. Several had improvised rain gear—black garbage bags with holes cut for head and arms. He sensed tension in the group, and a sense of urgency in their movements.

Gruaut pulled his phone from an inside pocket and pushed it out in front of him. Getting clean shots of the faces proved difficult. His first attempts were blurred by the rain. A drip splattering on the lens confused the automatic focus. He hoped the facial recognition software back at the office could compensate.

Tires crunched on the gravel from up *chemin* Blackwater to his right. He adjusted his position slightly to get a better view. A trailer was being backed down the lane to the launch ramp. Gruaut recognized the type of boat it was carrying: a black Zodiac with a powerful outboard motor attached. He had seen similar vessels on a training exercise he had attended near Quebec City. They were assault craft. Three of them had swept across the river to outflank his position on the Isle St. Jean. It had been a devastating move, and Gruaut's platoon had lost their flag.

The trailer rolled past, backed by a heavy-duty pickup truck. Gruaut shot a burst of pictures. "*Mon Dieu*," he thought. The *maudit* truck was painted in camo, in blotches of black and green. A figure, similarly camouflaged, stood on the back of the truck, holding onto a fixed stanchion. *Évidemment*, thought Gruaut, it was the mounting for a heavy machine gun. Gruaut had seen videos of truck-mounted weapons, combining devastating fire power with high mobility. He tried to make out the sign on the door of the cab, but mud splash obscured the lettering.

After twenty minutes, a puddle had formed under Gruaut. The rain poured down: he was soaked through. The activity in the lane paused, and someone closed the gate to the club. He could no longer see what was going on. Backing slowly away from his hiding place, the agent crept back up the hill to the cabin.

Gruaut stripped off and rubbed himself down with a towel. He put on his uniform trousers and shirt, and draped a blanket across his shoulders. Going to the kitchen, he switched on the kettle for a warm drink. He was still shivering with the chill when his phone rang.

"Sitrep?" demanded Pénard.

"They're moving an assault boat down to the river, *Capitain*. Besides that, there are *six* new boats in the bay, but I can't make out their markings through the rain. And there are twelve persons we haven't seen before: *des types para-militaire*."

"I need photos, Gruaut. Call me back if there are further developments."

Gruaut thumbed through the pictures he had taken on his phone. They would do for now. He pressed send.

For ease of surveillance, Gruaut had placed a table and chair in front of the big window that looked out across Blackwater Bay towards the island. He sat down, picked up the pair of high-powered binoculars that lay on the table, and scanned the island and clubhouse. Visibility was poor; curtains of rain slanted across the bay. At high magnification, he could see the raindrops pocking the surface of the water.

Movement near the clubhouse steps caught the agent's attention. He refocused his binoculars. Four figures, shrouded in their rain gear, who were struggling with a bulky object shrouded in a tarpaulin.

They were half lifting, half dragging the load along the path leading to the point. Gruaut watched them for ten minutes as they negotiated roots and rocks along the path, before they briefly disappeared behind the pine trees. They reappeared beside the lighthouse. It seemed to be their destination. One of them untied the cords securing the tarp. He removed it with a flourish.

Un canon! Mon Dieu, un vrai canon! Through the telephoto, the squat shape resolved into a long, olive-coloured barrel resting on a wheeled carriage. It was a field gun, without a doubt.

Never, in his career with the *la Garde*, had Gruaut felt so energized. For the first time, he was watching something that mattered, something that clearly threatened the security of the Republic. This was what he had signed up for! Glued to his binoculars, he began to scribble frantically in the notebook open beside him.

Gruaut thought himself an avid sports fan. Every year, he bought a season ticket for the *Olympiques* Junior A, and followed the golf on television. But, competitive sailing was a closed book to him. Now, through the washes of rain that blurred his view, he watched six sailboats align with military precision. This couldn't be for sport. Why, *pour l'amour de Dieu*, would any sane person venture out in this weather? It had to be a military exercise. Or, he corrected himself, a paramilitary exercise.

The movement on the water impressed the watching agent. The boats kept circling and coming back into line, just like manoeuvres on the parade ground at the *Garde* academy. Suddenly, in response to some command, the boats set off upriver, charging into the teeth of the wind. In silence. Until, seconds later, the boom reached his ears. They had fired the canon!

Now he understood. This was a test of readiness; practice for some landing on a distant beach. His phone ringing broke his train of thought.

"Gruaut?" It was Captain Pénard.

"*Oui?*"

"We have identified the men in your photographs. Michael Collins is the individual directing matters. He is second in command at the club. The one holding the rope is Garvin Bowter, and Harvey Kinnear is the short man in the green boots.

Our intelligence says they are all members of the Committee. The one waist-deep in water is Loess, Paul Loess. He was, until recently, a resident here in the city. We have an extensive file on him."

"One moment, *Capitain*." Gruaut had seen the assault boat speeding out of the bay, spray exploding from beneath its bow as it hit the waves off the point. It headed upriver, where, in the distance, two sails lay on the water. The boats had been blown flat, he supposed, by a gust of wind. *Non merci*, he thought, thankful that he wasn't out there in this weather.

The assault boat reached the capsized boats and was circling, its dark hull heaving up and down in the binocular's magnified circle of vision. "Like a shark," Gruaut thought with admiration. What a way to harden recruits.

"It's a race, *Capitain*," he said into the phone, suddenly comprehending. "Six boats set out. Two capsized, and now the leaders are coming back. It's very close. It looks as though …" The gun sounding again cut off Gruaut's explanation.

"What are you saying, Gruaut? You said an assault boat. Is this a paramilitary exercise?"

"*Mais oui, non, mais—*"

"Agent Gruaut, stay there! Watch and report."

"*Oui, Monsieur.*"

Over the next two hours, Gruaut sat at his post, immobile. The rain ceased, allowing him see more clearly. The boats returned to the shelter of the bay, reorganized and set off again, the gun sounding the start of another race. Eventually, as he ate his cold lunch, the activity across the bay moved to the patio behind the clubhouse.

Gruaut counted thirty-five people. With their rain-gear off, he realized that the group comprised both men and women. All wore blue T-shirts—a uniform? Collins—Gruaut put the name to the face he recognized him from the ramp—addressed the crowd. Beside him stood a grey-haired older man, obviously a person of importance. Perhaps the club commodore? Cups were awarded; hands shaken. Finally, Collins passed the Commodore a long object: a rifle, the sun glinting from its high polish. He gave it, with ceremony, to a young man, who raised a fist aloft.

Gruaut heard a faint cheer. He noted the time. The separatist-terrorists were distributing arms.

✧   ✧   ✧

"I THOUGHT THE regatta went well," said Harvey to Collins the next morning. "Despite the rain."

Chapter 18

SEVERAL COPIES OF the *Black and White* landed with a thump on the mess table. Paul looked up to see Florette Henderson standing in front of him, looking bothered. She carried a bundle of mail in her hand. It was much thicker than usual.

Paul knew several residents subscribed to the only English-language newspaper in the Noire valley. The club also got a copy of the *PR—la Presse de la République*. Florette delivered it every week along with the mail.

"May I help, Madame Henderson? Is there a letter for me?"

"*Mais oui*, Monsieur Loess. There is something for you. But I must speak with Monsieur Taggart first."

"The Commodore? I think he's in the clubhouse some-where." Paul got up and walked through to the bar.

"Florette is here looking for you, Taggart. She's quite in-sistent."

"Damn. One minute, Loess. I want to finish this," growled Taggart, his attention focussed on the wooden model of a boat clamped to the table in front of him. He reached forward with a drawknife and shaved another sliver of wood from the hull.

"It's starting to look like the *Bluenose*," said Paul encourag-ingly, getting a grunt in return. Everyone in the Mess knew that the Commodore had been working on this project for weeks, and was quite sensitive about his slow progress. Collins said that Taggart should have settled for plasticine as a medium, rather than oak. Paul waited as Taggart squinted along the hull.

"Good enough for now. Okay, I'm coming."

Taggart and Paul returned to the Mess to find Florette amid a circle of club residents come to collect their copies of the *Black and White*. Harvey was eager for news from his mother, and Tasker was expecting a part he had ordered from a chandlery. Hall was there simply to be with Tasker. Old Tom had clambered down the steep companionway from the crow's nest, and hoisted himself onto a stool at the bar beside Olga Wilk. Only Margret was absent.

Paul picked up a *Black and White*, his eye caught by the headline "Quebec Waves Fees for Secondary Re-education."

Doubtlessly it was a gaffe in translation—re-education; like *rebonjour*, just a way of saying "Hi" to someone that you had already greeted earlier that day.

"Well, Florette, I see you have quite a bundle there. More bills, I suppose?" said the Commodore, reaching for the letters.

"*Mais non*, Monsieur Taggart. These are from the government. There is one for all of you."

Florette slid the rubber band from the bundle and passed out the envelopes. She had them sorted alphabetically.

"For you *d'abord*, Monsieur Taggart. And one for *Messieurs* Bowter, Collins, *et* Countryman, *Mesdames* Delario, Crabbe and Wilk; *Messieurs* Hall, *et* Loess, *et* Tasker." She flipped through the stack of envelopes. "And Neely, Soy, Thurlow, and … *Eh bien*, there's one for all of you!"

"But where is Madame Mankie?" she added, looking around at the circle of faces surrounding her.

Harvey was the first to tear open the brown envelope.

"It's from the Ministry for Re-education and Culture. *Cher Monsieur*, blah blah blah. An invitation! It's free. Oh."

Harvey paled and looked round at his fellow club members. Paul had already discovered what "it" was. His sanguine interpretation of the newspaper headline had been, he realized after reading the letter, premature. "It" was a week-long residential course on "Values of the Republic," a requirement for all citizens at levels Two-B and below. True, board and lodging were free, but the downside was that it would be in French immersion. And it was compulsory."

"Well, I would welcome a change," said Philly Delario. "My letter says they hold these courses just down the road, a twenty-minute drive only. I know the place: it's the old high school, the one they converted into a training centre."

"This is nothing but another ruse to clear some of us off the island," muttered Old Tom.

"But, if we don't go, they might arrest us," said Harvey.

"And, I've always wanted to learn French," said Philly.

Collins drew the Commodore to one side. "A word in your ear, Taggart. They'll be calling for a vote next. Are you going to put your foot down?"

"Mike, if some of them want to go, I think we should let them. It is only for a week."

"That's bullshit, as you well know. You're twitchy because you think the GRs have you in their sights. So, make them come to us. Don't let people off-island."

"Listen, everyone," Collins raised his voice. He waited for the faces in the Mess to lift from their letters and turn towards him. "Things around here are coming to a head. You know it. I know it. They've forced us to live on this island. Now they want to get us off. I say 'No!' We built this part of Canada. This is our island. This is our land. Damn their free re-education! I am staying here."

Old Tom began a drum roll on the table, then burst into a fit of coughing. Paul noticed the bottle of club malt on the bar beside him was nearly empty.

"So I say stuff these letters," Collins continued. "I'm not about to leave the island for some phoney seminar. If you want to go, leave, and good riddance."

"That's not fair, Mike." Philly was close to tears. "You know what will happen if we don't go. The GRs will come and arrest us. It's only for a week."

"I don't believe it," snapped Collins. "Chances are you won't be coming back, if I know anything about the GRs. This is just another trick to weaken the club. It's as simple as that."

"Well said, Mike," said Old Tom. "Hear, hear."

"Hold on," said Taggart. "I think we should respect the decision of those who want to accept. Who's willing to go?"

Philly Delario raised her arm, and looked around for support. "You realize they say they have a spa," she said.

Tickles Dubois put up her hand, and nudged her partner Larry Soy. Duff Thurlow made up the fourth. He owned an aging Edel: cramped, and known to have a cabin roof which no amount of caulking could prevent from leaking.

"All right. I count four," said the Commodore. "The first session lasts for one week, beginning next Monday. The last paragraph of the letter says there are five spaces reserved for the club. Accommodation is limited, apparently. To show our willingness, we should send a full complement of five. I suggest we draw straws for the last volunteer."

"No point. Last in, first out, I'm afraid," said Collins. "That would be you, Paul. That makes five."

"Hear, hear!" cried Old Tom. "Five into the hot-tub, dear friends."

"Hear what?" asked Margret, coming into the Mess. "Is there any mail?"

Chapter 19

"IF I'D BEEN there, this shit would never have happened." Margret had been apologetic walking back to the dock. "I'll look after *Spindrift* while you're away. Don't you worry."

Paul tried to make light of it. It might be good to get off-island for a spell. Philly was good company; it might actually be fun.

"Oh, well," said Margret. You'll just have to watch out for yourself, Paul."

When Monday morning came, the sky was cloudy and spitting rain. Paul was apprehensive; his earlier desire to get off-island had evaporated. His breakfast of cold oats and coffee seemed to fuel his acid reflux. Now, he dreaded leaving the island, leaving his boat, leaving home. Yes, this was now his home. And he resented being forced away from it. Bloody Collins. Why hadn't Paul challenged him at the meeting? But then, there had always been something in Collins that Paul didn't dare challenge; a rock-hard will behind the smile.

It was a forlorn group of four that gathered at the gate at eight o'clock. Philly attempted to chat, but the others were little inclined to participate. Even the birds seemed to have given up on the morning. Harvey came to unlock the gate.

"Duff says he'll catch up," said Harvey. "Good luck to you."

The four walked up *chemin* Blackwater to the parking compound. None of them were particularly friends. Larry Soy looked particularly glum: a week at a re-educational spa retreat was not his choice.

When they arrived at the compound, Paul went to unlock the chain that held the gate closed. The key to the padlock was in a lockbox dangling from the wire mesh. The box opened with a digital code. Harvey had told him the code, but, as he tried entering it for the third time, he doubted he had heard right. As he struggled, Duff came panting up the lane.

"Let me try that," he said to Paul. "There's a knack to it."

Duff punched in the code and retrieved the key.

"Nothing to it, really," he said, removing the padlock and pushing open the gates.

The group entered the compound. Paul had left his vehicle under a poplar tree. This was a mistake, he now realized: the black-staining leaves had dropped all over his car. They stuck to the paintwork like disruptive camouflage.

"You should park on the other side," said Duff.

The group put their assorted bags, packed with enough spare clothes for a week away, into the back of the SUV. The driver's door was sticking with gum from the tree. Paul wrenched it open and got in. He turned the key in the ignition.

"Gets good mileage, does she?" asked Duff, sitting beside Paul. Larry, Tickles and Philly squeezed into the back seat.

"You should try high-test gas," Duff said. "It'll give you an extra fifty per tank, for sure."

Paul hadn't used the vehicle in weeks. Gas consumption was the last thing on his mind. He put it in drive and the car lurched forward. The brakes were binding. They screamed in protest as Paul turned out of the compound and drove up *chemin* Glen Rourke.

"You should move it every week," said Duff.

Paul reached the top of *chemin* Glen Rourke and turned left, more abruptly than he had intended. He accelerated jerkily.

"Sorry," he muttered.

"Look! I forgot today was market day," said Philly as they

rolled through Belltown. A line of stalls before the church displayed organic vegetables, dubious local wine, honey, and soap.

"It will be market day on our way back next week, Philly," said Tickles. "We can stop then."

Paul followed the road towards the city, entering the suburbs abruptly, where the country road from Belltown turned into a four-lane boulevard. To their left were apartment blocks; to the right scrubland, with a backdrop of forest.

They entered a school zone, with block after block of empty soccer fields, the white goalposts rising from the uncut grass like gallows. Paul crept along at thirty kilometres per hour.

"We're here!" cried Philly. The campus grounds came into view on their right. "It's really pretty when the crab apples are in blossom."

"Oh, that fence is new," she added quietly.

Paul turned into the drive and slowed to a stop before the main gate. Large signs warned against "coydogs."

"They're pests here in town," said Duff. "But really no danger at all, if you look them in the eye."

The security guard at the gate was friendly.

"*Bonjour, bonjour. Bienvenue!* Drive right in and follow the ring road around the back of the complex to reception. It's in the big red brick building. Follow the *signalization*, and *attention à la vitesse!*"

Paul drove towards the central buildings of the sprawling campus. To either side of the drive were strips of seldom mown lawn, flanked by tangled stands of sumac bushes. A scatter of taller trees stood isolated in the sea of rough grass. Most were leafless and stripped of bark. At a T-junction, Paul turned left and continued clockwise around the complex, forest to their left and buildings to their right. He had to slow every fifty metres for yellow-striped speed bumps. Even when taken with caution, they jarred the occupants at each encounter.

The parking area reserved for visitors was small; rows of portable classrooms—the kind once found in almost every schoolyard—occupied much of the asphalt. There was no sign of life. Paul found a parking space beside a brick wall. He glanced at his watch; it was just after nine. They must already be in class, he thought.

Everybody got out. Beside them was a row of blue bins standing more or less to attention, like a line of soldiers. A ramp led up to a door over which was suspended a large sign.

"RECEPTION," read Duff. "This must be it."

He pushed open the door, and the group followed him inside. They found themselves standing at the end of a long room. There were no windows; lighting was by fluorescent tubes hanging from the high ceiling. Posters were pinned to the walls: one invited tourists to ski Mont Tremblant, another to visit Quebec City—*la Capitale Nationale*. A stack of metal chairs beside one wall suggested that this might be a waiting room; black scuff marks on the floor spoke to past use.

Before them, a long counter divided the room in two. In the middle of the counter was an opening, and what Paul assumed was a security archway. At a desk behind the counter sat a young woman, intent on a computer screen. She glanced up.

"*Bienvenue.* Welcome to CEDRE," she said. "*Le Centre de Re-education.*"

✧ ✧ ✧

IT TOOK HALF an hour for the club members to register. Having the same address—the Blackwater Sailing Club—confused the young woman at reception.

"But you can't all live in the same place," she objected. She made each person write in the name of their boat.

"*Mesdames*," said the receptionist to Philly and Tickles. "You are in Cumulus, *Cabane* Number One. Jean-Guy will escort you."

The receptionist pressed a button, and a uniformed staff member—a security guard—emerged from a door behind her.

"Place your bag on the counter, *Madame*." The security guard opened the bag and searched the contents.

"Okay. Come through," he said, waving Philly through the archway. Nothing beeped.

The only hiccup came when Paul handed over his letter.

"*Monsieur*, I regret you are not registered."

"But the letter is clear about the dates. That's me."

"*Oui, Monsieur*, but we have you listed as a 'C' in our database. This course is reserved for class '2-A' on the *Régistre des habitants*. I regret there must have been an error; you should not have received this notification."

"But I..."

"*Désolé, Monsieur*. These other gentlemen are waiting."

Paul watched as the receptionist assigned the others to the care of guard who would lead them to their rooms. They were to go to Nimbostratus. Paul supposed they must have named all the different accommodation blocks after cloud formations.

"Bad luck, Paul," called Duff from the far side of the counter. "Thanks for the ride. I'll call you for a lift back towards the end of the week, but I expect they'll arrange transport for us."

Paul watched his fellow club members follow their guide down a corridor. He turned back to the receptionist, who shrugged.

"This way, *Monsieur*." Another guard appeared to guide him through the door. The door slammed shut behind him, and Paul stumbled down the ramp towards his parked car.

Frankly, he was glad to be back in the fresh air, despite the nagging wind. Paul started the engine and drove off. He followed the peripheral road back to the campus entrance. He had to wait a full thirty seconds while the guard stared at his face before the gate rolled open.

Paul stopped just outside to look back at the brown buildings, surrounded by their clusters of huts. He hadn't noticed the razor wire on top of the fencing before. The gate rattled back across the road behind him. Paul heard the clunk as it locked shut.

Chapter 20

PAUL'S REAPPEARANCE AT the club that afternoon caused a minor stir. Margret saw him standing at the bottom of the lane and came to open the gate.

"That was quick. You must be a star at reciting those Quebec values."

"I need a drink," replied Paul. "They didn't want me after all. Something about not qualifying."

Paul left Margret at the *Groaning Anne*—she had been fiddling with her statues—and walked up to the clubhouse. Entering the Mess, he found Mike Collins and Tom Forget at the bar.

"Look what the cat dragged in," said Collins.

Paul explained what had happened; how the others had gone through without a problem.

"And you only saw the person at reception? No other person?"

"Well, apart from the security guards. There were three of them, but they were friendly enough. They searched the bags. God knows what they were looking for."

"You must have been there for over two hours. Did you see any GRs?"

"I thought the guards looked like regular security people. What are you getting at, Mike?"

"Just curious," said Collins. "Old Tom here will keep you company. Listen, I must go; I have to check something."

Collins walked out of the Mess.

"Mike's a bit on edge these days," said Tom. "He doesn't like the idea of this 're-education'. Can't blame him. They gave him a hard time a few years ago when he was enrolled for French Conversation. Sent for immersion in Abitibi. Thinks they're out to get him."

"They?"

"Damn Government. Whiskey?" asked Tom.

Paul accepted the drink that Tom poured. He gulped half the glass.

"Thanks, I needed that."

"Must have been a trying time, this morning," said Tom, sympathetically. "Come up to the crow's nest. See my camp."

Old Tom had been the permanent resident of the crow's nest since long before Paul had arrived at the club. In his experience, Tom vehemently discouraged visitors. Paul was astonished by the unexpected invitation.

"Yes, of course. It's good of you to ask, I…"

"Best bring that bottle," said Tom, pointing to the remaining whiskey.

From the Mess, one reached the crow's nest that crowned the clubhouse by means of a steep ladder. Paul climbed after Tom, one hand gripping the rope that served as a handrail, the other the bottle. His head emerged above the rough, plank flooring, and he found his eyes level with a pair of embroidered carpet slippers.

"Welcome, Loess. Put on those slippers, if you would. Otherwise, the whole blasted Mess can hear our movements."

Paul stood awkwardly, exchanging his deck shoes for slippers as Old Tom lowered the trap at the top of the stairs. His host was wearing a pair of soft moccasins.

The sun was westering, and the crow's nest was bathed in yellow light. It imparted a warm glow to the well-varnished wood of the window frames and polished pine flooring. Paul ran his hand along a windowsill, fingering the deeply etched grain, and felt initials carved into the wood.

"T heart O?" he read aloud.

"Eh?" said Tom. "Oh that. Must have been kids back when we held summer camp."

The crow's nest was a veritable tower room at the top of a castle keep. Above their heads, four timbers converged on a central pillar, supporting the pyramidal roof. Paul could dimly make out small, dark bundles clustered in the apex of the roof.

"Blasted bats,' said Tom, following his gaze.

Large windows occupied all four sides of the room. Paul had expected to see far up and down river, but hadn't appreciated that the nest also overlooked the near shore of the river. He noticed buildings scattered among the trees—cabins, and smaller structures he supposed were sheds and garages. At ground level, he had not been aware of their presence.

Paul glanced around the room. An armchair, a recliner, two folding chairs around a wooden table, and a camp bed comprised the sparse furnishings. Above the bed was a long shelf of books. He ran his eye along the titles. "Better Borscht" was a cook book. Military history was well represented as expected, but the books on knitting surprised him. They ranged from a basic how-to manual to volumes illustrating elaborate art creations. On a side table, a tripod-mounted telescope pointed out of the north window.

"Take a look. The 'scope is aimed at the old Durkel cabin on the other side of the bay." said Tom, pulling forward a chair. "Try not to knock it."

"You can adjust this screw if you need to focus. Tell me what you see."

Paul placed the bottle he'd been holding on the table, then settled into the seat. He leaned forward on his elbows to look through the eyepiece. The front window of the cabin leapt into view. Paul had estimated the cabin to be over two hundred and fifty metres distant, but the high-power telescope made him feel he had entered an intimate, illuminated circle. The rough wood fronting the cabin was in sharp focus; Paul he could see the knots and grooves in the decking of the ramshackle veranda that ran around the building. Flowerpots, some broken and empty, others containing dead stalks, lined the sill of a wide picture window.

A slight movement—Paul thought he must have jogged the tripod—made him pay more attention to the window itself. He realized he could see easily into the cabin's interior. It seemed embarrassingly voyeuristic. It took Paul some seconds to make out a shadowy figure, hunched over a table by the window. Suddenly, the figure straightened and raised a hand in salute.

Paul recoiled abruptly, and Tom laughed.

"Ha, that gave you a start! It should be Pierre on duty over there. There are two of them, taking turns to watch us: a Pierre and a Jacques, but Pierre has the evening shift. We made up the names, of course. Mike asked me to keep an eye on them. Let's finish this bottle, and I'll tell you about our friends."

Old Tom sat down in a recliner and gestured Paul towards the ancient armchair. Paul imagined both must have required block and tackle to lift from the Mess below. Tom poured a drink into two glasses. Paul leaned back in the armchair, and looked around, astonished to see the walls of the nest hung with woollen tapestries. Old Tom tilted a lamp, the better for Paul to see.

"Yes, knitting is my passion, as you youngsters say. They're mostly nautical subjects. You can see, in this one, I tried to capture the wide sweep of a regatta."

Paul distinguished a large, orange spinnaker billowing in the foreground, and a line of white-triangle sails worked in pale wool against a dark, green backdrop—presumably, the forested slopes on the far side of the river. Sail numbers had been meticulously stitched on in black.

A washbasin and a small propane stove occupied a corner of the room. Wisps of steam were rising from a battered tin kettle. Beside the stove, attached to the wall, was a dispenser full of instant noodles packets that Paul recognized. He'd thought of buying something similar for the galley in the *Spindrift*.

"Can't offer much in the way of food," said Tom, rummaging in a wooden box beside the stove. "Ah, here's an old packet of digestive biscuits. Not too stale, I hope."

Old Tom settled back into the armchair, and Paul sat on a folding chair. He cautiously bit a digestive. He leaned back as best he could against the central post supporting the roof. There was a small wood stove between him and Tom. Its chimney pipe rose straight up to a hole in the rafters. It was lit and throwing out a welcome heat as the shadows lengthened and the evening grew chill.

"Glad you could join us," said Old Tom. "Mike Collins is very careful about who he lets into the club. You must have made an impression."

"The Commodore sponsored me, you know," said Paul.

"Ha! Taggart is for show. He does what Mike tells him to."

Old Tom had been fumbling around beside his armchair. He finally retrieved a canvas bag, from which he produced needles and a ball of wool. He began to knit.

"Work in progress," he said. "Now, Mike asked me to fill you in on club history. You're familiar with the rule book stuff— we grilled you on that previously. What you may not know is our true purpose. Yes, there's sailing, but Blackwater is much more than that."

Paul swallowed the remaining contents of his glass and reached for the bottle to pour them both another. Paul soon realized Tom spoke, not of the arcane rules of the club, but of the 'Triple-P' Committee and its manifesto. After half an hour, Paul had emptied the bottle.

"So, you say Blackwater is resisting the Republic. And you really believe that we can rejoin Canada? Keep the King and all that?"

"Well, lad, you know better than most. They forced you out of your house. There's this northward migration of people displaced by water shortages and excessive heat. We have to stick up for ourselves. Quebec won't."

"Here. Hold this."

Paul held out his arms to accept a hank of bluish-grey yarn.

"More socks," said Tom.

"Mike Collins," he continued. "Now, there's the man for you. Been a sailor here since he was kid, always up there in the rankings. Can give Taggart a handicap any day and lead him over the line. They're an old valley family, the Collinses," said Old Tom. "Been here for generations. Irish, of course. Came over after some famine or another."

"Mike has vision," said Tom after pausing to disentangle his wool. "And grip. He won't let go of this idea of a Free West Quebec. And the bugger's not all talk."

"Well, I suppose I agree, but surely there must be a way to achieve this peacefully: a political solution?"

"Mike says not," said Tom. "That's why we support the Pontiac Brigade. If you think good intentions will change anything, dream on."

Paul sympathized with Collins' vision. The initial idealism of the Republic—free from the tyranny of the King's Governor-General—had become the *diktat* of Quebec City. *Madame la Présidente*'s liberal idealism and pledges to diversity had soon withered, allowing the darker strains of populism to swell. True, the bullying of Quebec's giant neighbour to the south hadn't helped, but neither had cutting ties to the rest of Canada. Paul wanted to renew those ties; return to how things were before. But what sacrifices he was prepared to make, he still wasn't sure. Until he worked that out, the Blackwater Sailing Club was a comfortable harbour for would-be revolutionaries like him with a decent pension.

"Use the privy if you will." Old Tom gestured towards a curtain hung across one corner of the nest. "It's my secret *garde-robe*. Takes too long to get downstairs at night, and then haul myself back up. Just avoid walking under the downspout on the backside of the clubhouse. That's my advice."

Chapter 21

NO ONE COULD ignore the call for volunteers. The club had been postponing the project for years. Now the cess pit was so full that, as Phelim Neely expressed it, they would be recommissioning the Commodore's boat as a floating latrine if they didn't do something.

It was a fine morning, but the crew of resident members was in a surly mood. They had gathered by the island drawbridge to hear Bowter and Collins outline the morning's tasks. Barrows, picks, and shovels had been garnered from all corners of the island, including from beneath the clubhouse deck, where ancient barbecues went to die.

"The idea," said Garvin, "is to dig out the pit, put the—what the hell do we call it?—the night soil in the barrows, carry the loads across the catwalk, and throw it into that big, yellow container."

Earlier that morning, a contractor from Wasteau *et Cie* had backed cautiously down *chemin* Blackwater to deposit a twenty-foot dumpster at the top of the slipway. Beside it was a large stack of sacks containing fresh material with which to build a new filter bed. Wasteau's motto—"*À vos ordures*"—writ large in bright yellow letters on the side of the dumpster inspired confidence in no one.

"It's just like digging turf out of a bog. Not a big deal at all." Mike Collins picked up a long, curved spade and headed up the hill. "Follow me."

"As if he ever had to do that," muttered Margret to Paul as

they trailed Collins up the path to the septic field behind the clubhouse. "Mike's never been in Ireland in his life."

Collins stripped off his shirt and set to. His energy was contagious, and his intensity of purpose was such that the others followed him into the pit. They began to shovel dung into the barrows. The smell proved less offensive than expected, and the volunteers began to dig with greater enthusiasm. Even Old Tom was seen to wield a trowel for a few minutes before retiring to the clubhouse deck, all the better to supervise.

The crew developed an efficient circulation of barrows. They pushed loads across to the shore and emptied them into the dumpster, and returned carrying sacks. By noon, the old pit had been completely dug out, and the two hundred sacks were neatly stacked on the island. Half of the sacks contained peat destined for the new filter bed, and the other half contained sand.

Collins saw his crew's energy flagging. "Who's first into the water to clean off?" He ran down the dock and leapt into the water; a cannonball.

Others followed into the water, more cautiously using the steps.

"Ah, the boys," said Margret, standing on the catwalk with Paul, and appraising the near-naked form of Collins swimming nearby. "Here's some soap."

The crew, cleansed of shit, ate a brief lunch. Collin had further instructions for them. They gathered around. Paul felt the force of personality, his ability to command. No one disputed who was in charge.

"Fill the pit with the new medium following these instructions," said Collins, reading from the how-to sheets he had been given by the Wasteau driver.

"We'll leave the left-over sandbags beside the drawbridge. Two walls of bags on each side, three feet high."

"Isn't he wonderful?" whispered Margret to Paul. "Not only

is he improving the shitters, he's fortifying the island. Look at them lap it up."

An hour later, the club had a septic field replenished with fresh peat, and a low wall of sandbags. Harvey Kinnear leaned against the sandbags, and pretended to aim a rifle at an imaginary foe advancing along the catwalk.

"Let's get out the guns," he called to Collins.

"Yes! Bring out the guns, Mike!" called Dent Hall.

"No guns today," Collins said lightly. "Improvise."

With Joe Tasker and Dent Hall, Paul took up position with Harvey behind the wall of sandbags. They aimed shovels and spades, taking pretend pot shots at invading republican troops.

"You all look bloody absurd," said Margret. She strode back to her dock, stepped onto the *Groaning Anne* and drew her drapes, leaving Paul feeling foolish.

Later, Old Tom descended from the crow's nest to brief Collins. He had watched the observer in the Durkel cabin reacting to the day's activities. Pierre had run up the lane to return an hour later with Jacques. Together they had investigated the dumpster.

"Good. We stirred the buggers up," said Collins. "They'll be testing our dung for disloyalty."

Chapter 22

TO SLEEP IN the *Spindrift*, Paul would put his feet towards the bow, so his face was under the forward hatch. He'd tried various positions—the boat could, in theory, sleep three—but this seemed best, at least in summer, when he needed the air. Winter might be a different matter.

Paul had a small mosquito net he could tie over his hatch, but he rarely bothered. The bats that flitted across the water at dusk dealt with most of the insects. There was little light pollution on the island, and Paul liked to watch the satellites crawling west to east across the hatch opening. It was better than counting sheep. Most evenings, he would turn off his interior lights quite early, just to watch the sky.

The *Spindrift* lay in a complete calm after the daytime flurry of activity. She was the perfect sleeping partner, responding lightly to Paul's every change in position. A slight rocking would soon damp to stillness, solicitous of his smallest movements. She took some getting used to.

However, there were nights when the wind drove into the bay from the southeast. Waves would radiate from the lighthouse point, rocking the boat. Under such conditions, Paul found sleep difficult; the slightest variation in the up and down movement would lift him towards semi-consciousness, before a return to a more regular rhythm let him sink back into oblivion. If the winds increased, and if Paul had misjudged the tension on the spring line holding the *Spindrift* to the dock, the urgent bucking woke him immediately.

A week following the communal effort to refresh the septic pit, the afternoon became sultry and close. Old Tom reckoned there would be thunderstorm by evening, and the forecast warned of the passage of a cold front. Paul hated a storm at night, when he couldn't see the weather approaching. His imagination magnified his fear of his boat breaking free and being swept away in the tumult. By three in the morning, he had already gone on deck twice to check the tension on his mooring lines. He felt he wouldn't fall asleep again, but drifted back into unconsciousness.

Paul dreamed of worms rising from the flooded meadows below the boat. They gnawed at the hull, their multitude of tiny mouths rasping at the fibreglass. In his dream, a bead of moisture appeared on the inside of the hull, and then another, drip after drip. He desperately tried to stem the flow, but water began to gush through the holes. Paul awoke with a start. He was wet, and looked up to see that he had left the hatch slightly open, and the rain was slanting in through the gap onto his face. He closed the hatch, firmly tightening the latch.

Curled up in his bunk, Paul went back to sleep. He drifted into a second dream. Blackwater was attempting to flee some menace approaching from the land. Bowter had clamped the club's outboard engines to the edge of the island dock and was pulling the starters of each in turn. They would cough into life, run for a few minutes before cutting out, leaving Bowter fuming and impotent. And the island had not have moved at all. At which point, Collins took charge. He commanded all the residents to take up oars and, on his count, to pull, pull away. The island separated from the catwalk at the drawbridge and they rowed it out to the middle of the reservoir. As they rowed faster, the island began to rise from the water. It rose slowly, anxiously, like a heavily loaded float plane. The island lumbered into the air, skimming the tree-tops of a pine-clad promontory, and trailing skirts of dripping weed. After reaching a satisfactory altitude, the island banked and flew west. Paul and the other rowers rested on their oars, letting the island glided gently down onto a wide lake. There was light chop on the surface of the water. The island touched the crests of the waves as it lost the final inches of altitude: slap, slap, slap, before settling.

Lying flat, unwilling to rise, Paul had watched the dawn strengthen through the hatch. In the half light, he decided the dream was political. Collins was leading his flock to the promised land.

The drumming of boots along the catwalk woke him. The rules forbad running on the catwalk; it caused waves, disturbed the peace. Paul had learned quite early in his residency to yell loudly and menacingly at any perpetrators. Paul poked his head out of his cockpit to join the chorus of complaints swelling as the disturbance progressed along the catwalk.

"Lowder Pritcher, whatever you're after, slow down and walk, damn you!" Joe Tasker from two boats down was giving it full vent.

The object of his invective was a wisp of a man in his late fifties, distinguishable by his shortness and now by his heavy feet. His diminutive size allowed him to rent the *Last Sandpiper*, the smallest and cheapest boat on the club's roster. Paul couldn't have lain straight in the boat's minute cabin. By virtue of a shallow draft, it occupied the dock nearest to the club entrance, where the water shoaled rapidly, and where the weeds were thickest at this time of year.

Pritcher was the club expert on all things relating to accountancy. He had a knack for ensuring the bar never ran short of drink. Collins spoke of him with affection, calling him "that small fellah with the big head for numbers."

"Where's Taggart?" cried Pritcher, recovering his breath. He slowed to a stop as Tasker intercepted him on the catwalk. "The recycling truck has crashed the gate. The gate is open!"

A municipal truck collected the club's recycling every two weeks. Normally, it backed slowly down *chemin* Blackwater; an awkward procedure accompanied by loud beeping. This morning, it had rolled down the slope, swerved at the last moment before the water, and crashed into the gate.

Paul was standing at end of the finger dock beside the *Spindrift*, craning his neck to see what was going on. He could see the back of the truck, entangled in the partly demolished entrance to the club. The driver was standing on the boat ramp, his phone to his ear.

"Mind yourself, Loess."

"Jesus, Mike!" cried Paul, startled. Mike Collins brushed past him and walked swiftly down the catwalk to join Pritcher and Tasker. Paul turned to see where Collins had come from. The *Groaning Anne* was rocking beside the dock, and a clay statue that Collins must have knocked over, rolled across the deck and dropped into the water. Margret won't be pleased, Paul thought, but the curtains on her boat stayed tightly closed, and Margret did not emerge.

Paul hurried after Collins to join the growing group of residents on the catwalk near the club's entrance. Two men in grey uniforms were picking their way through the ruins of the gate and starting to walk towards the island.

"That looks like Jacques and Pierre. GRs." said Collins. "Lowder, go up to the club and fetch the Commodore. I'll deal with this."

Collins stepped forward to meet the two GRs before they could advance any further along the catwalk. Paul and Joe Tasker crowded behind him to listen.

"*Bonjour, Messieurs.*" The GR they knew as Jacques greeted them. "This is most unfortunate for you. The tow truck is *en route*, but perhaps we can be of assistance. We are renting the cabin over there—he waved in the general direction of the Durkel cabin—so we are neighbours, *des bons voisins.*

"It's good of you to offer, but we don't need your help," said Collins, forestalling Taggart, who had just arrived and was trying to regain his breath.

"*Mais*, one sees there has been a discharge of plastic into the river," injected Pierre, "which contravenes Quebec environmental law."

Looking towards the shore, Paul saw that one of the blue recycling bins had tumbled down the launching ramp, discharging its load of empty bottles and beer cans into the river. The contents were being carried offshore by the slow current.

"We'll get that cleaned up right away, officer." Collins turned to Tasker and Paul. "You two. Find some hip waders and a net."

It was unfortunate that Pritcher chose this moment to return. He came running down the catwalk clutching a rifle, the old three-oh-three from the trophy cabinet in the clubhouse that was awarded for exceptional service. He was aiming it vaguely towards the gate.

Although all in the club knew that the rifle lacked a firing pin, the GR men did not share this knowledge. Alarmed by the high colour of Pritcher's face, and by his unsteady waving of the gun, they backed slowly along the catwalk towards the gate.

"Okay, okay, *Monsieur. Calmez-vous*," said Jacques.

"This," said Collins, pulling the rifle from Pritcher's grasp, "is a club trophy. Look, it's not loaded." He held out rifle for Jacques to inspect.

"*Eh bien.* You have a right to your privacy, *Messieurs*, but it would be best not to threaten your neighbours with firearms."

Jacques turned to Pierre. "Okay. *On se bart.* Let's go."

The two agents turned and picked their way past the recycling truck, which was partly wedged in the broken gate. Having regained the shore, the GRs stood at the bottom of the lane watching the tow truck manoeuver. The driver, after a few attempts to find the best alignment, hauled the crashed vehicle free, trailing razor wire wrenched from the top of the gate.

"Best guard the entrance until we get the gate patched up," said Collins. "Garvin, think you manage that?"

"Joe and Paul, get those recyclables corralled."

Tasker had found a long handle net and was scooping flotsam onto the catwalk. Meanwhile, Paul had struggled into the hip waders. He reached for an elusive piece of plastic that was blowing into deeper water. The clammy grip of the waders gave him confidence. A mistake: another step and he felt a gush of water on the wrong side of the rubber. Under the gaze of the GRs, Paul stomped slowly to shore, unhooked his suspenders, and let the waders fall around his ankles in a green deluge.

Paul knew Collins was on the catwalk, watching him. Why did he have to make himself look a fool in these blasted waders? And what was Louder Pritcher thinking, waving the rifle around?

Paul wondered if the GRs were planning something. It seemed more than a coincidence that they had appeared so soon after the truck had crashed the gate. Pierre's comment to Jacques about Margret as they walked together up the lane from the smashed gate would not have reassured him.

✧   ✧   ✧

"I THOUGHT WE would see Madame Bellejoux," complained Gruaut to Pénard.

The captain shrugged. He knew that Gruaut had given nicknames to the club residents. Pénard had compiled a list of boats and their occupants; *Madame Bellejoux* was Gruaut's name for Margret Mankie.

Pénard had watched Margret through binoculars on several

occasions. She looked good wrapped in a towel. He had also been fascinated by the clay statues beside her boat, and wondered what they meant. Why the woman who lived in the bizarrely named *Groaning Anne* should create these objects, he had no clue.

A crazy bitch, he decided.

Chapter 23

"LACKING DISCIPLINE, LADIES and gentlemen," insisted Commodore St. James. "This morning was a fiasco. We need to be better prepared for this kind of intrusion. Cool heads in the face of danger, and all that."

The residents had gathered by the bar in the Mess to discuss the events of the morning. Mike Collins leaned back in his chair, gazing at the line of club pennants strung above the bar. The group was divided between those who saw the funny side and the others, who took their cues from their Commodore and were not about to suggest the matter be treated lightly.

"Was it really an accident?" asked Harvey. "The usual driver of the recycling truck has had enough practice backing down the lane, but this was someone new. I didn't recognize him."

"A setup by the GRs, then," put in Garvin.

Old Tom had descended from the crow's nest and was behind the bar. Most of the club members were standing, holding drinks: Tasker and Hall were on Dubonnet, Paul drank beer, and Pritcher, very subdued, was clutching a whiskey. Didier from the catamaran had intercepted the whiskey bottle and was pouring one for himself and one for Sebastian. Maude and Margret wondered whether to ask Old Tom to mix his famous margaritas. It was too late.

"Glasses for the girls," he said, presenting them with two glasses of white wine from the box in the fridge. "And you'll have wine, too Olga?"

"Not for me, Tomas," said Olga Wilk. She was clutching tall

glass of what could be water, but which was probably vodka.

Collins ran his eye over the group; almost everyone was present. The mood was almost festive. He glanced at Taggart, then banged a beer tankard on the bar for attention. He started slowly.

"Well," said Collins. "We do need to be more vigilant. A repetition of that farce this morning is unacceptable. The Commodore agrees with me."

Taggart nodded, and reached for his glass. He coughed, as if to clear his throat.

"Why we are living here at Blackwater?" continued Collins, before Taggart could speak. "It's not the most comfortable life."

"Hear, hear," called Old Tom. Several people laughed.

"I'll tell you what. We may be oppressed by this damned Republic, and spied upon by their Republican Guards. But here on this small island we are free. Free to swim, free to sail, and free to say what we damn well like!"

"Now, many of you won't be aware of what has been going on. Your Commodore here," he nodded towards Taggart, "has had to deal with months of harassment by the authorities. This morning's intrusion is only the latest example. The GRs want to drive us from the island. Go home, they say. Move back to Canada, they say.

"I say, 'No!' I say 'Enough!'"

"Our home is here, this island, this West Quebec," he said. He paused, surveying the Mess.

"I give you a toast, Ladies and Gentlemen, to union once again with Canada."

"Reunion, reunion!" shouted the Mess, banging glasses on the tables and bar.

"A rare talent for rabblerousing," whispered Margret to Paul. "Now watch, as he cools them down."

"There is a fair breeze from the west," concluded Collins.

"And the afternoon promises fine weather. I propose clearing the decks for a fun race. Taggart, do you want to add a few words?"

"Splendid idea, Michael," muttered the Commodore. He stood, and quickly left the room.

Paul sat with Margret watching as the Mess slowly emptied. Collins looked at them.

"How was that, Margret?" he said, a smile on his face.

"I have no idea, Mike, what you hope to achieve by sailing. I thought you had better things to do. Come on, Paul."

Margret stood up. They followed Collins outside, and joined the stream of club members weaving down the hill towards their boats. All were a little drunk on alcohol and *l'esprit de la révolution*.

André-Claude Sauveur, skipper of the *Goéland*, a twenty-two-foot Tanzer regarded as a dangerous contender, was walking in front of Paul. He was explaining loudly to Tasker that he detested those *gardes républicaines*".

"They are *maudits* born-again Jacobins. *Je suis pour la feuille d'érable, entendez-vous.*"

Tasker was nodding. "With you there, André."

✧   ✧   ✧

BACKING HIS BOAT out from the dock was an erratic affair. Paul was trying the three-horsepower outboard Old Tom had given him.

"No need for the bugger. Works perfectly, and I'll give you the old gas for it," Tom had said.

Paul pulled the starter hard. The outboard coughed briefly, then died. He tried again. A minute later, he knew he'd flooded the engine and he gave up. He got out, stood at the end of his dock, and pushed the *Spindrift*'s bow around into the wind. A light breeze was coming over his shoulder. He climbed back aboard, the zephyr of wind caught the jib, and he eased away from the dock.

Paul was alone, as Margret had flatly refused to be swayed by the general enthusiasm. The *Spindrift* wasn't a difficult boat to manage singlehanded, provided the winds stayed light. He kept a hand on each control sheet, and a knee on the tiller. He'd decided on caution, and raised the small jib, even though the current wind favoured the larger genoa.

"Sailing with that handkerchief, are you?" shouted Collins as he sailed past towards the start, his roller jib eased right out to give maximum pull. "See you on the way back."

Twelve boats were slowly sailing back and forth along the approximate start line. The breeze was intermittent: lulls followed by hot gusts.

"What's the start sequence?" called Joe Tasker. The Commodore waved vaguely up the reservoir.

"Go!" shouted Collins as he tacked onto starboard and powered up. Some skippers had been expecting such a tactic; others hadn't. There was confusion as boats that had been caught on port ducked and weaved to find clear air. By that time, Collins had a thirty-second lead. He was trailed by a chorus of futile curses from the field.

Paul, in the company of half the fleet, opted to try the east side of the reservoir. They tacked away from the start to work their way across the water, as Collins and the others kept near the western shore. The *Spindrift* was struggling between two boats, in the wind shadow of one and unable to tack out. Paul's speed was dropping. Where had the damn wind gone? In the middle of the reservoir, the water surface looked glassy.

Paul knew that an approaching storm was usually heralded by dark clouds building in the west, and the low rumble of thunder. Today there was little warning. One moment, the sun was shining and the wind was light; the next, a shadow crept across the water, and the surface of the water exploded with the first shots of rain. Each drop seemed to bounce, rebounding from the surface until hit by another falling drop, until the boundary between water and air was lost in the mayhem.

The rain clattered on the *Spindrift*'s cabin roof. Paul pulled the hatch closed and sat wondering whether to reach for a rain jacket. He was already soaked. All the boats around him were dead in the water, stalled by the rain. Tasker gave Paul a wry grin and a thumbs-up. Harvey, on Paul's other beam, was shrouded in an enormous, oilskin poncho and matching hat. The raindrops crashed down.

"Raft up!" called Tasker.

By now, the three boats were almost touching. It was easy to warp them together. The boats sat forlornly mid-river, sails drenched by the downpour. After a few minutes, the rain eased.

"Loess, what about a small rum?" asked Tasker.

"Watch yourself, Paul. Joe knows no such thing as a *small* rum," called Harvey from the starboard boat.

"It's a good rum," said Tasker. "Dent brought it back from our holiday in Cuba last winter."

"What's that, Joe?" called Hall from the cabin. He clambered slowly out of the hatch to join the company. "Did I hear my name?"

Hall, swathed in a silk robe, stood in the middle of the cockpit looking at the departing rain. It was a dark curtain withdrawing upriver.

"There should be a rainbow," he said. "Say, Harvey, do you want to come across? I think you can ditch the poncho now. Climb over Paul. There's plenty of room, and we can pull up the canopy when the sun emerges. Which I estimate is about now."

Paul scrambled awkwardly across the gap between the boats. He accepted an unbreakable tumbler designed to fit into the drink holders that lined the safety rail of *Olivier's Dream*. Two of the holders were already occupied, their contents sloshing gently to and fro. Tasker leaned back in his cushioned seat.

The sun broke thorough, sending coils of steam from the water's surface around them.

"I love the rain on the river—the sound, the scent," said Hall.

"Sure. I can't think why you went below after the first drop," said Tasker winking at Paul.

The four of them, each holding a cup of Hall's rum, gazed across the water at the boats that were still racing, sailing slowly close to the far shore where they had found a ghost of wind. Collins still held the lead, with André-Claude a crawling minute behind. Taggart and the rest of the fleet followed in a straggling line, all moving at the same, slow pace, keeping well clear of each other to benefit from every puff that wafted down the valley's sides. Poor Phelim Neely had opted for the wrong shore. He lay becalmed far down river, in danger of drifting onto the beach with the slight current.

"Collins will win, of course," commented Tasker. "He has to, really. Mike's ego would go into meltdown if André-Claude actually caught him at the line, even if this is a 'fun' race. He'll have to come back with the safety boat to fetch Neely, though."

"Are you sure Mike isn't going to dive off on one of his side trips?" asked Paul. "Last time out he gave up the lead, if I remember."

Harvey was quick to reply. "No, no. Not this race, Paul. Michael won't be making a delivery today. He would have told me. I have to sign out the merchandise from the club stores, after all."

"Mike doesn't tell you everything, Harvey," replied Tasker. "He was taking inventory in the cave last night, after you had turned in, tucked up and dreaming of the Milky Way, no doubt."

Harvey, who prided himself on his knowledge of the stars, looked put out.

"It was overcast last night, as you well know, Joe."

"Exactly, Harvey. The weather was perfect for Mike's business. You see, Paul, our illustrious Mr. Collins has hidden depths. You're new, so I suppose you haven't seen past the friendly and affable Michael. He's always keen to help out, the first to volunteer for the dirty jobs, and the first to organize others to finish those same jobs. So tall and clean shaven, who would have thought it? He's right more often than wrong, and he usually gets his way—I'll give him that. But he's pissed off a lot of people on the island. Being right around here doesn't endear you to everyone. Word to the wise, Paul: keep a pole handy to push him off if he comes too close. He has Margret besotted with him, of course."

Chapter 24

FOR CYNTHIA MAURICIE, the word "ambition" was for lesser mortals. She was bred to buoyancy: a pedigree and education that ensured her steady rise in the hierarchy of the Republic. If obstacles arose, family would deal with them. It helped that she was a colonel in the Intelligence Directorate of the *Garde républicaine*.

Here in *le Château* in Quebec City, at the heart of things, Colonel Mauricie was physically disconnected from the outposts of the *Gardes* scattered around the fringes of Quebec. It was from these fringes, she knew, that black swans sometimes flew—those unforeseen events that could derail a career.

It was, she reflected, time to stir up the commander of the *Gardes* division in West Quebec, an economically depressed corner of the Republic. The man should be more proactive against the small minority in that benighted region intent on rejoining the Rest of Canada. They were an irritant, but, in Mauricie's judgement, they lacked the organization to cause serious trouble. They were *Anglais*, mostly, encrusted to the land like barnacles, and tough to dislodge.

Madame la Présidente had, however, expressed concerns. And, one was wise to take her hints; Josée-Mathilde was ruthless with ineffectual subordinates, and in her determination to stay in the top job. Look at how she had repeatedly crushed the thin reeds in her opposition. But one day, she would surely slip and fall. And on that day, Mauricie might need to step smartly behind the rising power. She suppressed the thought that it might be herself. For now, she was happy to glide in the wake of her mentor.

Colonel Mauricie turned to the console at the side of her desk and pressed a button.

"Re-schedule my ten o'clock," she said to her assistant through the microphone. "I have a call to make."

♦ ♦ ♦

FIVE HUNDRED KILOMETRES to the west, Commander Brevet of Western Division was at his desk rereading his agent's report. The incident with the municipal recycling truck crashing through the club gates was most satisfactory: another turn of the screw. Captain Pénard had ensured the cooperation of the driver with a contribution to the man's wallet. Brevet made a note to commend his initiative.

Letters, ostensibly from the environment ministry, had the club scrambling to update their septic system. Brevet hadn't thought they would act so promptly. He was disappointed that defective sewage treatment hadn't been the *causus evictus* he'd been looking for.

Brevet put the report aside. He stood, stretched his back, and walked over to gaze out of his office windows. Streaks of grime on the exterior of the glass irritated him—Brevet had not seen a window washer dangling outside his window in months. He made a mental note to blast building management.

The corner office on the twentieth floor of Tower Three of the concrete maze known as the *Portalette* had windows facing east and south. The view to the east was towards the confluence of the Noire and the main stream of the newly international *Rivière de l'Outaouais*, where black water and grey mixed in swirls of eddies. To the south, below Brevet, an old iron bridge crossed to the midstream islands, thence to the Canadian border post on the far shore. Beyond were desolate flats, cleared long ago and now pocked with concrete foundations once poured in an attempt at rejuvenation. Discouraged, the developers had abandoned their projects long since. A giant graffito sprayed on a partly demolished wall proclaimed "Remember 1867", a wistful souvenir of Canada in fading red paint.

Traffic over the iron bridge was limited to commercial vehicles. Drivers of private cars—those with proper authorization—were required to make a detour over a second bridge several kilometres upstream. Today, Brevet saw that there was the usual convoy of vans—parcel couriers—queuing at the *douanes* on the Quebec side of the bridge. He supposed these were delivering medicines and other luxuries that were now hard to find north of the river. He smiled at the thought. The shipping companies paid a hefty duty that the Republic applied to such imports in American dollars. It was a good thing, too, since the Quebec *piastre* had been trading ever lower against other currencies. Senior ranks like Commander Brevet took a hefty cut of the profit from these border crossings; it was a perk of being posted to the back of beyond.

Brevet sighed; he had work to do. He returned to his desk, a sweep of mahogany veneer in the style known—so Accommodations assured him—as *Nouveau Napoléon*. It was uncluttered save the latest edition of *Extravagance Nautique*, the magazine for lovers of larger yachts. Brevet settled back in his orthopaedic chair and flipped through the glossy illustrations. Behind him, hanging on the wall, were certificates attesting to the Commander's qualifications. Several framed photographs showing Brevet with his hunting trophies: one with moose, others with the cadavers of other species at risk. There was also a picture of a celebratory group, taken after his famous victory—many years ago now—in the annual speed boat race held by the local marinas.

An electronic map on the wall beside Brevet's office door flashed live updates on incidents and developments across the Republic. A sophisticated scrambler unit beside his desk encrypted communications to and from headquarters. A light blinked on the unit, demanding his attention. Irritated, Brevet read the brief text on the screen. His superior in Quebec City required him to call at the earliest opportunity. *Madame Colonel Mauricie.* The bitch.

Brevet sighed and put aside the article on yachting in the Exumas. He pressed speed dial on the scrambler. After a series of clicks and whines from the machine, the call connected. He toggled the speaker phone to on.

"*Bonjour, Madame Colonel,*" he said respectfully. "Serge Brevet, returning your call. How is the temperature in Quebec City? We have it very mild here for the time of year."

"*Un instant, Brevet,*" came the reply.

Brevet heard muttering in the background; the bitch was clearing the room. He hated the woman. Mauricie had been promoted to her current rank the previous year, over—in Brevet's view—a more suitable candidate, a pragmatist who knew how things got done. Mauricie was a privileged child of Quebec's elite. What did she know about the realities of running a border town?

Although *Madame la Présidente* had vowed to eradicate corruption from the *Gardes* as a priority in her Christmas address, that, surely, was for public consumption? Mauricie, if she had a tenth of Brevet's experience of politicians, should know that. Yet, in her first directive as Colonel, the bitch required regional commanders to eliminate misconduct in the lower ranks. Brevet, proud wearer of the Order of Quebec on his lapel—the sword and *fleur-de-lys*—took this as a personal affront. There was no corruption in his West Quebec Division, he had assured her. *Point finale.* Brevet straightened in his chair, brushed a speck from the sleeve of his uniform, and gritted his teeth.

Patience, thought Brevet: just let her try something in his bailiwick. There were plenty of ways to slip and fall if you didn't know the complexities of the regional situation as he did. West Quebec had the potential to compromise the bitch. The thought of seeing Mauricie's nice arse flushed from her comfortable seat in *le Château* brought a smile to his lips.

"Brevet, are you still there?" Colonel Mauricie's voice disturbed Brevet's reflections about her suitability for her current rank.

"*Oui, Madame.*"

"You are aware of the growing pressures the central region is experiencing?"

"*Oui, Madame.*"

"*Madame la Présidente* is concerned about the border south of Montreal. There has been a surge of illegal immigrants from the USBAZ. Our American friends have been importing labour for the harvest. There is the inevitable spillover."

Brevet breathed more normally. So this was not about his use of operational funds.

"*Oui, Madame.*" He looked at his electronic wall map. Several pin lights were flashing at border posts along the St. Lawrence. "An orange alert, *Madame*. Indeed, I have been most concerned."

"Stop sounding like a blasted recording, Brevet.'

"*Oui, Madame.*"

Colonel Mauricie sighed. "Pay attention. Central region is looking for agents fluent in Spanish for temporary reassignment. I want you to list any under your command. I have here Agent Rojas. He will assist you in assessing your agents' fluency in this language. You can expect him tomorrow. I am sure you will be able to provide him with the necessary facilities."

Brevet reflected on his own attempts to master languages

other than French. In English he was officially proficient; although no longer a formal requirement under the new government, senior management expected officers at his level to be able to direct subordinates in the second language. Spanish was a different story. Once during a Mexican holiday, Madame Brevet had persuaded him to take Spanish lessons. It had been frustrating. Many of the words and phrases looked the same as in French, but he just could not get his tongue around them. In fact, the sole phrase he was sure he had mastered still came out as "*Dos bières, s'il vous plait.*" Provided he said it loudly and slowly, the waiters seemed to understand.

"*Merci, Madame Colonel.* But I must note that losing personnel must inevitably affect our surveillance capabilities. There are, as I have reported to Headquarters, subversive elements here in the western region who favour rejoining Canada. Our infiltration of these separatist cells is at an early stage, and I fear we may lose the progress we have made to date."

"The reassignment is temporary, Brevet. You must make do with the resources that remain to you. Draft in some regular police from traffic duty, or whatever they do. I have every confidence in you."

"*Merci, Madame.* I will expect Agent Rojas tomorrow."

"*Bonjour, Brevet.*"

There was a click. The light extinguished on the scrambler.

"Bitch."

Brevet looked across at a photograph of him posing with a magnificent buck. He wasn't born yesterday; this Rojas was obviously a spy. Still, he should attempt to comply with the Colonel's request. He might, he supposed, reduce his surveillance team at Blackwater. He suspected that Gruaut, at least, was fluent in Spanish. Wasn't his wife named Manuela? Not a Quebecoise name at all.

Captain Pénard would have to find someone else to watch

the club. But, perhaps, as the bitch had said, he could draft in some uniforms. Brevet pulled a file out from a drawer of his desk. He was sure he had seen a recommendation from Pénard—ah, here it was—about an Inspector Jules Laborde who the *Gardes* might recruit from the regular police, should the need arise. Pénard had known Laborde from hockey practice and vouched for him as a sound officer. Brevet made a mental note. He was running out of cousins.

Chapter 25

MIKE COLLINS FORBADE his network from using electronic means to communicate. Email was much too easy to intercept. He much preferred coded messages sent through regular mail; the authorities seldom scrutinized ordinary letters.

The message he had been expecting was overdue. Still, it surprised him to see Florette Henderson hurrying along the catwalk towards the club. He met her at the drawbridge.

"Not your usual day, Madame Henderson?"

"No, well, I...I have a priority delivery for you, Monsieur Collins." Florette winked heavily, and passed him a white envelope.

"Most kind of you, Madame Henderson. You really didn't need to make a special trip."

"But, Monsieur Collins, I was sure you would want this delivered personally." Florette touched his forearm.

"We have to stick together, these days," she added, mysteriously.

Collins escorted Florette back to the repaired gate. Garvin Bowter, as part of his duties as Harbour Master, had installed a new lock with a keypad. "Much more secure than the old padlock," he had assured the club residents. A week later, he was still having to remind people of the new four-number sequence.

"You have the new pass code, Madame Henderson?" said Collins. "Well, of course you do."

Walking back along the dock, he tore open the envelope and read the contents. It was as he'd expected but, damn it, he would have to hurry to make the rendezvous.

✦ ✦ ✦

HALF AN HOUR later, Collins was in the *Ring of Kerry*, steering along the western shore of the reservoir, the afternoon sun burning the back of his neck. He turned away from the light breeze and glided behind a rocky point into still water and the welcome shade of pine trees. The water was deep and a ledge along the shore made a natural dock. It was a perfect spot for diving, and a cottager had once built a spring board here. Only the stump of the diving plank remained.

Collins stood as he steered close to the ledge, then stepped lightly ashore holding the painter. Set into rock was an iron ring, a vestige of logging operations on the Noire—long ago abandoned—to which the logging company had once attached massive cables. Collins tied up.

A faint path wandered among riverside bushes and up through a screen of trees. After a brief climb up an embankment, Collins reached a ramshackle building: long and narrow with a steeply pitched roof. It had once been a shelter for passengers at a stop along the railway track which ran down the Noire Valley from Newbridge in the north all the way to Hull. The style was Canadian National from mid-last century. Long since abandoned, the railway and the wayside halts were falling into decay. He took the three steps onto the covered porch, hesitating before the entrance. It was hot, the intense sun beating off the wood siding. The paint on the door frame was peeling, and the wood streaked with black mould. The small window panes in the door were opaque with grime.

"You there, Donovan?"

Collins heard nothing but a cricket chirping from somewhere in the long grass.

"Major Pat Donovan?"

Again the cricket. The silence between its chirps seemed to deepen as Collins listened intently for a reply. He pushed open the door and peered inside. The dark interior was cooler, but stuffy, and smelled of rot. Collins walked across what had been the waiting room to a door on the far side. It opened onto a strip of weeds growing in the gravel of the old rail bed. He looked left and right, but the track curved out of sight, indistinct in the pollen haze of late afternoon.

He looked at his watch; his contact was late. After five minutes, he heard the crunch of wheels on gravel coming from down the track. A red pickup truck came creeping towards him, pushing aside stray branches of brush that had grown or fallen across the old railway cutting. The driver of the truck had the window wound down, a broad forearm resting on the sill. Something country was coming from the radio. A reaching branch scraped along the paintwork.

The truck pulled up beside Collins.

"Shit," said the driver. "The bloody weeds are taking over this track. I had to get out and move a fallen tree. You pick your spots, Mike."

"Let's get a crack on then, Pat," said Collins.

Donovan switched off the engine, and the music died. He got out of the truck, and followed Collins through the old station building and down the path to Collins' boat.

"I have two cases in the cabin," called Collins over his shoulder. "Five Armalite AR-15s in each."

"They'll be heavy enough," grunted Donovan.

With Donovan on the ledge and Collins standing in the boat, together they wrangled the long boxes onto the shore. Ten minutes later, both cases of guns were under a tarpaulin in the back of Donovan's truck.

"That's the last of them, then?"

"For now, yes," replied Collins. "The GRs have tightened inspections at the bridge, and deliveries have suffered. After you get these stashed, tell them that I'm arranging another route."

Donovan grunted and climbed into the cab.

"Be seein' you, Mike. Tell me when you get the ammunition."

Collins watched the truck turn around and start back down the track. A short distance past the bend, Donovan would turn off the old railway line onto the road leading north to Newbridge. Driving north and west, patrols were scarce. In an hour, Pat should be safely back on his farm. The rifles would join the arsenal of the Pontiac Brigade in the pig shed.

Then he noticed the maple leaf sticker on the bumper, the one that read "Free Pontiac Libre."

Jesus wept. This was supposed to be a covert operation. Would the Brigade never learn discretion?

Chapter 26

SPLIT RINGS AND turnbuckles were spoiling Paul's morning. He was re-rigging the safety lines on the *Spindrift*, a chore her last occupant had evidently not found necessary. Dirt encrusted the corroded threads, and the split rings that kept the screws from loosening threatened to split his fingernails.

"Morning, Loess!" Garvin Bowter strode past on the catwalk, distracting Paul and rocking the boats. Paul watched, helpless, as the screwdriver he had been using to loosen a turnbuckle rolled towards the gunwale.

Margret was watering her plants beside the *Groaning Anne*. She and Paul both heard the screwdriver plop into the water.

"Hard luck," said Margret. "So, you're going out on your own, then?"

Paul had by now sailed with various crews. He had wooed Margret and Harvey, and once—an error not to be repeated—asked Old Tom to crew. His head was still ringing with the advice Tom had shouted at him.

But Paul had yet to go solo on an overnighter. He had sailed the *Spindrift* single-handed before, but that had ended in the thunderstorm fiasco, when just about everyone except for Collins had been towed back to dock. Today promised to stay fine: almost perfect conditions, with a light breeze from the south-west.

"Yes, that's the idea," said Paul. "Once I get these lines tightened up, I'll sail upriver and anchor somewhere for the night."

"Do you have a chart? There's a good mooring just off the

mouth of Beaver Creek. The ground is firm sand. No one has lost an anchor there yet."

Paul tightened the final turnbuckle. It was calm at the dock. He pulled up the jib and untied the mainsail so it flopped along the boom, ready for when he got out of the bay.

"Push me out, will you?"

Margret stepped across the finger dock, and untied the *Spindrift*'s bow and stern lines. She gave the boat a push with her foot. The foresail filled and gently pulled the *Spindrift* into the bay.

"Thanks," called Paul. But Margret had already turned away.

"That was easy," thought Paul, steering towards mid-river. But now came a problem: how to raise the mainsail without a crew. He brought the boat into the wind, and the boat slowed to a near stop. Paul went forward to the mast. As he changed position, the *Spindrift* veered away from the wind. Heart pounding, he hauled the mainsail up as quickly as possible. The boat heeled, and Paul scrambled back into the cockpit to grab the tiller. He sat breathing deeply as the boat steadied.

With the jib sheet controlling the foresail in one hand, and the mainsail sheet and tiller bar in the other, Paul felt the boat surge, heading north. This was it. He was single-handed in a twenty-two-footer. Then he remembered he'd forgotten to put on his life vest.

An hour later, Paul decided to anchor near the mouth of one of the drowned side valleys that wound from the hills to the east side of the reservoir. The anchor was heavy, and lowering it over the bow required an awkward stretch. As the chain ran out, the weight increased until Paul felt the anchor touch bottom. He let out the remaining chain, then the length of extra rope recommended for water twenty feet deep. The boat gradually swung round on the anchor to face into the breeze. He planned to swim ashore and explore, light a fire, catch and cook a fish for supper.

❖ ❖ ❖

THE EVENING WAS cooling off. The sun had dipped below the skyline half an hour before, and dusk was creeping across the river from the shadowed western shore. No fish had bitten, so Paul opened a can to warm on his propane stove. It was almost a meat stew, with almost meat. Fortunately, he had beer. After supper, he lay wrapped in his sleeping bag, looking at the stars through the *Spindrift*'s front hatch. The boat was rocking gently, tugging at its mooring rope. Was the anchor dragging? Should he have noted his position relative to the shore? The worry kept him from sleeping, especially as the wind picked up after midnight. He imagined drowned trees in the murk beneath the hull, of roots snagging his anchor.

Dawn came as a relief. Paul crawled from his bunk and stepped out into the cockpit of the *Spindrift*. Low clouds scudded across the sky and a fretting wind made him shiver. He leaned over the side to splash water on his face.

Rubbing himself with a towel, he looked around. Surely he had anchored the boat further from shore? Peering over the stern, he saw rocks on the shallow bottom; the water level had dropped overnight. The previous evening, the rocky shore had been a hundred metres away; now the water's edge was at half that distance, wavelets lapping onto a broad band of grey mud.

Paul chewed a handful of muesli while waiting for water to boil. The wind was coming from the north, an awkward direction blowing directly onshore, and forcing Paul to motor out of the anchorage. He rehearsed the steps: set the throttle at its lowest speed, lock the tiller, go forward to the bow, and lift the anchor as the rope reached the vertical. Then, he'd have to pull rapidly hand-over-hand on the chain to bring the anchor on deck. It was a plan, thought Paul, as he sipped lukewarm tea. He felt keenly the absence of a crew. On the plus side, there was no one to comment if he messed it up.

Right then! Paul chucked the dregs of the tea overboard, and started the outboard. It ran on first pull! He let the boat creep forward into the wind. Paul made his way to the bow and un-cleated the anchor rope. He pulled up a metre of dripping rope and fed it down the slot into the bow locker. Pull, and coil the rope down. Repeat.

It seemed to take an age before the line was vertical and he was directly above the anchor. Now the heavy work began: lifting the chain and anchor towards the surface. Finally, heart pounding, he hefted the dripping anchor from the water and slotted it into place. He pulled up the jib and scurried back into the cockpit.

The north wind which had made leaving the anchorage difficult was now to Paul's advantage. He killed the engine and bore off to the south, letting the jib fill. It would pull the boat all the way back home.

An hour later, the *Spindrift* was nearing the point that marked the entrance to Blackwater Bay. The sudden narrowing of the channel with the drop in water level became more obvious. Blackened posts lined the margins of the channel: stakes driven into the mud to stabilize the banks of the reservoir. Long ago, the reservoir had sapped away the soil behind them, stranding the posts metres from the shore, devoid of purpose. Normally, their tops were under four feet of water. They led him along a sinister avenue towards the entrance to the club.

At the moorings alongside the catwalk, Paul saw that the masts of most boats were askew, boats tilting to port or star-board.

"Every damned boat is aground," yelled Taggart, standing awkwardly on the sloping deck of the *Cornishman*. "You can't dock. There's not enough water."

Of all the boats, only Margret's, with its twin keels, had settled evenly onto the mud.

Paul let the *Spindrift* drift in, carried by the boat's momentum. Margret was standing on their finger dock pointing to a newly emerged stump.

"There's just enough water for you here," she called. Paul let his bow nose towards the dock. Collins arrived beside Margret, armed with a boat hook. They were joined by Tasker, Kinnear and Bowter. Paul crept closer.

"It's the dam," said Collins. "They must have opened all the sluices overnight. It's time we had a word with the superintendent. Loess, we need your boat. Yours is the only one afloat."

"I've been out all night, I'd really rather—"

"Wait!" said Collins, ignoring Paul's objection. Collins hooked the *Spindrift* and pulled her close to the dock.

"Right, jump aboard now," said Collins. Kinnear and Tasker swung aboard Paul's boat, which swayed alarmingly. Collins stepped after them, while Bowter stayed behind.

"Pass me that," said Collins. He held onto a stay and reached out to take the long package Bowter was holding.

"Is that a—?" began Paul.

"No, Loess. It's a fishing rod."

Paul started the outboard and backed slowly away from the dock until he had room to turn. He headed back out, now with a cockpit crowded with passengers.

"Go south," said Collins. "Leave the sail down. It will be quicker to motor."

As they went down the reservoir, the water narrowed to pass between cliffs, then broadened again into a wide expanse dotted with rocky islets. After twenty minutes, Paul could see in the distance the buff, upstream wall of the dam.

"You'll have to take her to the shore before we get near those." Collins pointed ahead to the low sweep of high-tension hydro lines that crossed the river from the eastern to the western bank. Supported at both ends by electricity pylons, the lines sagged to within thirty feet of the water surface in the middle of the reservoir.

"Maudy got toasted there one time," sniggered Harvey. "Sailed underneath. Lightening came straight down the mast. Amazing."

"The lowest line is inactive," added Collins. "But I don't want to test that."

Collins undid the ties from around the package he had taken from Garvin. He pulled out a shotgun. He broke open the gun and pushed cartridges into its twin chambers.

"Useful for vermin," he said in response to Paul's look. "Maybe we'll find some at the dam."

"Take us over there," said Collins a few minutes later, pointing towards the shore. Paul steered closer and saw a tiny beach. He let the *Spindrift* glide into the shallows between two rocky ledges.

Collins went forward. "That's good enough," he called. "Give me a hand, Joe." Collins jumped off the bow into shallow water. Tasker, after a moment's hesitation, followed. Together, they heaved the bow of the boat onto the narrow strip of sand.

"I suppose she'll be safe enough," said Paul. They were standing on the beach looking at the *Spindrift*. Paul had insisted on throwing a light anchor off the stern into deeper water. He tied the bow line to a tree on the bank.

"Let's go," said Collins. He led the way uphill, away from the shore. After five minutes, they encountered a path.

"They made this track while they were building the dam back in the nineteen-twenties," said Collins. "It leads up to a viewpoint where people could watch the progress. From there, we can scramble down to the dam itself."

They reached a level area where bulldozers had pushed blasted rock across the hillside to create a platform. Standing at the edge, they looked down onto the full sweep of the dam, a bow of concrete stretching across the valley. To their left, waves on the reservoir splashed white, fretting against the upstream face. The deep valley below the dam was in shadow.

Behind them towered another pylon, the terminus of the high-tension corridor that crossed the reservoir. A hum filled the air. Hanging from a mesh fence, a sign threatened electrocution.

At their feet was a red-brick building, built where the dam abutted the valley side. Cables looped down the hillside from the pylon, connecting to massive insulators on the roof of the building.

"That's the generator house," said Collins. "We go down there." He pointed to the top of a flight of metal steps. Paul, Tasker and Harvey walked over to look. Rust wept from the corroded iron.

"Keep close to the wall," advised Collins over his shoulder. "Don't trust that guard rail!"

Their party regrouped at the bottom. Collins led them around the generator building and onto the service road than ran along the top of the dam itself. He pointed ahead with his shotgun towards a white portacabin.

"That's where we'll find the superintendent," he said.

✦　✦　✦

GUY LaMOLLE WAS having a quiet morning. He was sitting in comfort in his orthopaedic chair—standard issue for PowerBec employees—before two monitors. One was showing commercials during a break in an NFL game. The other was live-streaming the parking lot at the far end of the dam so LaMolle could keep an eye on his e-Buick. Not much of interest was happening on either. On the wall, beside his monitors, was a red telephone, the hotline to PowerBec Central Command. It never rang.

LaMolle's office in the portacabin was small. His tiny kitchenette in one corner comprised a propane stove and a beer fridge. The fridge was well stocked. A couch occupied the far wall, where he often slept. Although the decor in his office was spartan—he had taped a single poster of the Montreal Canadiens to the back of the door—LaMolle couldn't complain about the view from the window. It looked North, up the length of the reservoir to the blue hills of the upper Noire Valley in the far distance.

From his office, LaMolle monitored the reservoir level, sluice apertures, turbine speeds, and other parameters on an array of digital displays. Not that there was much need for him to do so, since they had installed an Artificial Intelligence called 'HYDRA'.

LaMolle was trying an easy sudoku while he waited for the game to resume. His title of superintendent was a slight exaggeration; he was the only PowerBec employee left at the dam. Quiet was normal.

His cousin Serge had called the previous day, telling LaMolle to open the sluices and drop the water level in the reservoir.

"*Seulement un metre*, Guy," Serge Brevet had said. "Let's not overdo it."

He didn't ask why. Whatever the Commander wanted, he got. It had always been like that in the family.

Opening the sluices required LaMolle to perform a manual operation in the turbine hall, a cavernous space deep in the concrete body of the dam. HYDRA could do everything except press a switch or turn a valve on the pre-digital machinery. Following his cousin's call, LaMolle had gone down to the hall. It was clammy and cold down there. He had pressed the necessary switches, and had hurried back to the warmth of his portacabin. The hockey game was only in the second period. LaMolle didn't feel like driving home.

Next morning, LaMolle looked at the gauge measuring the reservoir level. The water had dropped one-metre-thirty overnight. "Close enough," he thought.

✧   ✧   ✧

THE LOUD RAP on the door of the portacabin came as a complete surprise. LaMolle threw aside the sudoku, got up and shrugged on the jacket that had been hanging on the back of his chair. A surprise inspection from headquarters, perhaps? He was reaching to open the door when it flew outwards. A man was standing in front of him, a very large man, it seemed, who almost filled the doorframe. A minute earlier, LaMolle had thought his office was quite large, spacious even. Suddenly, it felt oppressive, the heating on too high. A strong smell of river wafted in.

"We are from the Blackwater Sailing Club. Are you the dam superintendent?" asked the man.

LaMolle looked at the expression on the man's face: cold, hard, angry. Then he saw the broken shotgun under the man's arm. He tried to speak, but all he could do was nod.

"Well, Superintendent, you dropped the reservoir level overnight, and that left many of our members high and dry. My name is Collins. We have come to ask you, politely, to raise the level back to normal. And, in future, to stop messing with it."

LaMolle noticed other faces peering over the shoulder of the intruder.

"Ah, well, *Monsieur*." LaMolle found his voice. He tried to remember the tips from the crisis management seminar he had attended. Somewhere, he had a small, plasticized card with does and don'ts, what to say and not say, in bullet form. It was perhaps in the desk drawer. It might as well be at home.

Collins snapped his shotgun closed.

"Euh, *Monsieur*, there is no need for that. Your situation is most unfortunate, but it is a question of public safety for the many thousands of people living downstream of the dam. We must anticipate surges coming down the river into the reservoir. There are so many thunderstorms these days. We monitor the entire watershed, and these decisions are made after careful analysis by our hydrologists at PowerBec Central. It is really out of my hands, *vous voyez*, and—"

"Out," said Collins.

LaMolle squeezed past Collins into the open air and almost fell down the two steps from the portacabin. One of the group assembled outside steadied him. There were three others, LaMolle realized, plus the big fellow behind him. Collins gave him an encouraging push.

"Take us to where you control the sluices."

LaMolle stumbled along the road that ran along the crest of the dam towards the generator house. Just before he reached the building, he stopped, pointing down some steps.

"It's down here, *Messieurs*, in the turbine hall."

"After you," said Collins.

They followed the superintendent down a flight of steel-grill steps, ending at a steel door. LaMolle pushed open the door. Strip lights suspended from the ceiling flickered to life, revealing a spacious chamber. Deep in the body of the dam, the turbine hall was walled, floored, and roofed by concrete. Water oozing from cracks in the ceiling dripped onto the floor, puddling in the dark corners.

Collins pushed LaMolle towards the centre of the hall where a white console housed a bank of heavy duty electrical switches. Beside each was a blinking light.

"Well?" urged Collins. Paul, Tasker and Harvey crowded behind Collins, their faces white in the fluorescent light.

"Below us here, *Messieurs,* are five giant pipes that bypass the turbines and lead out into the spillway. The red lights show that numbers three to five are closed: the green lights that one and two are open."

LaMolle fixed his gaze on the blinking lights. Better that than turn and confront the man with the gun.

"Close them."

LaMolle closed two of the switches. Electric motors hummed, and the background rumble of rushing water slowly eased. The green indicator lights turned to red.

"All five gates are now closed, *Messieurs.*"

"And those hand wheels against the wall over there." Collins pointed to the far wall of the turbine hall. "Are they for opening and shutting the gates manually?"

"*Oui, Monsieur.*"

Collins lifted the shotgun to his shoulder.

"Jesus, Mike," said someone.

All of them thought too late about backing away. The bang was shockingly loud in the confined space, reverberating for seconds afterwards. When the smoke cleared, they could see a blackened circle about a foot in diameter on the wall. The reek from the blast lingered in their nostrils.

Collins waited until their ears stopped ringing.

"Bird shot." he said. "Just a reminder, LaMolle, for the next time you feel like playing with our water level."

Chapter 27

IT WAS TUESDAY evening, and not much was going on at the Blackwater Sailing Club. The officers of the club had convened a meeting for seven o'clock. Observers were welcome. As it turned out, the entire membership decided it would serve as their evening's entertainment. The Commodore took his usual chair at one end of boardroom table with Harvey Kinnear by his side. Harvey had suggested St. James place his near-completed model of the famous racing schooner *Bluenose* in the centre of the table.

"It really is magnificent, Taggart," he whispered.

The other board members—Garvin, Maude, Benedict, and Collins—pulled up the remaining chairs around the table. Most of the onlookers had to stand, leaning against the walls of the room. It was the best crowd a board meeting had attracted in anyone's memory.

Margret had commandeered two stools from behind the bar. Paul perched beside her.

"Right, let's get this show on the road," said Taggart. "Harvey, you have distributed the agenda to everyone?"

"Excuse me, Commodore," interjected Collins. "Perhaps you could move item three up? I think many are here expressly for that item."

"Well, if no one objects." said the Commodore. "Item three becomes item one. Proposed? Seconded?"

Kinnear typed the names Maude Crabbe and Benedict Countryman on his laptop.

"Thank you. Item one: A proposed change to paragraph three of the club's constitution. As currently worded, it requires members, and I quote, 'to take an active interest in sailing, and to refrain from discussing politics on the island.' Garvin, you want to speak to this?"

"Thank you, Commodore." Bowter stood up. "For myself, I am against any change. These are hard times. We have lost homes—I myself a beautiful waterfront cottage. Our movements are restricted. The GRs watch us constantly."

"Intimidation," said Maude.

"But," continued Bowter, "the only response, in my view, is to keep our sailing tradition going, and to refrain from giving the GRs any more excuse to harass us here. If you ask me—"

"Well, that seems reasonable, Garvin," said Taggart. "Thank you."

Collins leaned back in his chair.

"Well, it's my amendment, Commodore," he said. "I would like a vote on it. But first, I note that most club members are here, if not all. We easily have quorum of the membership. So, in this case, a simple vote of the Board won't suffice."

"Er, I think Mike is correct, Commodore," said Kinnear.

"So, to reiterate, I propose the following: 'Members are to demonstrate a key interest in sailing *and* paramilitary activities.'"

"No, no, and no," said Bowter. "That is an absurd suggestion. We must remain, first and foremost, a sailing club, not your private army, Mike."

"The wording reflects the reality of our situation," replied Collins. "As you know, the Committee for a Free West Quebec has a paramilitary arm, the Pontiac Brigade. Whether we like it or not, the authorities already view members of the club with suspicion. They consider us terrorists."

"Garvin has a point, though," interjected Benedict Countryman. "The Committee is strictly political. We don't do bombs and whatnot, do we Mike? Leave that to the Brigade. You know, clean as a new sail on the surface, dark deeds below water. Eh, Mike? What's wrong with that?"

Collins pushed his chair back in a sudden movement. The legs scraped on the wooden floor: a screech of impatience. His face impassive, he looked at the model of the *Bluenose* in the middle of the table.

"I suppose, Taggart, that you still have some work to do on the rigging. And that bow sheer doesn't look right."

Everyone watched Collins, holding their collective breath.

"Let me see," Collins said, finally. "Harvey here has spent the day checking his inventory of jigsaw puzzles. Tom, you are onto your fifteenth pair of woollen socks, if I haven't lost count. Garvin, rubbing it again won't get a better shine off the silverware. Margret's got her damned gnomes. Gentlemen and ladies, I ask you, do you expect all this excitement to carry you through the winter?"

"But, Mike, you asked me to ..." began Harvey.

"Maybe you have been wondering why we have been filling the wine cellar with crates of firearms all summer. Perhaps it has escaped you that we have delivered over fifteen crates to the Brigade. That they now have some hundred and fifty AR-15s in-country, from Newbridge over to Shawton. Folks are getting a mite impatient. And what with the so-called Republic half-invaded by the Yanks, our chances have never been so good. Underground? Underground! It's time now to stand up and fight."

Collins slapped the table hard and looked around the Mess. He caught and held everyone's eye in turn.

Paul who was leaning back on a chair, suddenly overbalanced, and had to grab his neighbour's arm to stop himself from crashing to the floor of the Mess.

"For God's sake, watch it Loess," snapped Bowter.

"Shut up," said Old Tom. "Listen to the man!"

"I have a plan for a joint operation with the Brigade," continued Collins. "The Blackwater Sailing Club, ladies and gentlemen, is going to war!"

Chapter 28

HE HAD TWENTY-FOUR hours' notice. *Tabernac!* Commander Brevet had received the call from Quebec City the previous day. What had looked like a pleasant weekend with maybe a round or two of golf turned into a frantic rush to complete arrangements for a surprise visit by the Minister of National Culture.

Colonel Mauricie had adopted a collegial tone.

"Don't worry, Serge. He is just touching base. *Madame la Présidente* is sending all her cabinet on walkabouts. No reflection on you."

Mauricie never called him "Serge".

"What am I supposed to do with him? *Chrisse!*"

"The Minister has expressed keen interest in visiting Lac King in the *Parc national des collines*. I gather the Minister has a nostalgic interest: renaming the Gatineau Park was one of his first actions on taking office. He also considers himself a sports fisherman."

Good, thought Brevet: some common ground with the Minister. It gave him a reason to launch a power boat on Lac King, something he had wanted to do for years. The park authorities banned motors on the lake, except for official government business. Pénard would make the arrangements: the aluminium *chaloupe* the GRs occasionally used for river patrols would do nicely.

"I am wondering, Colonel, whether I could use the emergency fund for unexpected costs. We'll have to provide extra security for going into the *Parc*."

"That'll be all, Brevet. Have a good day."

The red light went out on Brevet's comms unit.

"After Quebec City shits on you," he thought, "they never pay to flush *la merde*."

✧　✧　✧

THE NEXT MORNING, Brevet was watching a speck in the sky. There was no way he could judge the distance. It could be a bird, perhaps a high-flying hawk? Brevet lifted his binoculars, finding nothing but blue. He had been waiting for nearly twenty minutes. With the short flight from Quebec City, you would think they could keep on time.

Brevet was standing beside a Chevy Suburban in front of the modest terminal. The airfield was half an hour's drive south of Hull Centro, connected by a stretch of highway that was kept in good repair so VIPs could drive downtown in comfort. When he went inside to check, he found the airport lounge empty, and the arrivals board insisted the flight had landed ten minutes ago. The smoked windows of the small control tower concealed any signs of life within.

Captain-Agent Pénard sat behind the wheel of the Suburban watching his Commander. He had—on Brevet's orders—requisitioned two vehicles from the motor pool at the *Portalette*. One was shiny black, without markings, and kept spotless for official visits. Pénard had two agents armed with submachine guns in a second Suburban that had followed them to the airfield: security for the Minister. The second vehicle pulled a boat trailer carrying the *Garde's* smallest patrol boat.

A sudden glint in the sky caused Brevet to raise his binoculars again. This time he held a small aircraft in his field of view. What had been a barely audible drone rose in volume and pitch as the plane banked to line up for its approach.

"Pénard!" called Brevet. "He'll be on the ground in two minutes. Tell your men to get over here, and to look smart."

The plane descended slowly, crabbing to the left in the light crosswind. It settled onto the end of the runway like a tired moth, puffs of smoke coming from the tires as they hit the asphalt. The engine sounds abruptly descended an octave as the plane swept past Brevet, then rose again with a snort of power as the pilot turned to come back towards the waiting group. The props fluttered as the pilot cut the engines.

In the sudden silence, Brevet ran his finger around his collar and glanced left at his three subordinates, who were standing in line at something close to attention. He felt exposed here in the middle of the bare tarmac. The door of the Bombardier ExecProp abruptly swung open and Brevet stiffened in anticipation. A uniformed crew member pushed out a short flight of folding steps. They slapped onto the ground.

Brevet's first view of the Minister was of his backside edging out through the door. The cramped interior of the aeroplane made exiting difficult, and Minister LeGros was a large man. He twisted awkwardly to grip the flimsy handrail, and descended the three steps to the ground. Brevet stepped forward and saluted.

"*Monsieur le Ministre!* I am Commander Brevet. Welcome to West Quebec. *Bienvenue!*"

Fat slob, thought Brevet, who valued neatness.

"*Chaulice*, Brevet. *Ces maudits petits avions.* These tiny planes skid all over the blasted sky. Véronique, pass me the *'osti* phone!"

Brevet gathered the last remark was to the young woman who was emerging from the plane behind the Minister. She deftly extricated herself from the aircraft, carrying a large document case in one hand, her boss's jacket over one arm, and holding a phone to her ear.

"*Un instant,*" she said into the phone, then passed it to the

Minister.

"*Oui?*" shouted LeGros into the device. "I can't hear. No. I'll be back in civilization tomorrow. Definitely."

Meanwhile, the co-pilot of the plane was extracting the Minister's luggage from the cargo bay. Two bags were already on the tarmac, but a long canvass bag had become wedged in the constricted space. She was struggling to remove it.

"*Attention!*" shouted LeGros. "Careful with that rod case!"

He handed his phone back to his personal assistant and turned his attention to Brevet.

"You have lousy reception here, Brevet. Get me out of this wind."

Pénard helped the co-pilot carry the luggage to the rear of the Suburban and load it into the trunk. He waved the security detail back to their vehicle and returned to hold open one of the Suburban's rear passenger doors. The Minister levered his massive body onto the rear seats, followed by his personal assistant.

Pénard got behind the wheel. Brevet sat beside him and fastened his seat belt.

"Let's go," he said, quietly.

Pénard checked in his mirror to ensure that the second Suburban was ready. He released the brake. The vehicles slowly accelerated, following a service road around the terminal towards the airport perimeter. They paused briefly at the entrance gate. Pénard rolled down the driver's side window and held out his GR badge. The guard saluted and lifted the barrier. Three hundred yards past the gate, they turned right onto the slip road leading to the highway.

From her rear seat, LeGros' PA leaned forward to speak to Brevet.

"You have the Minister's agenda, Commander. He has made one change." She passed Brevet a sheet of paper.

Brevet caught her scent and attempted a winning smile. He glanced down at the new item on the agenda, and his smile froze.

"The Blackwater Sailing Club? The Minister wants to visit a sailing club?"

"Just a brief visit this afternoon, Commander. The Minister is considering an addition to sites important to the national culture. The Minister makes it a rule to visit every candidate."

Brevet glanced at LeGros. The Minister was gazing out the window, seemingly fascinated by the succession of empty fields rolling past. *Shit de shit!* Brevet had heard that the Minister sometimes co-opted sites of so-called national cultural importance for his private use. Had he caught wind of Brevet's plans for the Blackwater Sailing Club?

"Of course," said Brevet. "It is only a minor detour from the route we take back from Lac King. We can visit this afternoon."

The highway curved east around the fringes of Hull. They crossed the Noire River over the high bridge, slowing only briefly for the checkpoint. The last twenty minutes had passed in silence.

"We are entering West Quebec now, Minister. *Le Pontiac*"

"Ah yes, Brevet. This Lac King business. *Madame la Présidente* insists. How long till we arrive?"

The convoy entered the village. "*LaCloche vous souhaite!*" proclaimed a sign beside the road. Written beneath in smaller letters "Belltown welcomes you" was barely visible. Brevet breathed a sigh of relief. The last thing he needed was for the Minister to rant about signage. He checked that the chase car was keeping close as they roared down the main street.

"We enter the *Parc national* soon, Minister. Then it will be another ten minutes."

They passed the last house in LaCloche and crossed a creek. The road narrowed, and they drove through forest. Dense stands of conifers bordered the road. After a kilometre, the road split to go around a building. It was in a rustic style, built with red cedar logs and roofed with green shingles. Brevet glimpsed a ticket window. A sign propped against the dirty glass read "*Fermé*/Park closed."

"The security is further on, Minister," said Brevet. "Just before we get to the lake."

This time, the barrier was substantial. Bollards driven into the roadbed guided the vehicles through a chicane to a gap in the high wire fence. A guard carried a machine pistol. Pénard lowered his window and again held out his credentials.

"*Avancez, Messieurs*," said the guard after a brief inspection. "You are entering the conservation zone. Please observe the regulations." He pushed a leaflet into Pénard's hand. It threatened dire consequences should he be tempted to pick wildflowers or chase fauna.

Once past the boundary fence, they were in the park proper. It was virgin forest, more or less, that extended uninterrupted north to the tundra. The southern end of Lac King appeared on their right, a jewel of brilliant green enhanced by a bloom of cyanobacteria. The road followed the edge of the lake. Although paved for some of its length, the macadam had disintegrated in many places, forcing the cars to reduce speed to negotiate the many potholes and washouts.

"Brevet. 'ow much fucking longer?" asked LeGros from the rear seat.

"You can see the roof of the lodge, Minister. Over there, among the trees at the end of the lake."

✧　✧　✧

A GRAVEL DRIVE led up to the front of the lodge, a two-storey wooden structure of rustic simplicity that nonetheless conveyed an impression of old money. The dark green of the decorative surrounds to the many windows perfectly accented the rich cream paint of the wood siding. Small turrets rose from the corners of the building.

Pénard stopped the car in front of a short flight of wooden steps that led up to a shaded veranda. The second vehicle, pulling the boat trailer, continued past and disappeared around the side of the house. Brevet got out and opened the door for the Minister and his PA.

The Minister stood on the gravel, examining the facade in front of him. Brevet took a flanking position to one side and a pace behind.

"Cottage gothic from early last century," LeGros said authoritatively, remembering the brief Véronique had passed him to read in the aeroplane. He adjusted his tie, and marched up the steps, trailed by his PA.

Brevet turned to Pénard. "Make sure the boat is launched while we are inside," he said, before hurrying after the Minister.

The permanent staff at the lodge comprised a caretaker and groundskeeper, and in summer two volunteers, one to prepare the teas offered at a modest price, and another to answer the questions of the occasional visitor. They were standing by the front door to welcome their visitors.

The volunteer guide, an elderly lady from LaCloche, stepped forward. "Hello, *Bonjour*," she said, in a voice used to quelling tour parties. She proffered a plasticized sheet, and a set of head phones.

"Our audio guide describes the history of this historic building: key dates, visitors and so on. It's for the self-guided tour. Kindly return it when you leave. Would you prefer English or French?"

"*Tabernac*, Brevet. What is this?"

"Madame," said Brevet, intervening. "We'll take three audio

guides."

Ten minutes later they had completed the tour of the ground-floor rooms, and were standing, silent, in one of the many bedrooms on the second floor. "And in this room," intoned the tape, "Winston Churchill is said to passed the night before his historic meeting with Mackenzie King—"

"*C'est assez!*" said LeGros. "*J'ai faim.*"

They trooped downstairs and out of the front door. The lodge staff had laid a table at the far end of the veranda with a white linen tablecloth. LeGros strode across and sat down heavily on a chair. His PA and Brevet sat opposite him.

The previous day, the Minister's PA, after making discreet local enquiries, had found a reputable firm to cater the Minister's lunch. Given the brief notice, she had agreed to the suggested menu, one that—she was assured—would be appropriate for the location and ambience. The crew from Wheelimeats had arrived at the Lodge early that morning to set up. The designated server, a youth more accustomed to door-to-door delivery, had dressed in black for the occasion.

"So, this was King's escape?" said the Minister. "This *cabane*? Well, Brevet, I'm not impressed. I shall inform *Madame la Présidente* accordingly. Take a note, Véronique. *The lodge building has minor heritage significance. The extensive work needed to renovate the building cannot be justified.*"

"With luck, it will burn down by itself in a few years," he added.

"*Tabernac!* What the hell is this?" exclaimed LeGros. The youthful server had placed a tray with a large, silver teapot beside the Minister. There was a basket of scones, silver dishes and jugs for thick cream and jam.

"The full English cream tea, *Monsieur*," he said.

Véronique went to the kitchen to have words with the caterer. Under protest, the chef warmed up a frozen pizza in the microwave, and served it, garnished with leaves of fresh basil, on the silver tea plates. Even so, the meal was not a success.

Brevet beckoned to Pénard.

"Have they launched the boat?" he whispered.

"*Oui, Monsieur*," replied Pénard. "The men moored it at the end of the wooden jetty. They filled the gas tank and have run the motor. All is ready for you."

"*Très bon*, Pénard." Brevet turned back to LeGros.

"Perhaps *Monsieur le Ministre* would care to fish the lake?" Brevet had waited until the Minister finished the crust of his pizza and sat back in his chair. He hoped that postprandial relaxation with a fishing rod might improve the Minister's mood.

"That, Brevet, is an excellent idea," said LeGros.

Véronique, the PA, leaned forward.

"You can change in the Lodge, *Monsieur*," she whispered. "I have placed your bag in the downstairs washroom."

Five minutes later, LeGros emerged from the Lodge wearing Bermuda shorts, a short-sleeved shirt in a flowery print, and a hat accessorized with fishing lures. The Minister had come fully prepared for this interlude in his busy day.

Brevet, feeling overdressed in his uniform, led the way down to the lakeside, followed by the Minister and his PA carrying the Minister's rod case.

"*Monsieur*," the PA reminded him. "You wished to visit the Blackwater Sailing Club this afternoon."

"Plenty of time, Véronique. Plenty of time." replied LeGros. He stood on the jetty, looking down at the waiting boat.

This was what Brevet had been waiting for: one-on-one time with the Minister. It couldn't hurt his career. He waited until LeGros had settled in the bucket seat near the boat's stern, then slowly opened the throttle to steer out into the lake.

"I will switch to the electric motor now, Minister," he said.

They were approaching the edge of the shallows at the northern end of the lake where Brevet hoped some decent fish might be lurking. The time of day and bright sunshine were not ideal, he knew, but for the first time since his arrival, the Minister wasn't complaining.

Half an hour later, Brevet was pleased. The Minister had caught two fish: a decent-sized bass and a smaller *brochet*. LeGros seemed content with the pike. It had put up quite a struggle, and Brevet had only just netted it as the fish twisted off the Minister's hook. So much for LeGros being a sports fisherman, thought Brevet. He steered back to the jetty where he saw the Minister's PA with Captain Pénard awaiting their return.

"Excellent. Quite a haul for such a short time," LeGros said, after they had tied up and clambered onto the dock. He held up the two fish he had caught. "Come here, Brevet."

The Minister draped his arm around the Commander and pulled him close. Véronique took photographs.

"Lac King, eh? We will have to change the name to something more suitable for the Republic," the Minister said. "I have it! *Lac Deux Poissons.* Perfect."

Chapter 29

PAUL WAS THREADING a kayak through a narrow channel bordered by tall reeds. He could just see the roof of the lodge above the vegetation, and he guessed he must have at least a hundred metres of marsh to go. It was the last obstacle before he could regain dry land. He had slipped across the eastern arm of Lac King just after dawn and paddled through the broad fringe of water lilies in the shallows to find the entrance to this channel. Well hidden in the reeds, he had tried to relax in the sun, listening to the rising hum of insect life as the morning warmed. At noon, he moved, as per the plan.

The last few metres, through dense scrub at the edge of the marsh, proved the most difficult. Then he was out on the sweeping lawn beside the lodge. There were ornamental bushes, which he used for cover as he skirted the rear of the building, making for the gravel parking lot on its far side. His target was in the shade of a large white pine.

Paul paused. He saw no one. He took the small bottle from his pocket and crept up to the nearest of the two SUVs. It was by far the dustier of the two vehicles and had a boat trailer attached, just as Collins had described. Paul opened the nearside door and felt inside for the gas cap release. Crouching on the gravel, he unscrewed the cap and poured the maple syrup into the gas tank.

Then he ran for it, around the back of the lodge and through the bushes, abandoning any pretence to stealth. Paul jumped into the kayak, pushed off, then glided back through the reeds. He breathed deeply, trying to slow his heart.

◇ ◇ ◇

WHILE PAUL WAS sabotaging the *Garde's* Suburban, the main body of the commando had crossed Lac King nearer to the park's southern entrance. There were four of them from Blackwater, including Collins, who assumed leadership. Two enthusiastic volunteers from Donovan's Pontiac Brigade made up the team. Taggart had excused himself on the grounds of arthritis, as had Old Tom. Many of the older club members had also demurred, arguing various ailments.

Margret, when asked by Collins, laughed. "You boys go off and enjoy yourselves. I've plenty to do on the boat."

The flotilla of club kayaks, led by Collins, crossed the lake under the cover of the morning mist rising from the water. One kayak towed an inflatable dinghy. After grounding the boats on a narrow beach, the volunteers pulled their kayaks beneath the overhanging cedars which screened the beach from the road that ran along the lakeside. They crossed the road, climbed into the woods, and waited.

"Relax," Collins had said. "Sleep if you want. They won't be along for a couple of hours."

Just before noon, they watched the two SUVs sweep past in a cloud of dust, the second pulling a boat and trailer. Collins waited until they were out of sight, before walking onto the road and waving for the rest of the volunteers to follow him.

The team had brought with them a variety of trenching tools, including a mattock and shovels. They stood where a stream passed under the road to flow into the lake through a large diameter pipe. Differential settlement had raised a pronounced hump over the culvert, creating a ridge across the road.

"We'll dig here, beside the culvert." said Collins. "We only have to enlarge this pothole. They won't see it until they come over the hump. It'll be too late by then."

✦   ✦   ✦

VÉRONIQUE LEANED OVER and whispered in the Minister's ear.

"*Oui*, yes, yes," said LeGros. "Brevet, whistle for your boys. We should press on."

Brevet nodded to Captain Pénard, who threw a quick salute and went to fetch the Minister's transport.

"A pleasant afternoon, Minister?" ventured Brevet.

"Yes, indeed. I assume the fish are on ice in that cooler?"

Pénard drove around to the front of the lodge and pulled up on the gravel. Brevet waited a few seconds, then went over to speak to him.

"Where is our escort, Pénard?" he asked.

"Something is wrong with their engine, Commander. They can't get it started. Should I tell them to join us in this one?"

Brevet thought quickly. The Minister would hardly notice that their chase car wasn't following. The last thing Brevet wanted was for the two guards to climb in with them.

"No. They can call a tow truck if they have to. We'll go on ahead. Just drive fast and raise plenty of dust."

✦   ✦   ✦

THE BLACK SUBURBAN came round the bend and roared into view, barrelling towards the members of the Blackwater Sailing Club hiding among the trees. It barged the air aside with sheer horsepower. Its rear tires sprayed loose stones in quantities that would have severely damaged the paintwork of any vehicle close behind, should any have been following.

The watchers saw the SUV brake as it approached the culvert. It drove over the hump, the front wheels dropped into the trench and the vehicle stopped dead. The rear rose upwards—it seemed to the observers in slow motion—to flip the Suburban onto its roof. The doors popped open. For a few seconds, the SUV rocked back and forth, like a black beetle trying to right itself. Then it stilled. Steam hissed from the damaged radiator.

"Pull on your masks," shouted Collins. "Let's go!"

He leaped from his hiding place and ran down the hillside onto the road. The others were slower to react, stunned by the violence they had witnessed. Then they, too, were running.

As he approached the SUV, Collins heard an angry voice from the interior. He peered inside: the occupants were hanging upside down, caught in the webbing of their seat belts. All were stirring feebly. Two were in the back, a large man and a younger woman. Collins assumed the man was the Minister. Two uniformed GRs—one the driver—were in the front seats pinned by the airbags.

"Pull the lever, Véronique, and get me down!" yelled the Minister.

LeGros' assistant struggled to find the release for the Minister's seatbelt. There was a click, and her boss slid abruptly to lie sprawled at Collins' feet.

The Minister stared up at the man looming over him.

"*Chaulice!* Who the hell are you?"

"Your saviour," said Collins. "Wait—I'll take those." Collins reached in and removed the pistols that had fallen from their belts of the GRs as they hung upside down.

"Garvin and Joe: get those two out of the front seats, and prop them over there." He pointed to the low bank beside the road. Brevet and Pénard were in mild shock, pale but otherwise unhurt.

"Tie them up, Garvin. Make sure you use the right knots."

"*Messieurs.* Wait!" protested Brevet. "I am a commander of

the *Garde républicaine*. This is ridiculous—"

"Quiet," said Collins. "And you *mademoiselle?*" He turned to Véronique, who had extricated herself, and was standing bewildered beside the upturned vehicle. "Not hurt? *Pas de blessés?*"

Véronique shook her head.

"Alright. You can go. Walk back to the lodge." The Minister's PA turned and hurried quickly up the road.

"Now for you, Minister."

The volunteers were standing in a loose semicircle around LeGros, unsure what to do next. The Minister leaned against the doorframe of the SUV, his face red, sweat pouring off him. He seemed deflated, in danger of slumping onto the road.

"Relax," continued Collins. "We aren't going to make you walk anywhere. We have provided alternative transportation."

Minutes later, Véronique had disappeared from sight. After Garvin had hobbled their ankles together with bag ties, Collins sent the two GRs shuffling after her.

"Now, down to the lake, Minister: it's only a few steps."

"*Attendez un minute,*" wheezed LeGros. "Evidently, you know who I am. If I am to be a hostage, please respect the dignity of my office."

"Of course. That is why you get to sit in the inflatable. The rest of us will paddle the kayaks. I should warn you, the valve to inflate your boat was leaking this morning. If you struggle, she might deflate. In which case, you will have to swim the rest of the way across the lake."

The inflatable, weighed down by LeGros, rode low in the water. Its sole occupant sat rigid on the rubber seat to ensure no water slopped over the sides. Bowter and Collins, in line astern, towed him across the lake, flanked by the remaining kayaks. They traversed Lac King without incident, except for startling a loon into a crash dive.

They paddled towards the eastern shore of the lake. Here, out of sight of the lodge, a forestry track led down to the water's edge and a short stretch of pebbly beach. It was a secluded spot, once well known to locals for nude bathing. A rotting picnic table under a spreading pine suggested that happier past.

✧ ✧ ✧

PAT DONOVAN HAD been there all morning. He and his men had driven in the red pickup three kilometres along a forestry road to reach the beach. Although clearly marked on his map, in reality the road was a mere track, uneven as hell: there were many rocks and washouts, and fallen branches frequently blocked the way. Donovan had driven slowly in low gear, fearing for his transmission. It had taken nearly an hour, with volunteers walking in front of the truck for much of the journey, cutting brush, and pushing larger deadfalls aside. When they finally reached the water, the sun was well up. After they had unloaded the kayaks, the commando left to paddle across the lake.

"Relax, Pat," had been Collins' parting comment. "I hope you brought a book. Don't expect us back until mid-afternoon."

Donovan resented Collins and his damn Committee. After all, it was he, Major Pat Donovan, who led the Pontiac Brigade. From the moment Mike had proposed this joint operation, he had had doubts. But an enthusiastic Mike Collins was hard to deny. He cursed the day he had agreed to lend two of his men to this scheme. Donovan was angry.

Mike and his elaborate plans: a simple post-office stickup would make the point just as well. Or exploding a small device. Or a night visit to the home of a GR. Donovan was sick of Collins' superior airs, his assumption of authority. The Committee was supposed to concern itself with the politics: operations fell to the Brigade. Keep it separate: keep it simple. That's how it was supposed to be.

And now Donovan, as designated driver, could do nothing but sit and wait. He felt like shooting something, somebody, anybody. Taking his rifle from its rack behind the seat of the truck, he walked across to the old picnic table. He sighted the gun across the lake, at an imaginary kayak.

By lunchtime, Donovan's neck was playing up: tension, he thought. He was in a surly mood. He shut Paul up smartly when Paul returned in his kayak, buoyed by his successful mission, and flooded with endorphins. For the next hour, Donovan sat in the cab of his truck, cleaning his gun, while Paul sat down by the water, both watching for the return of Collins and the commando.

Finally, at about three p.m., they saw the small flotilla round a point and paddle towards the landing place.

"You caught the bugger, then?" Donovan called to Collins as the kayaks grounded on the beach.

"Yes, *the* Seraphim LeGros, Minister of National Culture. A rare catch," replied Collins. "Paul, lend a hand."

Paul and one of brigade men helped LeGros clamber out of the inflatable and onto shore. They led him to Donovan's waiting truck.

"*Ceci est inacceptable,*" panted LeGros, trying to regain some dignity. "*Je suis—*"

"We know who you are," said Collins. "And, we have plenty of duct tape if you don't keep quiet. Lift him in the back, boys,"

"*Crétins,*" muttered the Minister, as he struggled, with Paul's help, onto the tailgate of the truck.

Collins turned to Donovan, who was talking with his men.

"Pat, put him in your Air B'n'B. But make sure you lock the barn door when you get him back to the farm. We wouldn't want our guest wandering."

Donovan shrugged and climbed in behind the wheel of his

truck. His two men squeezed in beside him on the bench seat.

"Jeez," muttered Donovan to his neighbour. "Next, he'll be telling us we have to exercise the bugger."

Chapter 30

THREE DAYS AFTER kidnapping LeGros, Mike Collins took Margret to inspect his prize. They had sailed in Collins' boat halfway up the reservoir. Pat Donovan picked them up at the abandoned railway halt. He was not happy: the brigadier had found the Minister a trying guest.

"Your man is a bleeding nuisance,"

"It's not for much longer, Pat," replied Collins.

"Easy for you to say. After you left, first thing he does is threaten to go on a hunger strike. So, I order the special from the *poutinerie* in Newbridge. You owe me, Mike: now, he gets through five a day."

They drove in silence. Five kilometers north of Newbridge, Donovan turned off the highway onto a gravel side road. Minutes later, they arrived. A pair of tractor tires painted red and white guarded the entrance leading to the brigade's secluded retreat. A mailbox clung to a post wildly askew. Beside it swung a sign announcing "Pat's *Gite* ..."

Donovan drove up the long drive between fences of barbed wire. The field to their left held a few brown cattle. "Bloody heifers," said Donovan, as the beasts tossed their heads and snorted from the dust raised by the passing truck. The field on the right was left fallow, and due for mowing.

The drive swung in a loop in front of the farmhouse. Donovan braked to a halt beside a row of tubs containing red and white geraniums.

"Red and white seems to be a theme," commented Margret.

"Damn right," replied Donovan.

They got out Donovan's truck and stood before the barn conversion.

"We put him in Tulleymore," said Donovan, leading Collins and Margret around the side of the barn to a flight of wooden steps.

"He's up there. Couldn't put him in Connemara on the ground floor. I have a booking coming tomorrow."

They climbed the stairs after Donovan. At the top, he took out a key and opened the door into the loft conversion. Minister LeGros was sprawled on a couch, eating and watching sport on television. He barely looked up as they entered.

"UN BUT!" he cried suddenly, and fist-pumped the air. Montreal had scored.

"He looks comfortable, Mike," said Margret.

"He's not supposed to be comfortable, blast it," replied Collins.

"Minister! Minister LeGros!" cried Collins, trying to catch the Minister's attention.

"Seraphim?" said Margret more quietly.

LeGros looked up.

"If it's about my ransom," mumbled LeGros, his mouth full of cheese curds. "Tell them to get on with it." He tossed aside the empty cardboard container. It joined the pile on the floor beside the couch.

"No ransom," said Collins. "We just want you to read our manifesto on the radio."

"*Jamais!* Never will I do such a thing. *Jamais* will I betray the Republic!" He belched loudly.

"Disgusting," said Donovan.

Margret laughed. "You really can't keep him much longer, Mike. In these conditions, he'll want to stay."

"I … damn." Collins scowled and went back outside. Margret and Donovan followed him down the steps. They stood on the puddled gravel in front of the barn.

"Is that where you keep the arsenal?" asked Margret, looking towards a low red-roofed shed, isolated among trees some distance from the barn. Donovan grunted.

"Well hidden from your other guests, I hope." She turned to Collins, and pulled out a folded newspaper from the bag slung on her shoulder.

"Did you read this? Inside page, the political column. It says that, although *Madame la Présidente* calls our kidnapping of LeGros 'an outrage' and 'unfortunate', in private she's delighted. It seems the Minister was a difficult colleague. I gather we merely anticipated by a few weeks his formal decapitation."

"But I was just drafting the Committee's ultimatum," said Collins. He looked around the yard for somewhere to sit. He found an upturned half-barrel that Donovan had yet to plant. Sitting there, he seemed less of a big man.

"You've made your point," replied Margret sympathetically. "No one, not even a cabinet minister, can feel safe into West Quebec now, not without a much larger escort."

"Shit! You're suggesting we let him go?" asked Donovan. "After all this trouble?"

Margret smiled at Donovan. "I suppose you wanted buckets of blood?"

"Fuck, yes!"

"When the time comes, Donovan," she said. "When the time comes."

"Bin him then," said Collins. Gone was Collins' usual amiable smile. He looked vicious. "Take him into town and bin him. Just make sure he can breathe."

"The blue bin, remember, Donovan," added Margret. "Recycling, not compost. They pick up on Mondays."

✧   ✧   ✧

COLONEL MAURICIE WAS at her desk by eight after a punishing workout followed by a shower. The warm glow dissipated as she opened the morning papers. She felt her chest tighten.

"*Ministre LeGros recyclé!*" screamed *La Presse*. "*Put out with the Trash*" said the English-language journal. She read how the operator of a municipal recycling truck had found the indignant LeGros, alerted by the Minister's cries for help. The separatist-terrorists had dumped the Minister on a residential street in Hull. The bin was a snug fit, and his extraction painful.

The call from *Madame la Présidente* came ten minutes later. Mauricie braced for fury, but got sympathy. She was unsure which was worse.

"Cynthia, my dear," said Josée-Mathilde. "We understand you were planning to visit your friends in the West tomorrow as part of our anti-corruption initiative. Now you can also speak to this Commander Brevet about—let us find the right phrase in English—his almighty cock-up. He is your subordinate, after all. If one didn't know better, one might think you arranged this, ahem, *ce embarras* for our dear colleague. *Félicitations, ma chère.*"

Mauricie put down the phone. She was relieved, but puzzled. How had *la Mante* known of her intentions? The previous week, she had arranged a visit to Hull Centro for a separate purpose. The timing was good. Do her other business first, and then in the afternoon, have the delight of reprimanding Brevet for losing a minister. The little crook would be squirming with worry all day, waiting for her. That *Madame la Présidente* would rather give him a medal for embarrassing LeGros was not "need to know" for Brevet.

Chapter 31

AGENT ROJAS WAS tired: he had been driving for three hours. He was at the wheel of a Cadillac CT sedan, one of the small fleet of luxury cars reserved for the use of senior cadres in the *Garde républicaine.* He glanced in the rear-view mirror. *Madame* Colonel, in the rear, was working on her laptop computer, papers strewn across the leather seat beside her. She saw his glance.

"Only another hour, Rojas. We'll be there in plenty of time," she said.

They had set off from Quebec City at six a.m., *en route* for Hull in West Quebec. They had made only one stop: for gas, at an official "rest area", where they had eaten a quick breakfast at a '*Triple B*'—the chain '*Bec Bonne Bouffe*' being the kind of roadside cafeteria where no one stayed for long.

It was now late morning; it was sweltering outside, and Rojas on straight stretches of road could see the mirage hovering above the blacktop. Most of the trip had been on empty highway, but a major bridge collapse forced them to detour. They were signed off the highway to join a country road that wound along the river. For kilometres, they drove on gravel and endured the juddering of washboards. Rojas supposed that, given time, the road would be re-asphalted. Next year or perhaps the year after that, depending on whose palm was greased.

On the left-hand side of the road, vast reed beds bordered the river. Rojas had read that it was an invasive tropical reed, a climate migrant from the South. He thought it sinister. To his right, strips of fields from abandoned farms stretched towards a dark line of trees. Rojas was nervous: this was his first time venturing into the distant and largely ignored western region of the Republic. The silence of his boss behind him did not reassure him.

After driving on gravel for half an hour, they began passing a succession of run-down commercial buildings interspersed with brownfield sites. A torn poster on a giant billboard promised—with an optimism shared by none—"*Nouveau projet* Coming Soon!" They were entering the outskirts of Hull.

Back on hard pavement, Rojas sped down a wide boulevard that shimmered in the heat. A giant *Petrobec* loomed at a major intersection, competing gas stations having long since decamped. They drove beside a mall, hyped as the longest in Quebec. Here, at last, was some activity. Outside the *Supermarché*, customers were pushing shopping carts towards their vehicles, laden—so it seemed to Rojas—with nothing but cases of canned drinks. Stopping at a four-way, Rojas pushed the button to lower his window. A mistake: the heat poured in. Aircons roared from the ranks of camper vans in the adjacent parking lot. The smell of stale beer wafted from the hot asphalt.

"Shut the window, Rojas," ordered Mauricie from the back seat.

They crossed the bridge over the Noire River into Hull Centro. Although highway signs still swung over the lane leading towards Ottawa, large concrete blocks placed across the road prevented passage south: nobody would be driving to Canada that way anymore. Rojas steered right onto the slip road that wound over, then under criss-crossing highways. The slip road ended, suddenly, at a traffic light. The light was flashing red. Probably had been for weeks, thought Rojas. He turned right, entering a grid of narrow streets, lined mostly by apartment blocks interspersed by an occasional older house that had survived redevelopment. They crouched between their tall neighbours, each house shaded by a dusty tree.

There was more traffic now. Official cars mingled with private micro-cars and delivery trucks. A long concertina bus belched fumes. Clusters of bicycles were chained to metal posts, benches, railings; their riders dispersed into the neighbouring buildings.

Directly ahead, at the end of the boulevard, was the grey massif of the *Portalette*. The vast agglomeration of concrete in brutalist style had once housed various ministries of the federal government. Functionaries of the republic now used the buildings, although they only occupied offices on the upper floors. The several tower blocks of the complex intersected at odd angles, connecting at various levels in geometries that baffled visitors. Unkempt vegetation sprouted from the green roofs, and vines tumbled down concrete from terraces perched high within the concrete maze.

"Go right," said Mauricie. "Take the ramp."

She folded her laptop and sat back as the vehicle coasted down a slope leading to the parking below the *Portalette*. Yellow lights set into the walls of the tunnel replaced daylight. Agent Rojas glanced behind him: *Madame* had slumped down in the seat, invisible to him.

A swing-gate at the bottom of the ramp controlled access to the underground parking. Rojas slowed to a stop just before the barrier. Beside him was a control box, in grey metal, with a loudspeaker and a security camera bolted to the top edge. He lowered his window and fed his security pass into an illuminated slot.

"Look straight at the camera," ordered a metallic voice, coming from the loudspeaker. Thirty long seconds passed before the slot regurgitated Rojas' pass.

"Welcome *Agent Rojas*, Commander Brevet is expecting

you," said the voice.

The barrier lifted open; Rojas edged forward, over a speed bump and beneath a metal beam; "Maximum 2.1 m" warned a sign in large red letters. He drove slowly, following yellow arrows painted on the ground, turned a sharp corner, and emerged into a vast parking garage. Receding rows of squat pillars supported the mass of concrete overhead. Roof and floor converged into the murk of the far wall.

"This will do nicely," said Colonel Mauricie. Rojas slowed to a stop beside an illuminated sign indicating the entrance to a stairwell.

"Meet me here at three o'clock and then you can take me directly to Commander Brevet's office. Tell him I'll drop in this afternoon. It will be a nice surprise. Now, you had best get to your meeting."

✦　✦　✦

MAURICIE STEPPED OUT of the Cadillac straight into a puddle.

"*Merde*," she muttered. "*Mer-duh.*" Mud had splashed her grey trousers.

She paused, adjusting her sling bag over one shoulder, and watched the tail-lights of the Cadillac disappear behind a pillar. Rojas was searching for his assigned parking spot. *Bonne chance* finding it in this labyrinth, thought Mauricie.

Splashing over to the door under the exit sign, she pushed on the aluminium bar. The door opened into a stairwell. The confined space felt oppressive compared with the echoing cavern she had just left. There was a vague smell of urine. From years of having worked in this complex—starting as a trainee in the Information Protectorate, from which she had thankfully escaped—she knew the unobserved exits, the doors leading to secret corners haunted by the smokers. Such knowledge was now proving useful.

Mauricie took out her Taser from the discreet holster at her waist and checked its charge. She might need to stop a two-hundred-pound male. She replaced the Taser, and to reassure herself, felt in her bag for the brown envelope. It contained two identical versions of a long document printed on legal paper. On the last page of each document, Mauricie had signed as Josée-Mathilde Papineau. *Madame la Présidente* had insisted that her presidential approval be deniable, that she could—should the political climate change—prove that some underling had forged her signature. The space for a second signature was empty.

Mauricie felt a tingle of excitement: today should consolidate her power in the corridors of *le Château*. It was an excellent scheme, meticulously planned, but today was critical: the document needed one other name.

She climbed two flights of steps, pushed open a fire door, and stepped out into a concrete canyon. It was like an oven and she walked quickly, keeping to the narrow shade cast by the high building. Coming to a street, Mauricie darted quickly across into the old quarter of Hull that surrounded the *Portalette*. She entered a maze of alleyways, leaving behind the towers of weeping concrete. It was only marginally cooler.

Turning onto *rue* Levesque, she walked swiftly downhill, past shabby low-rise buildings of wood and stucco. Fire, both accidental and arson, had left gaps in the once uniform frontage. Signs advertised monthly parking at rates well below what she paid in Quebec City. Several parked RVs seemed to have taken up permanent residence on the vacant lots. The surviving buildings appeared beaten into submission by decades of winters, their slow defeat evident in their sagging wooden verandas, flaking paint, and torn tar paper where rough campers had stripped the wooden siding for firewood. The few people on the street moved slowly, as if swimming through the heat.

Mauricie passed a *Tout pour une piastre*, the chain found everywhere in Quebec that guaranteed "everything for a dollar!" She sidestepped bins on the sidewalk in front of a charity shop filled with pairs of used ice skates. Getting a jump on winter, she thought. Through the grubby window of a bicycle shop she glimpsed road bikes dangling from the ceiling, like a mass execution. She wondered if they ever sold one. Since she had last been down this street, a Vietnamese pho shop had replaced the deli, previously run by an elderly Portuguese couple.

She hesitated at the next intersection. Further down the street, she recalled, was the Surplus Emporium, a bland, two-storey block to which government departments sent outmoded or unwanted furnishings—desks, orthopaedic chairs, filing cabinets—in the hope of recouping some value. The store also sold obsolescent electronics and a vast selection of smaller items, from staplers to paper stock with obsolete ministerial letterheads. As a young trainee in the Information Protectorate, Mauricie had found the emporium a treasure trove for furnishing her tiny apartment. She turned left on the side street.

A gust of air carrying the smell of fermenting yeast told Mauricie that she had reached her destination. The old brew pub had survived the wave of start-ups and micro-distillers that had peaked a decade ago, then crashed after exhausting the market for gastro-food, fruit-flavoured beers, and aromatic spirits. The brewery was still in the same building, barely updated. The interior walls were exposed brick—original concept rather than hipster revival.

The pub was beside the *ruisseau*, the creek that bypassed the Chaudière Falls on the Ottawa River and entitled this part of the city to call itself an island. Mauricie knew the pub had a shaded terrace by the water. If anywhere without air-conditioning might be cooler today, this would surely be it. She slipped through to the patio, ignoring a youth at the door who tried to offer her a menu.

She was wrong; it was even hotter on the patio. And it was empty. Mauricie went back inside, looked around, and saw a single ceiling fan turning at the far end of the bar. It was churning above one of the snugs that allowed for privacy. The barkeep, stripped to his undershirt, was wiping a glass with the untucked hem. He caught her eye, and nodded towards the alcove.

Silent on her rubber heels, Mauricie walked towards the end of the bar. She checked for other customers: the place was empty except for that one booth. She'd grant him that. But, apart from being almost deserted, the brew-pub wouldn't have been her choice for a rendezvous. She would have much preferred the air-conditioned wine bar on *rue Montcalm* owned by an award-winning sommelier. But this was, at least, a quiet choice for their meet. And they both sold alcohol.

"*Bonjour*, Monsieur Collins. Hot enough for you?"

✧   ✧   ✧

COLLINS LOOKED UP slowly, taking in the dried splashes of mud on Colonel Mauricie's boots. Her grey trousers had sharp creases; she wore three stars on the lapel of her smart jacket. Her hair was cut short to frame her face, familiar from Facebook. She looked older, of course, but hers was still a handsome face. Bleak between smiles, though, and hard as nails underneath. He put down his glass of draft beer—a summer special of the brew pub.

"*Colonel Mauricie.* I hope you had a pleasant trip from Quebec? Drink?"

"Christ, yes. Vodka martini."

Collins looked towards the barkeep. "You heard the lady."

She sat across from him in the booth. They waited in silence, Collins nursing his beer, until the server had placed a large vodka martini and a bottle of *Perrier Gaspésien* in front of the new arrival.

"*Félicitations* on LeGros, by the way. Josée-Mathilde was most pleased."

"It's still a deal, then?" Collins asked, quietly.

He watched Mauricie pull an envelope from her bag. It was one of those multi-use envelopes with little squares for the latest addressee. The flap had been closed with red thread. Mauricie pushed it over the table to him.

"Mike," he read in the last box. Someone had crossed out the names of all the previous recipients.

"I wasn't sure if you preferred Mike or Michael," said his companion. A joke.

He pulled out two identical documents, three pages each, printed on heavy-duty legal paper. The title on the cover spoke of an *entente*—a memorandum of understanding. Not a treaty, exactly, but the next best thing. Collins picked up one of the documents and turned to the last page, to the seal and the signature. He raised an eyebrow.

"We had it drafted in both English and French," said Mauricie.

Collins grunted and took out a pen. He read paragraph by numbered paragraph.

"Treating that part of the Republic known as the *Comté du Pontiac* in West Quebec, whereas it has unique geography and culture ... will be known as the Free County of Pontiac. Notwithstanding 'One-Nation' wording in the Quebec constitution, there will be ... recognition of language rights, control of education and selective immigration, the right to collect taxes, and representation in the *l'Assemblée nationale.*"

Collins ticked the key points off in his head. He had drafted most of them. "And the quid pro quo?" he said, finally. "Continued allegiance to the Republic?"

"It's as good as it gets, you know," said Mauricie.

"Yes."

Collins tested his pen on a napkin. Then, he called the barkeep.

"We need you to witness," he said. "Go dry your hands."

Chapter 32

PAUL WAS ELATED immediately after the successful raid on Lac King. Then reaction set in, and he became despondent. How would the authorities react? Would there be retaliation?

Margret tried to reassure him. "Don't worry. You all wore masks. You left and returned to the island after dark. As far as the GRs are concerned, you were here at Blackwater when the Brigade boys abducted LeGros."

Paul was less convinced that the late night celebration, however muted, had passed unnoticed. After leaving Donovan's farm, the jubilant volunteers had sailed back to the island on the *Ring of Kerry*. They had convened at the bar.

Now, a week after the raid, Paul discovered that the Brigade had released LeGros. He read about it in the *Black and White*. His solo effort at the lodge seemed to have been for naught. Why on earth had the Committee let the Minister go? He sought out Margret, who was on the far side of the island preparing to fire her kiln. She was splitting wood.

"Where's Mike got to now, Margret?" asked Paul, irritably. She had gone for an overnighter with Collins on the *Ring of Kerry* earlier in the week. They hadn't invited Paul.

"If you must know, it's 'catch and release' on Lac King," Margret replied.

"I'm serious, Margret. What was the point, if we just let him go?"

Margret brought the axe down abruptly, missing her aim, and sending a splinter flying from the log she was trying to split.

"Liaison," snapped Margret. "Committee business. So you can stop asking and stop worrying."

"But his boat is still at the dock," objected Paul.

"Then he took a club canoe. Now, let me finish this before the weather changes."

✧ ✧ ✧

PAUL WANDERED BACK to the *Spindrift*. Margret's curt replies had wounded him. And if Collins had really gone off in a canoe, then he doubted he would be coming back soon. Powerful weather was approaching. A hot wind was blowing from the west; gusty, it set the boats bucking against their mooring ropes.

Old Tom hadn't reassured Paul when he had paused beside the finger dock. Tom was the recognized weather guru in the club, largely, they said, because of the time he spent staring at the clouds from the windows of the crow's nest.

"No cumulowhatsits, young Loess. Not a mare's tails up high. Just this blasted wind. Makes one cough." To illustrate his point, Old Tom hawked and bent over to spit into the water. "Something's coming, that's certain. I'd say batten down the hatches."

When Margret returned from the island, she seemed to Paul in a better mood.

"I was going to light the kiln," she said, "to fire this big fellow." She nodded towards the clay figure she'd been working on, another recruit to join the figures lining the edge of the dock. "But the weather doesn't look great. Last thing I need is heavy rain."

Margret picked up a pallet knife and shaved a coil of clay from the figure's head. Its features were slowly emerging, and there was something in the jaw line that reminded Paul of Mike Collins.

By mid-afternoon, clouds were building in the west. Thunder rumbled in the distance. A single drop fell on the *Spindrift*'s deck, followed by a spattering against the canvas awning.

"I think we had better get up to the clubhouse, Margret."

She looked at the sky, and nodded. Several other members were already hurrying along the catwalk towards the island. The first of the rain was leaving dark slashes on the grey decking.

"Wait till I cover up Mike," she said, hastily tying a bag over the clay statue. "All right, let's run."

So it is Collins, thought Paul. He felt his face burn. He turned away in his embarrassment, and gave one last tug on the mooring rope, before sprinting after her.

The squall rushed on them from downriver. It was a straight-line wind, a cold punch of air from the base of the thundercloud. It hit Blackwater with fury. Paul and Margret made it onto the island and crouched behind the massive trunk of the white pine at the end of the catwalk. Hail was driving in from the bay, the gusts sweeping up grit and pine needles. Paul touched Margret's arm and pointed to the clubhouse.

"Hurry!" he shouted in her ear. "We have to get to shelter!" He ran, expecting Margret to follow. Flying detritus stung his exposed skin, as he scrambled to get under cover.

When he gained the clubhouse porch, Paul realized he was alone. He turned and looked back. Margret was still standing behind the tree trunk. He thought he heard screaming from the rigging of the boats tossing in the bay. Then he realized it was long, keening wail. Margret had moved out from behind the tree to stand in the teeth of the storm. Her howl went on and on. To Paul, it sounded half challenge, half lament. Should he run back and embrace her; lead her to shelter? He stood paralysed in the doorway.

When the wind finally eased, Margret turned and walked to the clubhouse. She mounted the steps and passed Paul, ignoring him. Her hair was slicked back, her face streaming wet. It was just the rain, he said to himself. Not tears.

Part III

The Ambush

Chapter 33

I NSPECTOR JULES LABORDE got the call while pumping his tires. It was his free Friday, and he had been planning a fifty-kilometre ride. His pride and joy, a new *vélo* by Pacino, was so light he could carry it one-handed up the cast-iron stair to his second-floor apartment in the shabby part of the *Isle de Hull*, once a ghetto for Portuguese immigrants. No one in their right mind would leave a bike like this unattended on the street. He slept with it in his room since parting with three months' salary to buy the machine.

Laborde's father had been a police officer, in uniform for his entire career and ending as a desk sergeant. Jules had followed in his father's footsteps, doing his time in patrol cars, before being promoted to detective constable. He knew he'd been lucky that, since independence, the recruitment of more senior officers to the *Garde républicaine* had cleared the way for his subsequent promotion to inspector. He felt he should have had more experience, but who was he to quarrel with the raise in salary?

"*Oui*, Laborde." He stood beside the bike, holding the phone to his ear. "Okay. The Blackwater Club outside LaCloche? Thirty minutes?" He ended the call. *Shit de shit*, there would be no ride today. Laborde stripped off his biking pants, and put on the trousers he'd abandoned at the foot of his bed.

The inspector's car, a drab Honda hybrid, was parked by the curb. It was nondescript and attracted little attention. But the appearance was deceiving: the mechanics at the police depot had added a battery booster, which supercharged the car's performance. Laborde got in and drove off through the narrow streets of Hull Centro. He turned onto the highway, going north, and put his foot to the floor. After fifteen minutes, he took the exit signed to LaCloche. He carried his speed through the village, going from *Bienvenue* to *Au revoir* in fifty seconds flat. Early morning traffic was non-existent, and Laborde felt no need to use the siren. He glanced at his GPS screen, slowed briefly at the *Arrêt* to turn left onto the *Route des Draveurs*, and followed the tourist route along the western edge of the reservoir.

His second right was onto a gravel road, *chemin* Glen Rourke. *C'est ça!* He let his vehicle coast down a long hill towards the flashing red and blue light of a police cruiser. He slowed for the T-junction at the bottom of the hill, and turned left onto a narrow lane, signed *chemin* Blackwater. An officer was stretching incident tape across the road in front of him. Laborde stopped beside a chain-link fence. He got out and looked around. Parked behind the fence were bulky shapes on wheels, shrouded by tarpaulins. Boat trailers, he decided.

"*Salut*, Martine," he called to the officer.

"*Bonjour, Inspecteur.* The team is already down there." She pointed down *chemin* Blackwater. "Two hundred metres, *un peu près*. It's a cul-de-sac, with little room to turn at the end."

"Have you notified the GRs?" asked Laborde.

There was a standing order to inform the *Gardes* should an emergency call come in regarding the Blackwater Sailing Club. He wondered whether they had the club under surveillance. Laborde was not happy to have them looking over his shoulder. The *Garde républicaine*, in his opinion, knew nothing of real police work.

"*Oui, Monsieur.*"

"*Merde! Merci, Martine.*"

Laborde turned and walked down *chemin* Blackwater beside a screen of dark cedars. Through their dying lower branches, he glimpsed a cabin. Judging by the tall weeds and mossy roof, it was abandoned.

At the bottom of the lane, he reached the water. Laborde paused and sniffed. A disagreeable smell was rising from a narrow band of black mud in front of him. Beyond was a channel separating the mainland from an island. Presumably, thought Laborde, this was the island home of the Blackwater Sailing Club. To his right was a substantial—if somewhat battered—metal gate. The gate was open, and beyond he glimpsed the masts of sailboats.

Standing in front of the gate, leaning against a railing, were two men: a uniformed officer, and a man wrapped in a towel. That would be the witness, thought Laborde. He followed their gaze, and realized that they were both watching activity at the water's edge some fifty metres away.

"Constable?"

"*Désolé, Inspecteur*," said the officer, turning swiftly and saluting. He pointed to where two figures at the water's edge were tugging on something bulky. "That's the forensic officer, *Monsieur*, with the *sergeant*," He gestured at a man beside him "And this is Monsieur Loess, from the Blackwater Sailing Club. He called the police."

Laborde showed Loess his badge.

"I am Inspector Laborde. I shall wish to speak to you, *Monsieur*. Please stay here with the officer."

One of the figures at the water's edge turned to look towards the bridge. He or she waved and pointed to Laborde's left, where he saw a pile of equipment. There was forensic gear—he registered a stretcher and body bag—and a pair of Wellingtons.

Laborde pulled on the rubber boots, walked down onto the shore, and began to trudge through the mud. The foetid smell he'd noticed before was now intense. It billowed up in waves from the decomposing weeds that lay in dank tangles on the exposed mud.

Approaching the water's edge, Laborde understood why the pair had remained so still: their feet were planted some six inches deep in mud. He nodded to the forensic officer—the *légiste*. She was wearing blue coveralls and hip waders. When last he'd seen her, at the Christmas party, she'd had on a sexier outfit, and hadn't smelled of disinfectant.

"*Bonjour*, Jules."

"*Salut* … Suzanne. *Ça va?*"

The forensics officer raised an eyebrow.

"A corpse in the a.m. and a Mac-something for breakfast. Sure, all is well in the bloody world."

Laborde took a deep breath.

"Okay then, show me what you have."

The sergeant, wielding a boat hook, held the body at the edge of the channel. The corpse was face-down, and all Laborde could see was a broad, naked back and buttocks, pale as cod fillet. It bobbed gently in water among a tangle of tree roots and plastic rubbish.

"Has the drone got all it needs?" Laborde asked.

Suzanne nodded. "*Oui*—been and gone. We can recreate the scene. No problem."

"Let's have it out, then," he said.

The *légiste* sighed, and unrolled a large, plastic sheet. She edged into the water, and she and the sergeant each got a firm grasp on the arms of the corpse. They dragged it out of the water onto the plastic sheet, leaving a long smear in the mud. Threads of red-stained water ran off the corpse to puddle in the wrinkles of the black plastic.

"The back of the head is a mess," Suzanne commented. "Uh-huh. That explains it."

They had rolled the body over. Laborde could see the hole punched in the forehead. The forensic officer bent close with her phone camera and took several pictures.

"Gunshot," she said. "Took the back of the skull right off."

Laborde had hoped for a simple drowning. As in 'Deceased' decides on an evening dip and is surprised by a heart attack far from shore, out of sight of witnesses or potential aid. 'Deceased' has failed to plan for sudden, accidental death. A regrettable lapse. *Point final.* Now, his day would be long and complicated.

"Time of death?"

"He hasn't been in the water long," said the *légiste*. "Six to twelve hours, my guess. I will get you a closer estimate after I get the body back to the lab. But, that's what we always say. Still keeping fit, are you?"

"Yeah, the bike, you know."

"Looks like you've put on weight."

"*Bon.* Okay. I'll take a selfie with our friend, and see if anybody recognizes him."

Laborde leaned over and took a picture of the dead man's face. He opened the edit function on his camera and pressed *autofix.* The software performed its magic: it filled and smoothed the bullet hole, arranged the hair in a probable style, and mopped the water and blood adequately away. After processing, the deceased would appear much as he had in life, if not somewhat improved.

"*Á la prochaine*, Suzanne."

"Afternoons are better. *Je m'excuse*, Laborde."

✧ ✧ ✧

PAUL, STILL WAITING beside the constable, watched the inspector plod back through the ooze towards him.

"Monsieur Loess?" said the inspector, as he scraped mud from the sole of his boots on the lowest railing of the bridge. "I understand you found the body? Do you recognize him?"

Paul looked at the camera-phone held out by Laborde. He had told himself again and again that it couldn't be him. He had braced himself for a gruesome sight, but the face was quite clean, the blue eyes open, the mouth frozen in a smile, or perhaps a grimace. There was also a mocking air to the corpse's expression that was all too familiar.

"Yes," he said, with only the slightest hesitation. "His name is Mike Collins."

Chapter 34

B Y TEN O'CLOCK, a curious group of residents had gathered on the catwalk. They stayed a cautious distance away from Paul and the police officers. Paul's yell on discovering the body had woken them abruptly. Many had dressed hastily: sou'westers over pyjamas, heavy pullovers and dressing gowns—anything warm that came to hand. It had been an uncomfortable night: a weather front had passed through in the early hours, rocking the boats.

The police officers, Paul and most of the Blackwater Sailing Club watched the ambulance back cautiously down *chemin* Blackwater. It stopped opposite the club entrance. Two paramedics got out and spoke briefly to the *légiste*. Then they hoisted the body into the back of the ambulance, and slammed the doors.

Now the actual work begins, thought Laborde, as he watched the ambulance drive off. The inspector could leave the taking of formal statements to his sergeant, but he was keen to get first impressions while people were still in shock. If they weren't in shock, that might be a clue. Laborde's sergeant had given him a list. He referred to his notebook. There were fifteen names. It would take all day to take their statements. Where were you last night? Did you hear or see anything unusual? When did you last see Monsieur Collins?

Laborde walked through the gate to the group gathered on the catwalk. For these initial meetings he would triage the witnesses into bystanders in blissful ignorance, witnesses of something they weren't sure about, and potential suspects. Then, probably later that night when he couldn't sleep, he would reverse the order. Keeping an open mind was always a challenge.

An older man—the sou'wester—stepped forward. He wore a nautical cap, with an anchor embroidered in gold thread at the peak.

"*Bonjer*, officer. *Je suis le commodore* of the club. Er, *le commandant du club*. This is a tragedy, a terrible tragedy."

"*Votre nom, Monsieur?*"

"Taggart St. James."

"Monsieur St. James. I am Inspector Laborde. It would be helpful if you could arrange a room in your clubhouse that we can use for interviews."

"Of course, of course. But is that…is that Mike Collins?" asked Taggart.

"Yes. The body has been identified as Monsieur Collins."

"My God. I mean, did he drown? How did this happen?"

"That, *Monsieur*, is why I need to interview all of these persons. Perhaps, Monsieur St. James, I can begin with yourself?"

Taggart led Laborde onto the island and up to the clubhouse.

"This is the boardroom," said the Commodore. "Will it do?"

"Very good. Now, *Monsieur*, perhaps you would tell me where you were last night?"

Ten minutes later, after finishing with St. James, the inspector installed his officers in the boardroom, ready to take statements. The club residents sat in the Mess, waiting their turns. Laborde hesitated as he passed the doorway, scanning the room. He could already imagine the outcome: a spreadsheet of stock answers to stock questions. They had all been asleep. Yes, they all heard something. Several would swear they had heard shots in the night: at midnight, at two a.m., at three, at five. Collins had been everybody's friend.

Still, amassing notes was progress and would make the case file respectably thick: something to give the GRs indigestion, should they take an interest. Laborde went outside, and stood at the top of the clubhouse steps. He felt a growing excitement: this case had career-boosting potential. He had an eccentric group of suspects, isolated on an island. One of them was probably the killer.

✦ ✦ ✦

THE COMMODORE AND another man suddenly emerged from the clubhouse behind Laborde. The second man was explaining to the St. James exactly when he thought he'd heard something in the night. Seeing the inspector, he fell silent.

"Ah, there you are Inspector," said Taggart. "This is Garvin Bowter, our Harbour Master."

"Monsieur Bowter," said Laborde. "Now Monsieur St. James, I need to see the layout of this island."

"Of course, of course," said Taggart. "Garvin here is the best person to show you around. I really should stay here, you know, in case the club members need me …"

"*Bon*," said Laborde, turning towards Garvin. "*Monsieur?*"

"Er, yes, This way, Inspector." Bowter led the way down the steps, and turned a sharp right onto a path leading around the clubhouse.

"I always do an inspection every evening," called Bowter over his shoulder. "Right round the island, the docks, and the gate, of course. Everything was shipshape last night."

"*Á quelle heure?* What time would that have been?"

Bowter stopped and looked at the clipboard he was holding.

"Four minutes past ten," he said. "I keep a register." He held out the clipboard for Laborde to inspect. "You can see here the time I finished. It's the exact time. I synchronize my timepiece with the radio every morning."

"Very thorough," said Laborde. "Now, perhaps you would show me the island. I need to understand the layout."

Bowter led Laborde around the clubhouse and onto the deck at the back.

"This is where we eat, when the weather is good," said Garvin, waving at the picnic tables. Laborde was struck by the faint smell of roasted meat, and noticed the row of barbecues against the railing at the far side of the deck. He guessed no one had cleaned the grills recently. On the nearest picnic table was a stack of unwashed plates. A few plastic chairs lay scattered about.

"It's a bit of a mess. Sorry," said Garvin.

Laborde walked to the corner of the deck and looked over the railing. The ground, dotted with juniper scrub and stunted pines, sloped steeply down towards the water.

"It's a scramble, but we can go down if you like," said Garvin. The inspector nodded.

Laborde followed the Harbour Master down the wooden steps that led off the deck onto smooth rock, covered with patches of moss. A track zigzagged down the slope.

The path ended at a concrete platform jutting out from the low cliff. The rocks to either side plunged sheer to the water. Laborde stood at the lip of the platform. Looking left, he could make out the masts of boats moored along the catwalk. To his right, the view was to the north up the reservoir towards the distant hills.

"We used to make people jump from here," volunteered Garvin. "It's only fifteen feet straight down into deep water."

He halted abruptly when he saw the expression on Laborde's face.

"I mean, I didn't mean…We stopped doing that years ago."

"Is there a current?"

"Yes, usually. But it's very slow round the island and through

Blackwater Bay. Most things get blown this way by the wind."

"Most things?"

"Oh, God, I didn't think. Well, they do, and they get caught underneath the catwalk."

The path continued along the cliff edge around the north side of the island, gradually descending closer to the water's edge. The slope was easier here, and the pine trees larger. Through the branches, Laborde glimpsed the clubhouse high above them. The path led past a dilapidated shack.

"Used to be a locker room," said Garvin, seeing the inspector's glance. "Now Margret uses it for her pottery kiln."

"Margret?"

"Margret Mankie. Lives on the *Groaning Anne*. That's the *Catalina* with the blue hull you passed on your way over the bridge. Slow boat with a big handicap. She never finishes better than fifth in the weekend races."

Laborde grunted. He had his notebook in hand. He wrote the word "*Catalina*" and underlined it as an aide memoire. Mankie, the handicap, and the groaning he would easily recall.

"And this is our lighthouse," said Garvin. They had emerged from the trees onto a ridge of rock that sloped off into the water. "It marks the entrance to Blackwater Bay."

The timber construct was painted in blue and white stripes, although the blistering paint suggested it had endured many seasons without a touch-up. The structure overlooked a small platform. At the edge of the platform rose a short mast with wires trailing from a cross piece. There was no sign of a light in the lighthouse.

"They're for the pennants," explained Garvin, pointing to the wires. "For the races. You pull up the red and the blue so the boats know there are five minutes to go. Then you pull down the blue after four minutes. Then you—"

Laborde wasn't paying attention. He was looking across the

water towards the far shore. There were no cabins among the trees that he could see; the forest rolled down to the water in a green wave. To both the left and right, the reservoir receded into the distance, its surface reflecting a few high clouds. The scene reminded Laborde of a poster he had in his office: *la vie en plein air*, from *les parcs nationaux du Québec*. He wondered if there was a bike trail along the reservoir.

"And you can swim all the way around the island?" he asked.

"Oh yes, we all do," replied Garvin. "It's eleven hundred and twenty-three metres. That's an exact measure. But, only if you get out at the dock. Starting from the boat ramp adds an extra hundred and ten. The club record is—"

Collins had been naked, thought Laborde. He was hardly likely to have been running through the woods like that, so he was most likely shot while swimming. A shot could have come from just about anywhere on this side of the island, well away from the docks and boats. It would have been easy to stalk a target swimming just offshore, and there were plenty of rocks and trees to provide cover. He would order a search of the shoreline for clothing, a towel or any sign which might show where Collins entered the water.

"… seventy-five circuits of the island in a season. That record belongs to Margret Mankie." Bowter paused to see if his audience required further clarification.

"I shall need a list of the boats and their owners, Monsieur Bowter," said Laborde.

From the lighthouse, the path continued along the shore, completing the circuit of the island. Laborde and Bowter arrived at the island end of the catwalk twenty minutes after leaving the clubhouse deck. The inspector looked curiously at the drawbridge mechanism.

"We rarely lift the drawbridge at night," said Garvin. "It might be a good idea now, I suppose. I will have to ask the

Commodore, and—."

"You have been most helpful, Monsieur Bowter," interrupted Laborde. "Please report to the clubhouse and give your statement to the officer. Make sure to include the smallest details."

Laborde turned away towards the water, a smile on his face.

The docks appeared deserted—all the residents were supposedly at the clubhouse—and Laborde walked slowly, examining each boat in turn. The inspector was not a boat person. He was unsure of his *babord* from his *tribord*, and he certainly didn't know the names of all the cordage. One thing he had been fairly sure of was that sailors were organized and tidy. The neatly coiled ropes and polished brass fittings on the boats closest to the island confirmed it.

Further along the catwalk, however, the boats looked more careworn. Varnish flaked from the woodwork, random lines stretched to support tarpaulins, and plastic boxes and sacs were piled on the decks. There was even a portable composter. This was more like a damp trailer park than a marina. Laborde came to a boat with a blue hull, the name *Groaning Anne* in silver paint on the bow. A dozen plants in pots were floating in the shallows beside the boat's hull. Grey statuettes lined the dock. Just like the *maudits nains*—the ugly gnomes his mother bought from the garden centre, thought Laborde.

The curtain in the cabin window twitched slightly.

"*Bonjour.* Is anyone on board?"

Margret uncoiled from the *Groaning Anne*'s hatch in one lithe movement. She stood in the cockpit, bare arms folded, looking at the inspector. Or rather, thought Laborde, past him, as if she was scanning the horizon for a distant hazard. He registered her browned and weather-beaten face, the red hair with streaks of grey. When she refocused on his face, he saw her eyes were green.

"So, the body in the bay was Mike Collins?" she said, fore-stalling Laborde. "I guessed it must be him. I heard nothing in the night, if that's what you want to ask, but *Anne* was rocking sometime after midnight—somebody driving up the river at night. There's more of that going on these days."

Laborde looked at the list of names in his notebook. "You are Madame Mankie?"

"He wouldn't have drowned, not Mike Collins," continued Margret, ignoring the interruption. "Shot, was he? It wouldn't surprise me if someone shot the bastard. He had a way of upsetting certain people. Have you found the weapon? I would guess not. It would be easy enough to dispose of. Just chuck it into deep water. You'll be doing a search, I suppose."

"Madame Mankie, one moment. You say Monsieur Collins had enemies?"

"Of course. In this pressure cooker, everyone has enemies. And Mike? Well, Mike had other interests ashore. Some agreed with what he was doing, others not."

"*Pardon, un instant.* Madame Mankie, what was he doing ashore?"

"Running guns to the rebels, of course. God, you're slow."

Laborde took out his notebook.

✧　✧　✧

TEN MINUTES LATER, Laborde left Margret, and walked along the catwalk to the mainland shore. He gazed back across the water to the island he had just left. It was bathed in the yellow light of late afternoon, in marked contrast to the mainland shore where Laborde was now in cool shade. The island could be a screen saver image, he thought: *féerique.*

"Focus," he muttered to himself. Laborde turned and walked up *chemin* Blackwater to where he had parked his car beside the

212

fence. He opened the door and sat in the driving seat.

Laborde shook his head. Stick with the facts, he told himself. The torn leather of his car's seat was a fact. The smell of the coffee dregs in the paper cup in the holder? Another fact. He took out his notebook. Whatever magic Blackwater had exerted to seduce him had evaporated in the short walk up from the water.

Laborde opened his notebook, and looked again at the names the Mankie woman had given him: a Donovan, an O'Brien, a McGuire, a Rourke. All Irish, thought Laborde. He'd asked where he could find these men.

"Are you blind, Inspector? They're standing right here beside you," she had replied. "This one is Donovan." She'd stooped to pat the head of one of the statuettes on the dock. "As for this wee one, I still haven't thought of a name."

In his car, Laborde sighed. He drew a thick, diagonal line through the list.

Chapter 35

THE POLICE FINISHED taking statements by late afternoon and vacated the boardroom. The Commodore called an emergency meeting. The remaining members of the Board sat around the table.

"Poor old Mike," Tasker said, looking at Mike's empty chair. "It won't be the same without him."

"Well, well," said the Commodore. "It's very sad, of course, but we can't dwell in the past. Perhaps a note of appreciation for Mike in the minutes, Harvey?"

"We will all miss Mike," added Garvin. "But, perhaps we need to focus on the club. Personally, I deplore it, but I suppose we have to cancel the race this weekend. Participation has been pathetic all summer."

"Of course, the political situation doesn't help," said the Commodore.

"Bloody Quebec," said Garvin, meaning the city and the Papineau government.

Old Tom interrupted, calling down from in the crow's nest. "Intruder alert! There's a truck driving on the old railway." He had spotted a pickup truck driving along the old railway line across from the island.

"Perhaps we should adjourn ..." began the Commodore, as the board members rose as one, and ran out through the Mess onto the deck. From here they could all see the vehicle, a red pick-up, heading south from the direction of Newbridge. It kept a steady pace, methodically pushing down the weeds, before disappearing behind a screen of trees.

"It'll reach the level crossing over Glen Rourke in two minutes," said Tasker. "Could be here in three, if it turns left."

"Go to the gate, Harvey," said the Commodore. "See if we have a visitor."

Harvey left the clubhouse and trotted down the path, and across the catwalk. He stopped and watched from behind the gate at the club entrance. The truck reappeared suddenly, coming quickly down the lane. The truck braked near the bottom, skidding the last few metres in the loose gravel. The driver got out.

"It's me, Pat Donovan," he called to Harvey. "Open the gate. I need to talk to the Committee."

Harvey felt a surge of panic. Since Collins' murder, he'd become extremely anxious. He hadn't slept properly in days and found it hard to concentrate on the simplest of tasks. Harvey recognized Donovan, but Donovan was definitely not a member. Frankly, thought Harvey, he would never pass muster. He found the man a rude brute.

"Er, we're not allowing any visitors on the island."

"Come on, man. Open up. I need to speak to Mike Collins."

"But, he's dead, Donovan. Shot. I thought everyone knew."

"Jesus. And what are you doing about that?"

"Doing about it? The police have been here. They interviewed all of us."

"Who's in charge, then?"

"The Commodore is up at the clubhouse."

"Open the damn gate!" Donovan grabbed the bars and gave a shove. The lock had not been engaged properly and the gate swung open.

"But wait, you can't just barge in here," protested Harvey.

Donovan brushed him aside, and strode along the catwalk towards the island, with Harvey trailing behind.

◇ ◇ ◇

THEY FOUND THE Commodore in the Mess, waiting for them. By this time most of the club members had gathered, alerted by the commotion. As Donovan entered, pursued by a panting Harvey, Tasker stepped forward.

"Pat," he said. "You heard the news then?"

"Terrible. Effing terrible." Donovan stood in the middle of the Mess, looking around at the assembled group.

"Commodore, this is Major Donovan," said Tasker. "Pat's Brigade was on the Lac King operation with us."

"I'll be needing the rest of the cases, Commodore," said Donovan abruptly. "Mike scheduled a last delivery last week, but he sent a message saying there was some delay. I guess he's not going to turn up now."

"Cases?" asked Taggart, thinking whiskey. "I'm not sure what arrangement you had with our Vice-Commodore but—"

"Who the hell is chairing the Committee then, if it's not you?"

"The Board has yet to nominate a replacement for Mike. You really can't expect to barge in here—"

"The guns, man. I need the guns. The things we use to shoot GRs. You've got another ten Armalites in the armoury, or whatever you calls it. Jeez, have you got no balls? The Chief has been shot, and here you are sitting on your island doing eff-all."

"No, they haven't." The voice had emanated from the old, leather sofa.

Donovan turned to look, but could see nothing but the back the sofa. "Haven't what?"

"Balls," said Margret, getting off the sofa, to stand in front of Donovan, hands on hips, looking him in the eye.

"Hello, Pat," she said quietly. "Welcome to Blackwater."

"Drink?" she added, and went to the bar.

"So, you're the new Chairman? Chairperson. Whatever." Donovan raised his glass to Margret.

"Yes. Mike left me your shopping list," said Margret. She turned to Tasker.

"Might as well give him two cases, Joe."

Tasker nodded.

"This way, Pat."

Tasker led Donovan from the Mess and down the corridor towards the galley. He unlatched the last trophy cabinet, swung open the door and flicked on the light switch.

"We store them in the wine cellar," he said. "I'll need a hand."

Five minutes later, they carried two cases into the Mess. Both Tasker and Donovan were breathing heavily.

"There's more down there," said Donovan.

"You can't take all our guns," said Harvey to Donovan. "Mike always said we might have to defend the island."

"Mike's dead," said Donovan. "You think you can stay on this island while the rest of us are out there fighting. Not going to happen. The guns go with me."

"Are you in need of volunteers, sir?" Old Tom had lifted the lid of one of the cases and now stood at attention, a rifle to his shoulder.

Chapter 36

"ANYTHING?"

"*Pas grande chose, Inspecteur,*" replied Laborde's sergeant. "We completed the interviews of residents of the island. Fifteen in total. I've entered the results on the incident spreadsheet."

"A spreadsheet?"

"*Oui, Monsieur.*"

They were in Laborde's office, a ten-by-ten space, made to seem even smaller by his bulky sergeant. A half wall of frosted glass separated his office from the cubicle-land within the open-plan core of the building. Looking past the sergeant's shoulder, Laborde saw the tops of heads: three balding, reflecting the strip lights overhead; one with dark, neatly cropped hair; and one blond and pony-tailed. Nearly a full house, then.

Beside his desk, a narrow, window slit gave him a view of the car pound, a view that competed with the view of the Italian dolomites that his computer screen saver currently displayed. Laborde sighed and pulled the keyboard towards him.

"Did you run the AI?" he asked the sergeant.

"*Oui, Monsieur.* As you know, the program pulls the data from the spreadsheet. It looks for anomalies: where people were and when, weighted by the degree to which others corroborated their alibis."

"Was there a clear winner?"

"*Malheureusement, non.* But forensics narrowed the time of death. Between eight p.m. and two a.m. Here is the report."

Laborde scanned the folder. Suzanne had done a thorough job, but apart from a more accurate time of death there was nothing new, except for one comment under miscellaneous. She noted a dark stain on the victim's fingers had turned out to be oil, of the type used to lubricate firearms. Had Laborde's team somehow contaminated the scene? If not, the victim had been handling guns recently.

"Did the search of the island turn up anything?" he asked.

"*Pas grande chose*: a broken canoe, a dead beaver, and a paddleboard. We found the board floating against the shore on the far side of the island. We brought it back for analysis."

"And the clubhouse, and the boats?"

"Apart from pornography on certain boats, the only suspicious items were in the clubhouse. We found a shotgun behind the bar and a rifle in one of the trophy cabinets. Both are at the *labo* for testing, although the rifle is lacking a firing pin. Monsieur Bowter told us that it is a sailing prize."

"Do we know who won the prize last?"

"*Eh bien, non.* Monsieur Bowter—he has much to say that one—told me he couldn't have the prizes inscribed with this year's winners. Trophy World in Hull Centro is closed, *évidemment.* But the year before, the winner was the victim, Monsieur Collins. His name is engraved on the silver plate screwed to the mounting board."

"Well, he hit the jackpot," muttered Laborde.

Chapter 37

ALL FIFTEEN RESIDENTS were in the Mess. They were a subdued gathering. A week had passed since Paul had found Collins' body, but all had watched the police lift the corpse from the water, and the memory was hard to erase. No one had swum around the island since.

"It's still a murder inquiry," said the Commodore. "And the inspector told us we had to remain on the island and not take the boats out."

"Yes, but they have no suspects," said Garvin Bowter. "No one at the club has even been taken in for questioning. They can't think it's one of us. After all, Pierre and Jacques have been watching the club for weeks now. The inspector must have talked to them and ruled us out. I think it's time we got back into our routine."

"Meaning what, Garvin?"

"Well, you know, it's October now, and we need to think about rigging the club for winter. We need to install the storm windows, hang the heavy, velvet drapes, and pull out the rugs from storage. We need to clean the wood stove, move firewood to strategic locations, and carry the barbecues under the deck. How about some Halloween decorations around the bar?"

"Good idea, Garvin," said Margret. "A few more ghosts floating around the clubhouse might cheer us up."

"No need to be sarcastic, Margret. It's about boosting morale."

By the end of the morning, despite the muttered complaints

of members who felt they had volunteered enough, the club-house was transformed from the bare decks of summer to a degree of winter comfort. Paul was exhausted. He flopped on the vast leather sofa that he just helped pull into the middle of the Mess, revealing thick dust and tangled nests of hair. He stretched out, feet up, on the sofa.

"Mice," said Old Tom, from the armchair opposite. "They pull it out of the sofa stuffing. Mind you, that's nothing compared with …"

Paul tried to tune out Tom's story of an infestation he had once dealt with in a field kitchen in—Cyprus or Bosnia, he couldn't quite remember—which had involved an array of improvised traps.

Margret came into the Mess from the deck and stood in front of Paul.

"Frankly, I would be leery of this old sofa," she said, looking down at him. "In summer, it's pushed against a wall and offends nobody. But in winter, we pull it out so lazy people like you can lie down in front of the wood stove."

"What's wrong with that?" asked Paul.

"That sofa eats people. They fall asleep, and get rolled up in its leather lips. Their remains are in the folds behind the seat cushions, flesh stripped and bones crushed. Last April, I found a plastic biro, a handful of coins, and bone grit."

"Oh, pull the other one," said Paul. Still, he sat up, leaving room for Margret to join him on the sofa.

"What do you think of that Inspector Laborde?" he asked, after she had sat down.

"Out of his depth," replied Margret, abandoning her bantering tone. "He has more suspects than he can handle. Look at his problem—every one of us is a potential murderer. We all have motives, although I grant you, they may be of various strengths. All of us had opportunity. As to means, I gather he hasn't found the murder weapon. And no one is going to mention that we have two crates of rifles still hidden in the wine cellar. And that's just the possibilities on-island, poor man."

"Well, who do you think did it?"

"I *know* who shot Mike."

"Christ, how do you *know*?"

Their conversation was interrupted by the Commodore. Taggart coughed loudly. He had emerged from behind the bar with Harvey where they had been in deep conversation. Harvey held his clipboard ready to take notes.

"I thought you would ask 'who'," whispered Margret, before turning her attention to the Commodore.

"Attention, everyone," called Taggart. We need more supplies again. Harvey has made a list. He says we're low on corned beef, coffee, and olive oil. I'm sure you will want to add your own requests. Remember that we're only going to the minimart in LaCloche, not Costco, so let's keep the list short. Harvey will leave it on the mess table for your additions. I'll take my car, and Garvin and Harvey will come with me."

"Not a great idea, Taggart," said Margret. "Not only are the GRs watching us after Mike's shooting, the police are on high alert too. It's no time for off-island shopping."

"She's got a point," said Tasker."

"We can't let the GRs bully us," said the Commodore. "We've agreed to forego our sailing races. What more do they expect?"

"I'm with you, Commodore," said Harvey. Bowter hesitated, then nodded.

"Good. That's settled then. Tomorrow morning."

"Fine," said Margret, turning to walk out of the Mess. Paul followed.

"I do need some supplies," he said to Margret, as they walked together down the clubhouse steps. "I'm awfully low on marmalade."

"For God's sake, you and your jam. It's Taggart who needs something special, I expect. Glue for his model boats, I expect."

✧   ✧   ✧

"WHAT'S THE SPEED limit in the village?" asked Harvey, the following day. He was sitting in the back of the Commodore's Volvo station wagon. Bowter was beside St. James in the front passenger seat. Taggart's driving always made Harvey nervous.

Entering Belltown-LaCloche, they passed an electronic sign flashing a sad face.

"It's a Saturday," replied Taggart over his shoulder. He was driving fast, one hand on the wheel. "No one cares on a Saturday. School's out."

They drove past the church to the end of *rue Principale* and turned left at the gas station. There was one pump still functioning, and a line of vehicles waiting their turn to fill up.

Across the road was Henri's Shawarma. Sunshine was breaking through the clouds after an overcast morning. Diners had ventured outside to sit on the wooden benches beside the small parking lot, eating lunch from paper wraps dripping shawarma juices. It seemed the liveliest spot in town.

"We'll treat ourselves after we get the supplies," said Taggart. "Haven't had a takeout in ages." He swerved into the forecourt of the minimart, and pulled into the slot reserved for the handicapped or pregnant.

"Maybe we should park somewhere else, Commodore," suggested Harvey. There were only a handful of other vehicles in the lot, and plenty of options.

"Don't fuss, Harvey. We'll be in and out in no time," said Taggart. Then he glanced in the rear-view mirror.

"Oh, bugger," he said.

The police cruiser had turned into the parking lot after them. It pulled across the rear of the station wagon.

The officer made them wait several minutes before getting out of the cruiser. Taggart lowered his window.

"*Bonjour, Messieurs.*" said the officer. "Turn signals are not optional, *vous savez?*"

Taggart saw that the officer wore the blue uniform of the regular police. That wasn't so bad: being pulled over for a traffic infraction was a damn nuisance, but better than being stopped by the GRs. That would have been more serious.

"*Bonjer*, Officer." He held out his licence and registration. "It won't happen again."

The officer peered into the car. Beside the Commodore, Bowter stared straight ahead, his hands in plain view on the dashboard in front of him. In the rear seat, Harvey sat frozen, white as a sheet.

"You were distracted by these persons, perhaps?"

"No. I mean yes, Officer."

"I will see your identifications, *Messieurs*." The officer waited while Harvey and Bowter searched their wallets for their documents.

"Wait," the officer told them. He walked back to his cruiser with their papers. He spent the next five minutes on his computer, then strolled back.

"*Bien*, Monsieur St. James. In future, ensure to use your turn signals."

"Yes, of course, Officer."

"And, I am giving you a ticket for speeding in a school zone."

"I think it's Friday, not Saturday, Taggart," whispered Harvey from the back seat. He shut up when he saw the back of the Commodore's neck turning red.

"... that you must pay at the detachment post in LaCloche

by the end of the month."

"Two hundred *piastres*? Only ten dollars? Thank you, Officer. Now, if that's all, we—"

"And, I regret, *Messieurs*, that the *Garde républicaine* has notified me that an agent wishes to speak to you. He wants to know why you have all ignored the request to attend re-education."

Chapter 38

COMMANDER BREVET GLANCED up from the papers on his desk, and looked at the man hovering in the doorway of his office in the *Portalette*. The inspector was five minutes late for the meeting. A hint of disrespect? Brevet pushed the thought aside.

"*Entrez.* Come in, Laborde," said Brevet, gesturing towards a chair.

"So good of you to find the time," he continued. "We always like to collaborate with our sister service."

"Of course," said Laborde.

No "*Monsieur.*" Brevet tried again.

"And how are the police making progress on this homicide at the Blackwater Sailing Club?"

Laborde pulled a folder from his attaché case.

"This is the forensics report. It confirms what we suspected: a fatal gunshot to the head. No residue, so a shot from a distance with a three-oh-three calibre bullet. The *légiste* found residues in the victim's lungs, which included micro-algae. Apparently, this suggests he was in the water when shot. The man was naked, and enquiries confirmed that nude swimming was a common practice among club members. The victim was known to swim in the evening. A search discovered a towel beside the shore on the far side of the island."

"Suspects?" asked Brevet.

"Any of the club members seem to have opportunity. Around the island, there is plenty of cover for a sniper. Analysis by our drone survey showed that sixty percent of the shoreline is out of view of both the clubhouse and marina. The search has not found the weapon but, from the striations on the bullet, the *légiste* believes it to be an older model, possibly vintage. Given that evidence, and the accuracy of the single shot, I believe it must have come from relatively close range."

"Ah, so one of the club members with a grudge?"

"Possibly. But no one had seen the victim for two days. We cannot be sure where he was shot. It could have been close to the island or further up the reservoir near the mainland shore. The body could have drifted down in the wind. Are you familiar with the Noire reservoir, *Monsieur?*"

That's better, thought Brevet. "Yes, *Inspecteur*," he replied. "I have fished there many times. There is, as you must know, a slight current running south through the reservoir."

"So," he added, "what about motive?"

"Nothing is clear yet, Commander. For instance, the descriptions of the victim vary widely. He seems to have been popular as a senior officer of the club, yet several hinted that others detested him. No specifics. I would like to interview the club members again."

Brevet smiled. "It's your lucky day, *Inspecteur*. We have just rounded up three of them. They were stopped by a traffic cop in LaCloche. I've put them in secure isolation cubicles on floor seventeen, here in the *Portalette*. One they call the Commodore seems to be the ringleader. The other two are nobodies. I expect to release them. Now I'll wait until after you've finished with them."

"*Bon*, thank you, Commander. I wonder if you would also make available agents Pénard and Gruaut. I would like to take their witness statements."

✦ ✦ ✦

LABORDE FINALLY LEFT Tower Three at seven that evening. He felt he had narrowly escaped being locked up in the *Portalette* himself. Commander Brevet had not taken kindly to Laborde's request to question the two GRs.

Laborde had learned to be patient when interviewing a suspect. At first, Taggart St. James had blustered, Garvin Bowter had complained bitterly about the low water levels, and Harvey Kinnear, to Laborde's surprise, actually cried. Collins had been everyone's friend, a great vice-commodore, an enormous loss to the club.

By the end of the afternoon's questioning, he had a picture of a very different Collins. A martinet, according to Bowter; insubordinate, said St. James; always chasing the girls, sobbed Kinnear.

The subsequent interview with Réjean Pénard had been unsatisfactory. Laborde had hoped for a frank exchange; they were colleagues of sorts and knew each other from hockey.

Oui, Pénard had confirmed that the *Garde* had the club under surveillance, but only intermittently. They simply didn't have enough men to watch it round the clock. Alas, *non*; on the evening in question, Pénard had been filing expense reports back at headquarters. And, regrettably, Agent Gruaut had been away on special duty.

LaBorde wished he could have wiped the smirk off Pénard's face—the superior air of the GRs infuriated him—but that would have to wait until their next practice. Instead, he had shut his notebook.

"I'm to escort you out of the building, Jules," Pénard had said.

He led the Inspector through a maze of corridors to the

elevators. Pénard punched the button to descend to the main floor. They stepped out into a vast atrium.

"Through the glass doors and turn left," Pénard had said. "Oh, and Jules? You know how it is. I'm sorry."

Laborde knew of a place in Hull Centro that served decent food at all times of day. He pulled into the St-Hub, went to the bar, and ordered the *quart de poulet*.

"A pint of draft," he said, pointing to the *Ruisseau* on tap. "And a whiskey."

Chapter 39

THEY HAD THEM lined up on the barbecue deck, all fifteen of them: a grey battalion ready for inspection. Joe Tasker stalked along the line. He grabbed the one on the end, lifted it off the ground, and shook it.

"No: completely empty," he called to the group of prospective diners who had assembled on the deck for supper.

The club had feared this moment. Although not unexpected, Tasker's verdict was devastating.

"But, surely you can go for refills at GasCo?" Maude Crabbe asked hopefully, putting her plastic dinner plate down on the nearest picnic table.

"If you imagine I'm going to risk a trip into Hull to line up with all those people from the camper vans, think again," said Joe. "Just ask Garvin and Harvey."

Bowter and Kinnear had arrived back at Blackwater the previous day. After Captain Pénard had escorted them out of the *Portalette*, they had walked to the club all the way from Hull. It had taken most of the afternoon. Commodore St. James, as they had announced to those assembled in the Mess, was still helping with enquiries.

"I ruined my shoes," said Harvey. "It's hard walking on the old railway line."

"What do you say, Garvin?" demanded Maude. "Surely we can drive to GasCo?"

"Don't look at me! Anyway, the GRs said the club could expect an inspection soon," replied Bowter. "There are still concerns that our septic may be *non-conforme*, apparently."

"And, they told me that our project to replant the banks of the reservoir with natural vegetation is not moving fast enough," added Harvey.

Old Tom Forget emerged from the Mess onto the deck. Paul moved aside to give him room: Tom walked with a cane and used it vigorously to clear the way. He used it now to rap against one of the empty gas cylinders.

"End of the road, damn it," he said. "Club's not what it was. I counted three GRs over at the cottage just now. They're planning something. Still, who cares? Let 'em come, I say."

Old Tom, who used to regale the bar with war stories, had grown morose over the past week. His response to Paul's offer of help to climb the steep steps to the crow's nest had been savage.

"Bugger off, Loess! I can manage," he had growled.

Still, thought Paul, one had to make allowances: Old Tom was a victim of the fluctuations in the reservoir's water level. When the level was last dropped at the dam, a sharp rock had punctured the hull of his boat. When the water rose, the boat had failed to rise with it, and foundered. Its deck was now awash, the keel driven deeply into the bottom mud.

André-Claude had been waiting to one side, holding his plate. He cleared his throat, drawing people's attention.

"*Pour moi, ça suffit,*" he announced. "*C'est impensable, vivre sans propane.*"

"We agree. It's just no fun anymore. We're leaving," said Sebastian Gann, nodding to his friend Didier.

"Tomorrow, I take *Zdrowie* upriver," said Olga Wilk.

"It's the Committee's fault," blurted Harvey. "If it wasn't for the Committee for Free Pontiac, they would leave us alone. It's your fault too, Margret. It's all coming apart. They said they would send me to re-education next time they caught me. I don't think I can take that. I'm not brave, not like you Margret.

I don't want to, I won't ..." Kinnear collapsed onto the nearest bench, his face buried in his arms, sobbing.

Everyone stood around, embarrassed. "I think they gave him a hard time in the *Portalette*," muttered Bowter.

Paul nudged Margret. "Say something!"

"Garvin," she said, after a pause. "You are notionally in charge in Taggart's absence. Should we vote on abandoning the club? If people are leaving, we need to know how many. This place can't keep going if too many members leave."

"Well, I... Yes: I suppose we need to vote on it. It's whether to leave Blackwater. That's a big decision. No refunds on annual membership, I'm afraid. I want to make that clear. So is it a show of hands? For leaving?"

Paul counted eighteen in favour. Following Margret's lead, he abstained.

"So the vote is for evacuation. How disappointing," said Margret, quietly. "I suppose you all have some idea of where you are planning to go?"

The assembled club fell silent. Most suddenly realized had nowhere to go: migrants from the USBAZ now occupied their former houses, cottages, condos or apartments. For some, Blackwater had been home for years.

"Okay," said Margret, after waiting in vain for suggestions. "Newbridge has a dock on the river. You could sail up there in a couple of hours. The town is staunchly free Pontiac: there will be no hassles from the GRs up there."

"Yes!" cried Garvin. "Newbridge is the obvious place. I can't think why I didn't think of it. There are plenty of moorings along the river bank, and a boat launch. The river there is deep, and the bay wide enough: perhaps even wide enough to have a decent sail. I think that—"

Tasker expressed everyone's frustration. He dropped the empty tank he was holding and kicked it. It rolled along the deck, down the steps, and began to career down the slope towards the reservoir. There was a faint splash.

"Newbridge it is, then," he said.

✧   ✧   ✧

NEXT MORNING, BLACKWATER hummed with activity. The clubhouse was in uproar: favourite pictures and photographs were taken down; mementos collected; bar supplies consumed or removed; club trophies surreptitiously transferred to boats. Along each finger dock, sailors hurriedly prepared their boats for departure. Joe Tasker phoned a friend in Newbridge with a tow truck.

"He'll be here at ten o'clock," announced Tasker through the bullhorn. "Dent and I intend to tow *Olivier's Dream* to Newbridge. If anyone else wants to take their boats out of the water, you'll have to wait. And my friend only accepts dollars, not *piastres*. The rest of you will have to sail."

"Over here. No, over here!" Garvin was directing boats jockeying to be first in line for hauling out. "Tie up just in behind the *Last Sandpiper*. I said *behind*!"

"Wow," said Paul to Margret. "I've never seen so much action, even during the regatta. Aren't you going to get the *Groaning Anne* ready?"

"I'm not leaving. At least not yet," replied Margret.

"I'll stay, if you do. Dock buddies for ever?"

"Oh, for Pete's sake, Paul ..." Margret snorted. But secretly, she not displeased by his choice.

Chapter 40

COLONEL MAURICIE'S PLAN A was dead—as dead as Collins, since the fool had got himself shot. She needed a Plan B. More urgently, she needed the second original of the signed agreement. If Brevet found it, he would have leverage. He might use it as proof that Mauricie had conspired with Collins against the Republic. If he made that known in certain conservative circles within the *Gardes*, Josée-Mathilde would insist that Mauricie resign. Deniability was *La Mante*'s survival strategy.

Mauricie had asked Brevet directly whether he had ordered Collins' assassination.

"*Mais non, Madame Colonel,*" he had replied. "Of course, if you had given the order … I am a professional. As to the identity of the culprit, *l'inspecteur* Laborde suspects one of the club members, but I regret to say the police investigators are living up to their reputation for incompetence."

A professional joke Brevet certainly was, but a potentially dangerous joke. Mauricie wished she could invite Brevet to level P3 at *le Château* back in Quebec City. Parking lot three was sixty feet underground and informally called the "*Oubliette.*" A few hours viewing the consequences of betrayal would bring him to heel. Unfortunately, Brevet was five hundred kilometres away in Hull Centro.

Mauricie thought hard. She rejected several options on how to proceed: one was too subtle, one too slow, another too uncertain. That left her with the one she first thought of: she would have to remove Brevet permanently; rub him out so that no possible trace could lead back to her. It would remove the immediate risk, and—if spun right—signal stern action against corrupt officials, in line with *La Présidente*'s anti-corruption drive.

Colonel Mauricie got up from behind her desk, and walked over to the window of her office, Plan B forming slowly in her mind. She could see far-off birds circling over the estuary—gulls maybe, or geese. One of the distant specks suddenly plunged into the water. Not a goose, then. Could it be a gannet? Mauricie wasn't sure how far up the St. Lawrence the birds came, how far from the sea proper. As she stood watching, sunshine broke through a gap in the clouds to fall golden on a distant patch of water. Of course! She came to a decision: Colonel Mauricie would request a favour from the Americans encamped on the south shore of the St. Lawrence.

The spooks had been there since the border adjustment and were the eyes and ears for the USBAZ, monitoring suspicious movements up and down the seaway and further north. Everyone pretended not to know that they flew their surveillance missions across most of Quebec. The compound was "black ops" and stuffed to the brim with gadgetry and ordinance.

The favour would come at a cost, however, and the currencies she had to offer were limited. She could already hear the condescending tone of her male counterpart in US intelligence: "Well, anything for you, *Cherie*."

His price would probably be dinner at one of the better restaurants in *le Vieux Port* and, inevitably, arranging for an additional quota of Spanish-speaking migrants to be admitted to Quebec from the USBAZ. Under the President's pet "People the North" policy, Mauricie knew nothing moved in the way of requisitions unless that executive order had been satisfied.

Mauricie sighed and picked up her phone. At the end of the call, she asked, "And when can you get it done?"

"Shit, *Cherie*, just send me the coordinates, and we'll get the bird up and away in no time."

✧   ✧   ✧

TWO DAYS LATER, the drone was circling lazily on a thermal, two miles north of the Blackwater Sailing Club. The Pontiac spread beneath it, a patchwork of farms and forest, the reservoir a long finger of black water between the hills. The drone had launched three hours before. Now it was waiting for a signal, impatient for its promised transformation into holy white fire.

Chapter 41

THE LAST FEW days had been highly satisfactory for Serge Brevet. His months of deliberate provocation had born fruit: he had succeeded in demoralizing the Blackwater Sailing Club. The Re-education program had proved a great success: only one club member had successfully passed the exam and returned to the Blackwater. He flipped open his notebook to check his memory: a Phelim Neely. Delario, Dubois, Soy and Thurlow had elected to continue their studies in Quebec values. Brevet knew that the time it took to reach competence was—how to put it?—elastic. And now, he had arranged for Commodore St. James to join them. The Commodore was well and truly on the beach: it was most gratifying.

True, he had released Bowter and Kinnear on Laborde's recommendation. They were mere pawns, released to carry the news to Blackwater of Taggart's detention, sowing fear and confusion prior to a muscular visitation by the *Garde*.

Now, Captain Pénard was standing in front of him describing how his force had successfully invaded Blackwater. They had circumvented the locked gate entirely, simply by wading around it and climbing onto the catwalk on the far side.

"It was a textbook operation, *Monsieur*," said Pénard. "The *connards* scattered like ducks. Some fled up the reservoir in their sailing boats."

"Is there anybody left, Pénard?"

"Only two, *Monsieur*. They showed no resistance."

I'll deal with those few squatters in due course, thought

Brevet.

"*Bien.* Well done, Pénard! A feather in your cap. Dismissed."

Brevet sat back in his chair and swivelled around to gaze out of the window. Now he could assure Headquarters he had quashed the separatist terrorists' dream of a Free State of West Quebec. He had cleansed the nest of radicals who had styled themselves as the Committee. But, as he emphasized in his report to Colonel Mauricie, outrages would doubtless continue. There were still elements—members of the so-called Pontiac Brigade—who remained to be dealt with. They had taken to the hills, hiding in the remote fastness of *le Parc nationale des collines.* Alas, he anticipated further attacks against the new settlements, those housing *les migrants de souche*, the true *Quebecois* escaping from the Yanqui occupation of the south shore.

Brevet smiled. In truth, he welcomed the idea of the occasional terrorist incident. If some of these could be directed towards the competitors of Brevet's commercial associates, all the better. The *Garde* would investigate, if not too thoroughly. Perhaps he should ask Quebec could send another unreliable minister to visit? Brevet had concluded his report with a request for a substantial increase in his operational budget.

The only slightly disagreeable matter concerned Agent Gruaut, who had returned from his month-long assignment in Montreal. He had arrived driving a minibus. Inside were five Spanish-speakers, transferred, it seemed, from farm camps on the south shore. They were, according to Gruaut, assigned to help with the harvest: a gesture of friendship from the USBAZ administrators.

"Orders from *Madame Colonel*, Commander," Gruaut informed him. "We are to find ways of occupying these people." Brevet told Gruaut to put them in temporary accommodations in the *Portalette.* Then he put the matter out of mind.

Later that afternoon, Commander Brevet found time in his

busy schedule to visit the Blackwater Sailing Club. It had been three years since he had last been near the island. That was the last time they had rejected his application to join. The interview had been brief, and conducted by the club secretary from the far side of the locked entry gate.

"No, Mr. Brevet," Kinnear had said at the time. "It is quite impossible: this is a sailing club and your sea-doos are simply unacceptable." Now, after his recent visit to the *Portalette*, Kinnear had learned to call Brevet "Sir".

Captain Pénard drove Commander Brevet from the *Portalette*, through *LaCloche* and turned onto the road leading to the club. Pénard drove straight down *chemin* Blackwater and stopped at the bottom, beside an old sign which said "Commodore Parking Only." As Brevet got out and looked across the water to Blackwater Island, it occurred to him that he might use the migrants that Agent Gruaut had brought from Montreal. Surely some were experienced in serving at table, cooking, and so on? He remembered the Caribbean cruise he had taken with Madame Brevet some years previously. The standard of service on board had been exceptional. The GRs should expect comparable luxury at their new retreat on the island.

Someone had left open the gate to the club. Propped against the gatepost was a board with the name Blackwater Sailing Club. He made a note to order a new sign. "*Club Nautique de la Noire*," he thought, had a European feel.

Brevet walked with Pénard along the catwalk towards the island. They passed several empty finger docks, and a few moored boats, their cabins shuttered and padlocked. As the pontoons bobbed up and down, he felt he was already getting his sea legs. They were passing one of the finger docks, one littered with plants and pottery, when a figure appeared.

"Madame Mankie," whispered Pénard to his superior. "The mad woman I told you about. *La folle!* She, and that neighbouring boat, a Monsieur Loess, are the only ones who haven't left."

Brevet checked his stride. He looked at the *Groaning Anne* and addressed the woman who had just emerged.

"Ahem. *Bonjour*, Madame Mankie. My name is Serge Brevet. I am taking charge of this island in the name of the Republic. You might say that I am your new commodore."

The woman was dressed in overalls. She glanced at Brevet, then bent towards a column of clay placed on a plastic mat on the wooden decking. She was holding what looked like a knife. Brevet felt a frisson of alarm.

"Welcome," she said. "I've been expecting you."

Margret took the sculpting tool and returned to working on what Brevet realized with a start was a human figure emerging from the clay. Brevet felt disappointed. He had expected to see some emotion on the woman's face: surprise, or even fear. Still, no matter. The task at hand was to choose the best berth for his boat.

"*Alors, Madame.* You must excuse me. I must complete my inspection."

"You were right, Pénard," he muttered as they continued past. "*Complètement folle.*"

When Brevet crossed the drawbridge at the end of the catwalk and stood, finally, on the island, the thought occurred to him he should have brought a flag. He would claim the Blackwater Sailing Club for the Republic. But that would have to wait. Time was short: a quick reconnoitre of the island would have to do for now.

"Pénard!" said Brevet. "*Un selfie avec moi.*" Brevet recalled an image from an article he had scanned on the sailing history of the Caribbean. The artist had imagined Columbus landing on the beach of the new continent, posed with knee thrust forward and hand on sword hilt. *Exactement comme ça*, thought Brevet.

✧　✧　✧

DURING THE WEEK, Commander Brevet liked to set a good example to his juniors. He always ensured that his trousers had knife-edge creases, and a spare uniform hung, wrapped in plastic, behind his office door. Each morning he paused to have his boots polished at the stand in the atrium of Tower 3. He seldom left his office before six in the evening on weekdays. Now, on the Saturday following his reconnaissance visit to Blackwater, Brevet was out of uniform. The day promised to be sunny and warm. He wore golfing trousers and his favourite barbecuing shirt, the one patterned with hibiscus flowers over a background of vibrant, Hawaiian blue.

Although he liked his staff to think he was never off duty, today would be an exception. This was the day Brevet would launch his Neuport Cruiser on the Noire reservoir. He had found the boat advertised for sale in the back pages of *Canadian Powerboater* magazine. The seller lived near Toronto. Brevet had pointed out the obvious difficulties of importing to the Republic, and had negotiated a much reduced price in consequence. To his great satisfaction, the arrangements to bring the boat across the frontier had gone without a hitch. He had ensured that the border agents waived the customs duty.

Brevet had temporarily stored his purchase in the secure compound behind the *Portalette.* It had arrived swathed in the blue cling-wrap that had protected the boat during the long road trip from Toronto. Brevet had ripped off enough of the plastic to make sure that there had been no damage in transit. Now that he had resolved matters at Blackwater, he was impatient to see if the Neuport's twin one-hundred-and-fifty horsepower outboards lived up to their promise.

Brevet drove into town from his residence in the upmarket

Blue Hills sector of Hull in his new Bighorn 2500. The truck was fully loaded with extra wide tires, chrome running boards, and with—essential for this morning's mission—a fully adjustable tow hitch. He was to meet Captain Pénard at the gate to the compound.

On seeing his commander's personal vehicle approaching, Pénard pushed open the gate, and Brevet swung into the lot. His boat was parked at the end of a row of camper vans, held in the compound pending payment of fines by their owners. Brevet backed down the row, watching in his side mirrors. He crept to a stop aligned directly in front of the trailer. Pénard wound down the boat trailer onto the truck's tow ball. Perfect first time, thought Brevet. This is going to be a good, no, a great day.

"*Allons-y!*" said Brevet, and drove off, making an extra wide turn out of the *Portalette* compound to keep his boat well clear of the gatepost. He stopped outside the fence and waited for Pénard to climb into the truck beside him. Brevet glanced at Pénard and grunted in approval. His subordinate was wearing Bermudas, T-shirt and baseball cap; perfectly suitable for this mission. The automatic rifle the agent was holding between his legs was the only sign that a morning's boat trip on the reservoir demanded more security than in the past.

Brevet planned to launch his boat from the ramp just up-stream from the Noire dam. He had arranged for his cousin, dam superintendent Guy LaMolle, to unlock the chain at the top of the ramp. The chain prevented random boaters from launching on the reservoir. Brevet pressed the horn as he approached the ramp and lowered the driver's window.

"*Salut, Guy!*" he called to his cousin, pulling to a halt. "*Une belle journée.*"

"*Bonjour, Serge. Ça va?*"

"*Ouais. Ça va. Ça va.*"

"Pénard, help me turn this thing around, so Monsieur La-

Molle can back her into the water."

After reversing, moving forward, and reversing again under Pénard's direction, Brevet had the trailer positioned at the top of the ramp, poised for launching. He pulled on the emergency brake but left the motor running. He got out of the vehicle.

"Don't just stand there, Pénard. Help me pull off the rest of this plastic wrap." It took five minutes to remove the covering from the boat. The three men stood back to admire the boat, revealed in all its splendour.

"*Un beau bateau, Serge,*"said LaMolle. "How is she called?"

Brevet went to the bow and stroked the perfect white finish. He pointed to the name "*She's a Lady*" picked out in blue letters beside the motif of a mermaid.

"*Mais, c'est en anglais!*"

"*Bon Dieu, Guy!* Everyone knows that it's unlucky to change a boat's name. Now, I want you to get in the truck and reverse down the ramp. Just wait until we climb aboard."

Brevet lifted a short ladder from its storage hooks on the side of the trailer. He placed it against the boat and climbed up into the cockpit. Pénard followed, his weapon slung over his shoulder. Brevet pushed the ladder away so it fell back onto the ramp. He turned and gave LaMolle a thumbs-up.

"Back her down, Guy," he called.

LaMolle released the brake. He let the trailer roll down the slope into the reservoir until the wheels submerged and the Bighorn's exhaust gurgled in the water. Pénard went forward and reaching over the rail, unlatched the restraining hook from the bow of the boat. The *She's a Lady* floated sweetly off the cradle. Brevet reversed away from the trailer and let the boat back into the bay in a smooth arc. He waved to his cousin, pushed the stick into drive, and turned away from the boat launch.

"Stand up front and keep a watch for deadheads, Pénard," he called. Partially submerged logs were still a hazard in this part of the reservoir, even though years had passed since the last logging run.

Brevet sat in the captain's chair, one hand on the wheel, the other caressing the throttle control beside him. Dials on the dashboard showed engine revs, fuel, speed and bearing. He headed due north, the dam receding behind him in his rear-view mirror. Once away from the shore and clear of the danger of floating logs, Brevet waved Pénard back to sit down in the cockpit. He opened the throttle. The boat surged ahead, sweeping beneath the power lines that sagged over the middle of the reservoir. Brevet breathed deeply; this was worth the wait! The sun, the spray, the growl of the twin engines perfectly tuned! A deep wake fanned out behind them. It slapped, after long minutes, along both forested shores of the broadening water.

Fifteen minutes later, Brevet sighted the lighthouse marking the eastern entrance to Blackwater Bay. *Une phare sans lumières*, thought Brevet. That would change when the club was under his management. He laughed: a lighthouse without lights, how ridiculous.

A line of masts was visible, and Brevet could just make out the clubhouse on the hill behind, its windows glinting amid the pine trees. He spun the wheel and the *She's a Lady* swung in a graceful curve towards the mouth of the bay.

Brevet put the engines in neutral and let the boat glide towards the shore and a floating dock he had scouted on his visit earlier in the week. He had probed the bottom with a stick to ensure that the water depth was enough for the Neuport. Her draft was only half a metre, but one couldn't be too careful with a new boat. The dock was moored to the rocks near the point, and had seemed ideal. But now, as he approached, Brevet realized that it was exposed to the south. There were more sheltered docks further within the bay; closer to the catwalk might be a better choice.

"*Attention*, Pénard! Hang the fenders over the side."

The boat bumped hard. Pénard jumped, half falling onto the dock.

"*Chaulice!* Watch the paint!" shouted Brevet, as the boat ground along edge. Pénard grabbed the stern of the boat, bringing it to a stop. Brevet switched off the ignition. He stood, and stepped lightly onto the dock.

"Tie her up well, Pénard," he ordered. "We can't have her rubbing."

A short gangplank led to the shore and a well-worn path. Left, he knew, led to the clubhouse. If he went right, he expected to arrive at the point beside the lighthouse.

"Wait for me here, Pénard."

Brevet turned right. The path wandered between pine trees, a thick carpet of needles underfoot. It emerged after a hundred metres onto a rocky promontory. He was, as he had guessed, beside the old lighthouse. Brevet paused, breathing the scent of the pines. In the quiet, he could hear ripples lapping against the shore. In the bright sunshine, the water danced with sparkling reflections. For once, *La Noire* was blue, really blue. Brevet sensed something he rarely felt nowadays. He felt connected. Like when he hit a glorious drive at golf.

Suddenly, it came to him: what all his efforts had been for. He knew what he would do. He would build! Right here on the point. It would have to be in reinforced concrete, of course, to withstand the winter ice. He would install a hot tub and an infinity pool. Brevet had no idea he was overlooking what had once been the Eaton Chutes.

✧   ✧   ✧

STROLLING BACK FROM the point, Brevet found Captain Pénard.

"We'll go straight to the clubhouse. Bring the hamper from

the boat."

He waited while Pénard fetched the beer and food before continuing along the path. The agent trailed behind, his rifle slung over his shoulder and carrying the hamper in both hands. The path led to the drawbridge at the end of the catwalk. Brevet had no wish for a renewed encounter with that Mankie woman, so continued on the path leading up the hill to the clubhouse.

Near their destination, the pine trees were higher. Brevet noticed a row of overturned canoes smothered under deep drifts of needles to the right of the path, and a strange single pole, upright in a circle of sand. He climbed the wooden steps to the clubhouse entrance. There should be some ceremony, he thought: a piping aboard of the new commodore. But all he could hear was the abusive chatter of a red squirrel from a branch of the nearest tree.

Inside, he wandered from the Mess to the committee room to the bar, looking at the pictures of past regattas and the navigational maps displayed on the walls; at the string of pennants from rival clubs, the knot work, and the embroidered cushions on the old sofa and armchairs. There was an office of sorts, crammed with sailing paraphernalia. It was clutter, but historical clutter. It made Brevet feel quite the *seigneur*.

The place would have to be cleared out and renovated, but he would, as commodore, preserve some of the storied atmosphere of the club. Perhaps he would keep the knot work, if cleaned and varnished. And the staff would need some tradition-al standards to aspire too. There was nothing wrong with exclusive traditions once you were on the inside. He would need club rules to keep the lower grades of GRs in order when they came for R&R. He was sure there must be a list somewhere. The Anglos were good at that sort of thing.

In the corridor with the glass cabinets, Brevet looked closely at the inscriptions on the silver trophies. He would be doing the awarding in the future, *bien sûr*, but perhaps he could have the name Brevet engraved on something. His eye rested on the old rifle, resting on its highly polished backboard. It was, he read from the engraved plaque, awarded for the most audacious act of the sailing season. Last year's winner was a Michael Collins. Brevet wondered what his audacious act had been.

Half an hour later, Brevet was installed in an Adirondack chair on the deck beside the clubhouse. The sun was pleasantly warm, and Brevet was relaxing under the influence of the single malt that Pénard had found behind the bar. He wondered vaguely if the club had a stock of wine. Adding a *cave* for his vintages would be on his to-do list.

Brevet suddenly realized that LaMolle had allowed the reservoir to fill back to its normal level. Perhaps Guy had been right to do so; he was relieved that a veneer of shining water again covered the stinking mud exposed when his cousin had dropped the level. It would remain like this—picture perfect—now that he, Commodore Brevet, was in charge. From this high point of the island, the view upriver was pristine, the river calm with tendrils of mist rising off the water under the heat of the late morning sun.

He looked forward to taking his young nephews and nieces wakeboarding.

✧ ✧ ✧

IN THE AFTERNOON, although a few puffs of cumulus appeared in the blue sky above the Blackwater Sailing Club, the wind remained calm and the visibility exceptional.

From its cruising height of two thousand feet, the drone recognized its target on the clubhouse deck, and locked on. It banked in a tight curve, and began to descend along a zipline trajectory, accelerating all the way to impact. The image of the island grew and grew in its forward camera, the drone confirming every detail of the target to the last pixel, until nothing else remained but hibiscus and Hawaiian blue.

Chapter 42

MARGRET MANKIE WAS on the dock beside the *Groaning Anne* when she saw a flash and then a ring of black smoke shoot into the sky. The report of the explosion came a second later. Burning debris hissed into the bay.

Paul poked his head out of the cabin of the *Spindrift*.

"What the hell was that?"

He ducked as a fragment hit the dock and skittered towards his boat. It was triangular, like the dorsal fin of a shark.

"Hold on to that, Paul," said Margret. "Could be a souvenir."

⋄   ⋄   ⋄

WHEN THE FIRE had mostly died, and with the smoke dissipating in the light breeze, Margret and Paul picked their way along a catwalk cluttered with fallen debris, and crossed the drawbridge onto the island. They stumbled uphill through charred pine trees towards the clubhouse.

The explosion had demolished the crow's nest, leaving the ruined building open to the sky. The layout of the ground floor was still recognizable, but the bar was reduced to smouldering splinters. Glass shards and congealed spatters of metal from melted trophies covered the floor of the corridor by the display cabinets. Margret recognized the Commodore's Cup, which had rolled across the floorboards. Bending over to set it upright, she caught the reek of cauterized flesh. There were shreds of colourful textile mixed with carbonized fragments. Whether parts of Brevet or Pénard, it was impossible to tell.

"I'm going to check out the wine cellar," she said to Paul. "That, at least, is blast-proof. See if you can find any bits that are recognizable while I'm gone."

"God, no." Paul was afraid of what he might find sticking to the wreckage. He found the mess sofa—miraculously unscathed—in the rubble. He felt the seat; the leather was scorched and faintly warm. He sat down carefully.

"I'll wait for you here," he said to Margret's disappearing back.

Shifting his feet, Paul felt the crunch of broken glass. It was a framed group photograph that, until half an hour ago, had hung above the bar. The faces of the Board members who had grilled him when he joined smiled up at him from the floor. Now, Mike Collins was dead, Taggart interned, and the others had fled.

"RIP," he muttered to himself.

✧　✧　✧

MARGRET PICKED HER way towards where the kitchen used to be. The cabinet that had concealed the door to the old mine lay on the ground, torn from its hinges. She brushed aside the debris, and walked the few steps to the end of the shaft.

Standing in the circle of faint daylight that angled down the shaft, Margret waited for her eyes to adjust. After two minutes, she hauled a wooden case from against the wall and levered open the lid. Resting on top of a row of five Armalites nestled in their bubble-wrap, was a buff utility envelope, designed for reuse. Mike Collins had crossed out his name on the distribution list and written Margret as the next recipient.

"In case of my untimely death," he had said to her their last night on the boat.

Chapter 43

IT WAS THIRTY kilometres from the Blackwater Sailing Club up to Newbridge. The first half of the journey was plain sailing, with a south wind blowing at Paul's back. When he reached the bend where the upper section of the River Noire flowed into the reservoir, the valley narrowed and the current became noticeable. Continuing under sail was impossible: Paul had no option but to lower the sails and start the motor. The *Groaning Anne* glided alongside.

"You'll have to tow me from here," called Margret. "My damn outboard has given up."

Paul kept a tow rope handy in one of the cockpit lockers. He coiled the rope and threw it across the gap between the boats. Margret caught it and wrapped it around a bow cleat.

"Okay, then."

Paul let in the clutch, and let the *Spindrift* pull slowly ahead until he felt the rope jerk taut. He twisted the throttle, and the boat surged forward, towing the *Groaning Anne* in its wake.

Upstream, past the northern end of the reservoir, the Noire began to behave like a proper river. It flowed through the undrowned valley in a succession of gentle curves and straight reaches. Paul was alert for signs of shallow water: weed streaming in the current that betrayed a shoal ahead, the forests of reeds on the inside of each bend. Paul steered well clear of both, hoping to keep safely within the deepest channel.

They entered the last reach before Newbridge, where the valley narrowed, and the river cut straight and deep through a notch in the hills. Progress became painfully slow against the faster current.

After half an hour of making little more than half a knot, the *Spindrift* with the *Groaning Anne* straining behind, emerged into a broad bay. The river's flow slackened, and Paul relaxed. Ahead, along the western edge of the bay, he could see a straggle of houses and other buildings: an obvious church, and a larger building which he thought might be a hotel. As he got nearer, he realized that the village was built on a low terrace, only a few metres above the water level. The river bank might be stabilized but even so, Paul decided, the town must be prone to flooding. So this was Newbridge. They had arrived without incident, for which he was truly thankful.

Paul steered towards a line of wooden docks where several sailing boats were tied up. Most he recognized as club boats from Blackwater.

"Put us beside those," called Margret, pointing to a line of houseboats moored along a boom.

A man was standing on the dock staring at them. Then he waved and pointed to a space where Paul and Margret could berth their boats.

✧   ✧   ✧

"WHERE'S MANKIE?" CALLED Donovan as he caught the rope tossed by Paul, and pulled the *Spindrift* alongside the dock.

"And, hello to you, Donovan," said Paul. "She's back there, in the *Groaning Anne*."

Margret's boat was gliding in behind Paul's. Donovan ran to catch its bow.

"Good morning," said Margret, standing up in her cockpit.

After both boats had been secured, she said, "We'll need a hand later, to carry a heavy box and the remaining supplies from my boat. Where is everybody? I don't see any life on these boats."

"Municipal bylaw: no overnighting on the river," replied Donovan. "We had to put them in the back room of the pub."

Donovan led the way up the wooden steps from the dock to the embankment. Paul paused at the top. He was surprised to find that they were standing on a railway line. It stretched in a long curve beside the river, bordering the main street of the village.

"Is this the same railway that runs past the club?" he asked.

"Haven't you been in Newbridge before?" said Margret.

"Well, I ..." began Paul. "No."

"You are correct. This line went all the way down to Hull. It was abandoned in the 1980s."

The Newbridge town council had converted the old railway into a riverside path. Weeds sprouted from between the red bricks which had been laid between the rails. Paul noticed two collapsed flower boxes flanking a bench: *in memoriam*, and an illegible name.

"Come on, Paul," called Margret over her shoulder.

Donovan and Margret crossed from the path to the other side of the main street. Paul hurried after them. They continued along the sidewalk, past a succession of shuttered shop fronts, an abandoned chapel, and a building that had once housed a bank. A cash machine had been inserted into its stone portico. Several people were in line. A large sign reminded customers that withdrawals of the new million *piastre* notes were strictly limited to five per daily session.

They stopped in front of the old hotel, *les Draveurs*, which was a coffee shop in the mornings and a pub from lunchtime onwards. The hotel showed no sign of life. Only a poster in the window promised activity—Talent Night was on Fridays from seven p.m.

Donovan paused, and turned to Margret.

"Have you replaced Collins on the Committee, then?" he asked. "He said he deputized you."

"Yes," replied Margret. "Mike left me instructions about the ammunition."

"Good: it's about time the Committee delivered the ammo. The brigade boys shot off all the complimentary clips in an afternoon. And, just so you know, you won't be ordering the Brigade around anymore. Not like bloody Collins. I'll have no more of that Lac King nonsense."

"We'll go round by the bins," added Donovan, pointing to the alley alongside the building.

At the back of the hotel was a fire door, wedged open a crack with an old sneaker. Donovan pulled the door wide open. Paul caught the whiff of bacon, and felt the vomit rising to the back of his throat. It was the same stench that permeated the blasted clubhouse.

Donovan led Paul and Margret down a corridor. The wood panelled walls were decorated with posters of acts that had played the hotel. They passed two doors: one for *Guys* and one for *Gals*. The bacon smell became stronger and stronger. At the end of the passage was a large room with a high ceiling. It was dimly lit: the windows were covered with heavy drapes, and the only light came from a row of bulbs dangling from a central beam.

"There have been some wild dances in here," said Donovan. "That's where the bands used to play," he added, nodding towards the stage at the far end of the hall.

Paul looked around. Along the inside wall of the hall was a row of twin bunks. Boxes, chests, and other luggage were piled between the beds. Clothing hung from hooks lining the wood-paneled walls. Half way along the opposite wall was a cooking range, its metal chimney rising to near the high ceiling, before angling out through the side wall. Several people were clustered around the range, most sitting on a motley collection of wooden chairs. Paul recognized Harvey standing at the stove, wielding a large frying pan.

"I asked 'over-easy or sunny-side up'." Harvey's voice rose in pitch. "Well, if you can't make up your mind ..." Paul gathered that bacon and eggs were on the menu, even for supper.

Donovan coughed loudly.

Eight faces turned to look at the new arrivals: Garvin, Harvey and Maude—all that remained of the Board—plus Neely, Old Tom and Lowder Pritcher. Tasker and Hall seemed to be quarrelling about who should have the top bunk, and barely noticed the new arrivals. These, thought Paul, were the residue from the Blackwater Sailing Club.

"Look who I found down by the docks," said Donovan.

Harvey's frying pan clattered onto the stove top.

"It's Margret and Paul! You made it!"

✧   ✧   ✧

"HARVEY, PERHAPS YOU would help Paul with the cargo in my boat. You can bring it up here," said Margret.

"Of course," said Harvey, and scurried off. He knew exactly where to find a trolley.

Paul looked at Margret, who nodded, and he followed Harvey back down the passage.

"What's the Brigade up to these days, Pat?" she asked Donovan.

"Jeez you're nosy. The answer is not much. No ammo. We ran a *Gardes* truck off the road last week. We do the odd ambush."

"What about republican snitches here in Newbridge?"

"Aye," said Donovan. "The boys caught an informant only

last week. Had a phonebook with all our names highlighted. They dangled him off the old, covered bridge."

"Thank you, Pat. Ah, here they are, back. Put the case over here, Paul," said Margret, "and pass me that hammer." She took the hammer and levered the lid from the box.

Donovan, Garvin, and the others crowded round. Margret pulled away layers of bubble-wrap to reveal one of her clay statues.

"Good," she said, "it looks like they've survived the trip."

"You … you've brought your bloody gnomes from Blackwater?" stuttered Garvin.

"What the fuck?" said Donovan, staring.

"Don't worry, Pat. I've ordered the ammunition. We're just waiting for the shipping confirmation before going to collect it."

Chapter 44

Despondent after abandoning Blackwater, the continuing absence of their Commodore, and the murder of Mike Collins, the club members had spent the past week in uncomfortable accommodation at *les Draveurs*. The locals regarded them with suspicion, the Newbridge authorities threatened eviction, and they were growing tired of Harvey's insistence on cooking eggs. They needed leadership.

Accordingly, a much-thinned board of the Blackwater Sailing Club convened—in exile—around a table in the lounge bar of the hotel *les Draveurs*. Garvin Bowter, Maude Crabbe, Old Tom Forget, Phelim Neely, and André-Claude Sauveur were at the table. The secretary, Harvey Kinnear, began briskly.

"The first order of business is to welcome two members onto the board. I propose we acclaim Margret to replace Mike Collins. Objections?"

"I assume you will also take on Mike's position as chair of the 'Triple-P' Committee?" continued Kinnear. "Yes, of course you will."

The board chose Paul as Youth Member. Benedict Countryman, it seemed, had lived up to his name: he had abandoned the club and gone to stay with his aunt in the back country past Shawton.

"Are we going to elect a new commodore?" asked Margret, speaking for the first time. "I doubt if Taggart is returning, and we certainly don't need to recognize the brief reign of Commander Serge Brevet. He called himself 'Commodore' when I met him at Blackwater."

"Bloody nerve," said Old Tom. "Now I come to think of it, he would now be a past-commodore. And, in accordance with club tradition, his ashes are floating in the reservoir. Damn good place for 'em."

"Are there any nominations?" said Kinnear, hesitantly. He rather liked the idea of himself as commodore.

"Okay, I propose Garvin," said Margret. "Seconded? Paul?"

Paul raised his hand slowly, unused to the brisk pace of board meetings.

"Well deserved, I say," said Old Tom. "Got my vote."

"I'd say that's unanimous, Harvey," said Margret, looking at the others around the table for dissent.

"Well, ahem," said Bowter, standing up. "I would just like to say that, after years as Harbour Master, I never expected to become commodore. It's only while Taggart is away, of course."

"Congratulations, Garvin," said Margret. "Perhaps, you can think of some projects to engage the members—I know Taggart deferred safety courses, for instance. Those would be doable here at *les Draveurs*."

"Well, yes. I always thought we should consider First-Aid." He sat down abruptly.

In the matter of chairing the 'Triple-P' Committee, the board agreed on Margret, respecting the wishes of Mike Collins.

"We must re-establish communications," said Margret. She saw blank looks around the boardroom table. "Look: we lost all our radio equipment in the attack on the island. Mail addressed to Blackwater is being diverted God knows where. We are currently *incommunicado*."

"But Margret," said Bowter, "that may be a priority for the Committee, but, I mean, I think we should focus on club matters. I like to restart our Sunday races, for instance, and—"

"But Garvin, a committee priority *is* a club priority. Surely you remember Mike put that to a vote at the plenary meeting last summer?"

"Well, I—"

"Good. Now, are there volunteers to go down to the Surplus Megastore in Hull Centro to pick a communications unit? A scrambler model that masks its transmitting location would be nice. I have the specifications."

Silence followed. White noise from the public bar poured into the void.

"That, er, seems like a good start, Margret," ventured Paul. Then everyone spoke at once.

"But how do we avoid the GRs? And the police have check stops everywhere." This was from Neely, who had been released from re-education after two weeks with the news that Philly, Tickles, Larry and Duff had elected to stay, for *perfectionnement*, so they said. Neely seemed unaffected by the experience, bar a slight stutter. But he kept pulling at his fingers, as if trying to remove surgical gloves.

"Cow-a-choo," he explained. "Can't get them off."

"Take Maude's Leaf," said Margret. "They never pull over a Leaf. Provided, Maude, it still has enough range?"

"Yes, it'll take us down to Hull Centro and back, no prob-lem."

"Good. Then you go with Paul. Okay? The second matter I think we should discuss, Commodore, is what to do with the boats."

Beside *les Draveurs*, several club boats resting on their trailers. Their owners had towed them from the club in the rushed exodus. Others, who had left matters too late, had sailed north to Newbridge. Only the *Ring of Kerry* and Old Tom's sunken hulk had been abandoned.

"Is there any hope of going back to Blackwater?" asked Maude.

"No," said Margret. "The place is a ruin, and the GRs seem intent on taking it over. We are orphans, I'm afraid. Joe, you have a comment?"

"We might launch on one of the northern lakes. There's another friend of mine, runs a hunting camp up North on the Baskatong Reservoir. It not bad water: a bit cold but few nasty rocks. On the whole, I think it would suit us."

"But it's far for people to come for the regatta," Bowter added, doubtfully.

"Your boats can't stay here, that's for sure," said Old Tom. "Maude already got a damned parking ticket."

"Over to you, Commodore," said Margret, standing up from the table. "Convoy the boats out of Newbridge by the end of this week. Move the whole club up to Baskatong."

"Excuse me," interrupted Harvey. "Baskatong isn't Blackwater. We'll have to change our name."

"Please make a list of suggestions, Harvey," said Margret. "So clever of you to think of that."

✧ ✧ ✧

THE FOLLOWING EVENING, Maude and Paul returned from their shopping expedition to Hull Centro. As Maude pulled into the lot beside *les Draveurs,* the Leaf looked as though she had driven through thick vegetation.

"Mission accomplished," Maude said proudly as she struggled out from behind the wheel. She had the front seat pushed as far forward as possible so the rear could fold down to accommodate their bulky purchases.

"Oh that," Maude added, seeing Margret eyeing the mud and scratches on her car. "We had to take a shortcut on the way back to avoid a check stop."

"One communications unit with all the bells and whistles,"

said Paul, pointed to a cardboard box in the trunk. He opened the flaps of the box, revealing the equipment packed around with protective foam. Cables, coiled and secured with plastic ties were on top, together with an instruction manual.

"The salesperson at the store said these communications units are on a staged surplus program," he added. "Which means it is still in operation with the GRs, and its scrambler unit uses the same codes."

"Well done! Now, we can get back in business," said Margret. "Let's set it up in the hall."

The box was light enough to be manageable for one person. Paul lifted it out of the trunk and carried it into the building.

"Put it over there on the stage," said Margret.

Paul hefted the box onto the stage and climbed up beside it. A table against the wall seemed a good place. It was beside an electrical outlet, where Paul assumed they plugged in the microphones on concert nights. He pushed a box of empties to one side and placed the box on the table.

"It's a custom model," he said to Margret, as he removed the communications unit from its box. "Look at these side panels of walnut veneer and the chrome casing. It must have belonged to some executive."

Paul glanced at the instructions. They seemed simple enough: "First, remove the packaging and protective plastic film from your new unit." The previous owner had already done that. "Second, connect the unit to your power outlet." He plugged in and heard a faint hum. He touched the finger pad and a screen appeared, challenging him for a password.

"Shit," he muttered.

Margret put her hand on his shoulder, then leaned forward and peeled off a small square of paper that had been taped to the side of the device.

"Try 'Neuport'," she said.

✧   ✧   ✧

GARVIN BOWTER HAD been annoyed when Joe Tasker suggested his friend up North with the camp on the Baskatong. Moving the boats there would be a major step, but returning to Blackwater was out of the question. There would be compensations, he thought. The lake was large, certainly big enough for cabin boats to race. Their course could be more triangular than in the Noire, where the races had been up and down the reservoir. And, from a sailor's viewpoint, the lake had advantages. There would be less fluctuation in water levels, no current, and the prevailing wind from the northwest blew straight across the water.

Joe had explained that there was an island across from his friend's fishing camp, with ample shelter to moor all the remaining Blackwater boats. A small cove on the south side of the island was a natural harbor. It had a hard, sandy bottom, if Joe remembered rightly. Yes, on reflection, perhaps it was a good idea. A pity he hadn't thought of it first. And with no Collins around to interfere, they could focus on sailing and there would be no call for all this paramilitary business. Bowter decided to take immediate charge of preparations. The trek north would require thorough preparation and a firm hand.

The following morning, it pleased Bowter to see the club members imbued with new energy and purpose. Responding well under his direction, he thought. They purchased supplies and topped up with gas at the *dépanneur* without much grousing about the exorbitant prices. They greased trailer hitches and cinched tarp straps.

"Make sure they are really tight," Bowter advised Joe Tasker, as he inspected the preparations.

"Eff off, Garvin," Joe and Dent replied in unison.

By Friday, all were ready, packed, and happy to leave behind the dismal barracks at the back of *les Draveurs*. Barely warrants one star, was the general verdict. The only dissenter was Old Tom, who had found a double room on the top floor of the building with fine views up and down the river.

"No point." he said. "Not bloody moving again."

Further discussion was interrupted by the barkeep from the lounge bar of the hotel.

"There's a Ms. Milk at the bar, looking for a Mr. Forget."

Old Tom went bright red.

✧   ✧   ✧

"WHAT ABOUT YOU and Paul?" Bowter asked Margret later that evening. "Both your boats are still on the river."

"They'll be staying there for the time being, Garvin," said Margret. "We won't be joining you immediately. There are matters I have to see to here."

"But—"

"But nothing, Commodore Bowter. You lead the convoy. Set up camp."

"He'll have them sailing in circles around that lake in no time," Margret said to Paul later, when they were alone. "That's not my idea of retirement."

Part IV
The Drying

Chapter 45

S INCE HIS COUSIN'S violent demise, Guy LaMolle had let the reservoir fill back to its normal level. This, he tried to tell himself, was because he found exposed mud around the shores of "his" reservoir displeasing. Old stumps, heaps of boulders draped with slime, and mysterious mud-shrouded shapes emerged when he let the level drop. To be honest with himself, LaMolle knew that abandoned houses and traces of old farm buildings lay below the surface. That meant things buried that would be better undisturbed. He hated ghosts.

LaMolle felt light-headed, directionless. He spent much of each day sitting in the portacabin, gazing at the water through the scratched windows. He had paid little notice to the water's moods before; it had been his job to take a professional interest, but otherwise he had ignored its changing beauty. Now as he watched the reservoir, he saw the colours change: from a mirror reflecting the silver clouds, to dark green when the sun was vertical and the algae were in bloom. To his mild surprise, it was seldom blue. Last evening, the setting sun had set it aflame, before turning to black.

But when the wind whipped the reservoir surface from placid to choppy, LaMolle grew morose. When a rain squall blew across the reservoir, streaking his window with smears of rain, quite uncontrollably, he began to cry. Why, after years of service, was his career to end?

It was not his fault! For weeks, LaMolle had been diligently monitoring a fissure in the downstream face of the dam. A month ago, only a trickle of water seeped from the crack; some seepage was normal, but he couldn't deny that the flow had been increasing. Now, he had to admit, the seep qualified as a gush.

LaMolle had dithered, putting off the inevitable. But two days ago, he had reported his observations to PowerBec Central Command. That had, he gathered, triggered a code orange. Central Command texted him that they would dispatch an assessment team as soon as one became available. There were, so he was told, grid issues in high-priority areas that needed urgent responses. So, no, they couldn't be more precise. They suggested LaMolle use the PowerBec app to see when a team might arrive. It could be morning or afternoon, this week definitely.

Consequently, the following morning, it surprised LaMolle to see a vehicle driving slowly towards him along the curve of the dam. A Ford F-550 truck halted beside the portacabin. The corporate logo—*Plus vert que jamais*—in bold, yellow letters stencilled on the side panel, emphasized the green priorities of the company. With their ladders and a cherry-picker folded on the roof, one could hardly mistake a mobile PowerBec team. A trailer towed behind the truck carried an inflatable boat.

The driver's door opened, and a young woman in overalls clambered down from the cab. Two men emerged from the crew seats behind her. They went to the rear of the truck to unload equipment.

"Ashley Daigle, from Central Command," she said to La-Molle when he came to meet her. "I'm the team leader. Those are my technicians, Yves and Carlo. You reported leakage on the downstream face?"

LaMolle wondered how recently Daigle had graduated from the technical school.

"*Mais, oui.* I just thought that—"

"So, when did you first notice this leak? I take it you do daily inspections? No? Huh."

Daigle turned to her crew. "We'll fly the survey first. Get the mini-copter ready."

"Now, Superintendent LaMolle, tell me roughly where to find your problem."

"*Bien sûr.* If you want to follow me—"

"That won't be necessary. Just show me on this plan." She held out a tablet showing a schematic of the dam.

LaMolle took and held the tablet awkwardly.

"The fissure must be about here, I think. I'm not sure, but—"

"Good. I won't need your assistance further, Superintendent. But perhaps coffee later in the office?" Ashley Daigle strode to the parapet above the downstream face of the dam, and looked down the long concrete slope to the tumble of rocks and straggly bushes in the deep valley below.

LaMolle stood outside the portacabin and watched Yves climb into the back of the truck. He re-emerged seconds later, carrying what looked to LaMolle like a large metal suitcase. He put it down and unfastened the lid. Inside, nestling in protective packaging, was the mini-copter.

"Yo! *Toi-là. Viens m'aider!*" called the technician.

LaMolle was about to protest, but thought the better of it. He had lost all confidence since his encounter with the Blackwater Club. He helped the technician lift the machine out of the box and place it carefully on the ground. It was laden, he supposed, with sensors.

"*Une belle, eh?*" said Yves, fondly.

LaMolle watched Yves connect a slim computer to a handset, and test that the mini-copter responded to the controls. He made some last adjustments, then gave Daigle a thumbs-up. Seconds later, the machine lifted off, then flew over the parapet to hover above the downstream face of the dam. Yves, holding the handset control, and with his gaze riveted on the 'copter, followed slowly to the parapet. He adjusted the control, and the 'copter began long sweeps back and forth across the dam. LaMolle watched with envy. He regretted having never taken the training, but then, management had never suggested it.

Daigle, after watching to see that the 'copter was performing as expected, walked across to opposite side of the dam, and leaned over to look down into the reservoir.

"Now for the fluorescene," said Daigle to her second technician. "Dump the end of the hose over here and we'll work along."

Carlo went to the truck and opened a side compartment. He pulled a hose from a reel, and dangled it over the wall into the reservoir.

"*Bon*, that's enough," said Daigle. "Go and turn on."

LaMolle leaned over the edge to watch the green, fluorescent dye billow out in the water below. He felt ignored—useless—and retreated to the portacabin. From here, he could, at least, check the levels in the reservoir. It would be something to do. He switched on the coffee machine.

An hour passed before Daigle rejoined LaMolle in the portacabin. Yves and Carlo crowded in behind her. Daigle carried the laptop which had recorded the minicopter's survey.

"*Bon*, now we have the data. Let's see how bad this is," she said, after LaMolle had poured three coffees, cream and two sugars, and passed them around. Daigle sat in LaMolle's swivel chair, placing the computer in front of her on LaMolle's desk.

LaMolle and the two technicians looked over her shoulder at a map of the dam, a digital model in to-the-millimetre resolution. The green dye had wriggled its way through the body of the dam to highlight the weeping fissure, now surrounded by a braid of ramifying cracks.

"We'll just flatten that to horizontal and boost the anomalies," said Daigle. "Okay, there we go."

A large, red bloom appeared in the middle of the screen.

"*Tabernac, c'est beau!*" said Yves.

"That, Monsieur Superintendent," said Daigle, ignoring her technician, "is a bulge in the downstream face of the dam."

"Not good?" asked LaMolle.

✧ ✧ ✧

TWO DAYS AFTER the visit of the PowerBec team, LaMolle received a copy of an email to the Director of Operations (West). The assessment of the Noire *barrage* led by Daigle had revealed a structural issue. Although the dam was not in immediate danger of failure, it was over a hundred years old, and repairs would require major reconstruction. Remediation was, LaMolle gathered, out of the question budget-wise. The reservoir would be drawn down, and the dam mothballed. The grid had plenty of capacity to compensate for the loss of the feeble amount of electricity that the Noire still generated.

LaMolle prayed that decommissioning would be a slow process, one that could see him through to retirement. He was soon disillusioned. The following week, a fall thunderstorm dumped heavy rain far to the north in the Noire watershed. Central Command predicted the flood would crest at the Noire dam within forty-eight hours. The senior hydrologist thought it possible that the reservoir might overtop the dam, an unacceptable risk for such a weakened structure. LaMolle got the order from the Director himself on the red telephone in the portacabin—ringing for the first time—to open wide all the sluices.

"Do it now, LaMolle. And leave them open."

The Director told him to report to headquarters after emptying the reservoir.

"There is an early retirement program you might be interested in," he added.

After putting the phone back in its cradle, LaMolle looked at his watch. It was getting late in the afternoon, but he supposed there was still time. He put on his official jacket and went outside. He walked along the dam to the steps leading down to the turbine hall. Reluctantly, he descended to the cavernous room. Before him, on the central console, an array of switches controlled the electric motors that opened and closed the valves in the giant pipes beneath his feet. He pressed the five buttons to open them all. One motor refused to start: number three, up to its usual tricks.

"*Typique, absolument* par for the course," muttered LaMolle.

He turned to the wheel to open the valve manually. Gradually, the rumble of water through the pipe below increased in volume. Once the pipe was fully open, the green light flickered on.

LaMolle didn't linger. The clammy damp, the metallic taste of the air, and the hollow echo of his boots on the metal stairs triggered his memories of the shotgun blast.

Back in the open air, he leaned over the parapet to gaze at the water thundering down the spillway. The concrete vibrated under his palms, and the pulsating air buffeted his ears, making coherent thought impossible. He was still there an hour later. But, as the dusk gathered, the wheeling starlings returning to roost saw no human presence on the dam. Absent LaMolle's supervision, the wild was already repossessing the fractured mass of concrete.

✧ ✧ ✧

THE SURGE ARRIVED from upriver, a pulse of turbid water laden with silt. The level of the reservoir peaked two metres below the top of the dam—a fair safety margin, nicely calculated by the hydrologist—then dropped back slowly as the water flushed downstream through the open sluices.

Over the following weeks, the Noire River retreated towards its original bed, withdrawing—reluctantly, it seemed—from the land, leaving behind a landscape of shallow ponds separated by glistening expanses of mud. As the waters withdrew, the rejuvenated river tumbled over newly re-exposed ledges, recreating falls and rapids last seen in yellowing photographs of a century past.

Chapter 46

PAUL LOESS WAS fiddling with his rudder by the town dock in Newbridge. A raft of weed, carried by the current, had caught on the blade. He had to lean far over the stern to reach the tangle. The water gurgled past; the murmuring of a real river. Following the rain of the last few days, the flow had increased noticeably. The flow had not, however, returned to normal, and the river continued to carry down branches and other flotsam from upstream. This was despite a drop in the water level. The Newbridge town council had set a measuring post in the river bank to warn of impending floods. Calibrated in feet and marked with red and yellow bands, it showed a drop of six inches.

Paul eased the mooring ropes on the *Spindrift*. When he had finished the adjustments on his boat, he did the same for the *Groaning Anne* and the two other club boats still tied up at the dock. Satisfied, he returned to the *Spindrift*, and stretched out on the cockpit cushions. The sun came out, and it was pleasantly warm.

"Not taking a nap are you, Loess?" Garvin Bowter had come down the steps from the embankment, and stood on the dock beside the *Spindrift*.

Paul woke abruptly. Surely he had only been asleep for a few minutes? He had been dreaming of Margret.

"Don't worry about the mooring ropes, Garvin. I have just checked them," Paul replied. He watched as Bowter walked past the line of boats, giving a tug on each line.

"Can't be too careful," called Bowter.

Paul had thought himself inured to Bowter's officious manner, but it had become even worse now he was the Commodore. Picking up the Le Carré that he had been rereading for the umpteenth time, he finished half a page before putting the book on his chest. Paul shut his eyes again, hoping to resume his dream.

No Margret.

He tried to resume *Tinker, Taylor, Soldier, Spy*. Was he soldier or spy? What had he achieved in the half year he had been living at the club? Yes, his occasional successes at the Sunday races had earned respect. His role in the kidnapping of LeGros had been a high point. But, he admitted to himself, as the weeks turned into months, the monotony of life on the boat—the little club rituals, the bickering around the communal meals—had lulled him into a torpor. Was he happy? The answer, without Margret, was no.

Enough! He sat up and ducked down into the cabin of his boat. He had the missile fin that fell onto the deck of the *Spindrift* wedged above the book rack. It had become a talisman for Paul, and he rubbed it for good luck.

Paul lifted the grate under his feet and felt for the package he had hidden where once he'd found Randolph's bottle of wine. He pulled out an old three-oh-three calibre rifle. Luckily, the police search hadn't found it: the officer had been fascinated by the contents of the sail lockers. He had told Paul that he was a keen sailor too: "Lasers, *bien sûr*. I have just one sail!"

Mike Collins had presented the rifle to him on the day he had offered to coach Pauls' swimming. Paul had been taken by surprise: in their previous encounters Collins had been gruff, verging on rude. Now, Paul felt the power of Collins focussed attention. It made him uncomfortable.

"Well, I'm not sure. I have this thing to do with Margret

later ..."

"And, I have something for you, Loess," Collins had said, standing beside the *Spindrift*, and holding out a long object wrapped in canvas. "WW1 vintage from our stock in the wine cellar: it's amazing how they look as good as new. It's in recognition of your service on Lac King. Treat her well."

"I ... Thank you, Mike."

"After supper, then," said Collins. "Bring a towel, and I'll meet you at the lighthouse."

✧   ✧   ✧

THAT EVENING, AFTER their swim, they had sat together by the water on the far side of the island. It was getting towards dusk. Collins was close; Paul could smell his sweat, feel his warmth. He was showing Paul how to break down and re-assemble the rifle.

"Easy does it, Paul."

Paul had fumbled trying to close the breach on the bullet. He had fumbled lifting the rifle. He had aimed at a floating log, and stumbled on a loose stone. Mike got up and went to the water's edge, preparing to throw a bottle into the water.

"Just breathe out and squeeze the trigger. Here, try and hit this." Mike tossed the empty into the reservoir.

He had fired only once, missing the bobbing target. Mike fell back into the water with barely a splash.

Paul had dropped the rifle and rushed to the water's edge. He waded in, but Collins was already a dark shadow among a shoal of dark shadows, slipping into deep water. Paul had stood stock-still and thigh deep, his heart pounding.

"Missed me!" Collins had called thirty seconds later, emerging from the water behind Paul. "You'd better practice when the light is better."

"Christ, Mike. You gave me a scare."

"Huh. If anyone's allowed to shoot me, it'll be one of the Brigade boyos. Here, give me your towel: I'll dry your back."

"No, Mike. I can manage." Paul had picked up the rifle and put it in the crook of his arm. He turned and started walking deliberately along the path leading to the boat docks. He had felt Collins watching him until he was swallowed by the deepening gloom beneath the pine trees. Then he had begun to run.

✦   ✦   ✦

SINCE THAT EVENING, whenever the memory seeped back into his consciousness, Paul retrieved the rifle from its hiding place. He practised obsessively: the breaking down and re-assembling. He could, by now, do it in the dark.

Paul slid the rifle back into its canvas sheath. Yes, he decided: he was happier. Mike Collins had made life too complicated. Now, since Mike's death, he could focus on winning Margret's affections. Paul had volunteered as the Club's new Master of Arms. He had rescued the club's miniature starting canon, and lashed it to the *Spindrift*'s bow.

Paul climbed out into the cockpit of the *Spindrift*, and stepped off his boat onto the narrow plank walkway along the riverbank. Margret had arranged her remaining figurines along the shore beside the *Groaning Anne*, and he stepped around them carefully. There were fewer now: Taggart was at the bottom of the reservoir, plus several others who Paul couldn't identify, and had not dared to ask. Margret had pitched them over the side when they left Blackwater. Now only half a dozen remained. How would Paul feel if he saw himself, a caricature of his face carved into clay, as the latest in Margret's collection? He didn't want to think about that.

"Paul!" Margret called from the embankment above him.

He looked up to see her silhouetted against the westering sun; her face in shadow, but her hair a golden halo. The breeze blowing off the river tugged at her skirt and jacket.

"We have to go," she shouted. "Neely is here with the Leaf. Donovan is bringing the truck. We have to collect something in town, if you remember."

Chapter 47

MO, THE DRIVER, was sweating in the stifling cabin of the delivery van. He took his thermos from its holder and drained the last of the iced coffee. It was now tepid, and he regretted adding the extra cream. He was still thirsty.

Getting through customs on the Quebec side of the bridge to Hull Centro was taking ages. The border guards on duty at the barrier were diligent this morning: he expected a lengthy search and—Mo expected—a thorough shakedown. He guessed their zeal came from a change in management: some big cheese officer must have been replaced. Whatever, he thought. He was well prepared: he had two envelopes containing different sized wads of dollar bills. One he had pushed down his boot, and the other, thicker bundle tucked behind the van's visor. He reached up to make sure it was still in place.

Van by van, the line of white delivery vehicles advanced towards the frontier. Mo eased the brake, and let the van crawl forward onto the metal grating of the bridge. He was now above the Ottawa River. The structure trembled as the turbulent water bucketed past beneath his feet. Mo rolled down his window and damp air blew into the cab. It was like being spritzed.

From his driver's seat, he was up high enough to see over the guardrail. It gave him a dizzying view of white water streaming away from under the bridge, rushing so fast that waves cresting downstream seemed to stand still. Mo spat out the window and watch the gob arch into space, to be lost in the spume. Foot off the brake, the van edged forward again. Now in Mo's view was a massive girder. He looked at the flaking paint and the rust, and felt vaguely apprehensive.

He could see his first destination: the *Portalette*—the ugly building complex the drivers called "the Concrete Palace." Mo could push his old grandmother in her wheelchair there faster. Sighing, he looked again at his nav screen. He had one pickup and nine deliveries to make: the first stop here in the downtown, the rest out in the new settlements west of Hull where many homes had been allocated to migrants from Montreal's south shore.

The inhabitants of the new settlements had keen appetites for making online purchases, usually ordered from the States and shipped via Ontario. Although the delivery business was booming, the company paid their drivers miserly rates. True, there were ways for drivers to supplement their incomes. Using dollars to buy alcohol on the Quebec side, and running crates back in the otherwise empty vans was one. It worked out at five bucks per litre for vodka, plus a little peace offering to the border control. The price of a bottle of *Botteleggeur* was nearing five hundred *piastres*. Mo did not approve of alcohol and left this lucrative trade to others.

Finally, Mo reached the front of the line. He glanced at the photocopy of his diploma that he had taped on the dashboard, together with a passport photo of his wife-to-be, whom he had never met. He muttered a quick prayer. They were reminders of what life might still offer. But the immigration authority had already rejected her application twice. And driving for ParcelFirst was far from the bright career his online college had promised when he had enrolled.

"Contributions to Centroaide, *Monsieur*?" said the customs officer.

Mo passed him the thinner of the two envelopes.

"*Merci, Monsieur*," said the officer. "And what's in the back?"

Mo passed him the second envelope. The GR lifted the barrier, and Mo drove over the end of the bridge into a wasteland of redevelopment. The concept had originally been for high-end condos: lofts converted from old industrial buildings. Mo had seen the promotional videos that offered luxury and an active lifestyle, with the city's attractions at your doorstep, and prices in the stratosphere. Now, the closest thing to a destination was a four-hour drive to the west, the accommodations were the scattered clusters of camper vans parked amidst the rubble, and the active lifestyle was running contraband across the river.

His first stop was a regular delivery and pickup. Mo signaled right and turned into an alley which sloped down to a metal roller-door set in an otherwise blank concrete wall. *Livraisons* was painted in bold letters on the door.

All ParcelFirst vans were fitted with official transponders for speedy delivery to government sites. He knew he would only have to wait. And wait. After a delay which seemed to Mo interminable, when he began to wonder if he would have to reverse the van back up the slope, the roller door lifted. It jerked to its full opening, and Mo advanced slowly into the unloading dock.

They were waiting for him: two GRs, one big, one small, both in uniform. Fats and the Rat, thought Mo. He pulled on the emergency brake and switched off the ignition.

"Hi, *Bonjour*," he said. "I have a delivery for the *Garde*, and a pickup. I need a signature here, please." Mo held out the pad for the electronic signature. Fats stared at him.

"Open the *maudit* door," he ordered.

Mo scrambled out of his seat and slid open the side doors. He pulled out two boxes and hefted them onto the dock. Both were labeled "Care of Commander Brevet."

"Children's toys" read the customs label on one; "Kitchenware" the other.

"Toys, eh?" said Fats. "Fucker won't need them now."

"Er, I'm supposed to make a pickup, too," ventured Mo.

The two GRs turned and stared at him.

"Over by the wall, *tabernac*," said Fats.

Mo climbed onto the platform and went over to a long crate. It looked heavy. There were no labels of any kind: no sender, no list of contents, no addressee.

"But, where am I supposed to take this?"

"Just load it and go," said Fats.

"*Oui.* Back where you came from, *'osti*," So, the Rat could speak English after all.

Mo dragged the crate to the edge of the platform, jumped down, and heaved it across the gap into his van. He climbed back behind the wheel, the two GRs still watching him from the loading dock. He switched the engine on and drove slowly away, keeping his eyes firmly on the yellow lines leading to the exit. The roof of his van scraped the closing roller-door as he gunned the engine to go up the slope to the road.

"Fucked if I deliver down that hole again. Fuck the Concrete Palace. Fuck," he thought. Back in the open air, he tried to swallow, tried to spit out of the window. He had, while underground, forgotten he was thirsty.

Mo drove quickly away from the *Portalette* through the streets of Hull Centro. His remaining stops were all in the new settlements northwest of town, known as the *Plateau*. Mo hadn't been that far out before: bandit country, other drivers had kidded him. But ParcelFirst ran a slick operation, and would have paid off any organized gangs. He hoped.

The nav screen showed his optimal route: eight addresses, shortest distance, minimum time. First, Mo needed to refill his thermos and buy some lunch. Any fast food would do, a *dépanneur* even. The strip malls peeled past as he drove: dreary, half-shut enterprises, places to buy used furniture, tires, and discount gas; places to store furniture once you had used it.

Finally, he saw a *HubExpress.* It seemed to be the only place to eat along the six kilometres of road leading to the new settlements. Mo turned in and followed the drive-thru lane around the building to the self-service window. One of those tiny, electric cars was in front of him. It stopped at the order microphone. In the rear-view, Mo could see a large, red pickup crowding the back of his van. Some people.

Mo knew what he wanted to order: a tall coffee and the churro combo. Why, he wondered, did some people need to read the entire menu? This seemed to be the case with the driver in front of him.

"Oui, Madame?" crackled the speaker, but the driver made no attempt to order. Mo felt his shirt sticking to his back. How long does it take to decide between the double and the triple patty? He was glad he was vegetarian.

The loud rap on the side of the van startled Mo. In the side mirror, he could see the driver of the pickup had got out, and was coming forward to speak to him. It wasn't his fault; it was the car in front.

Pat Donovan slid back the door beside Mo.

"We'll be having that package now," he said. "So you can shift your arse."

✧   ✧   ✧

PAUL HELPED DONOVAN carry the box and lay it across the back seat of the Leaf. There was no longer room for Paul in Maude's Leaf, so he walked back and got into the truck cab with Donovan. They watched the delivery van in front start up, then drive through without ordering.

"I'll be having the combo. You want anything?" asked Donovan.

"Sure," replied Paul. "That sounds good."

"Two combos with two root beers, darlin'," called Donovan into the order mic. Then he rolled forward to the window.

"You know, Loess. I asked that driver if he had any trouble coming across the river."

"So?"

Donovan reached out to take the two brown paper bags.

"He said 'no problems'. So, I asked how he'd stashed the crate. If it was in some kind of secret compartment or whatnot. You know what he said?"

Paul shook his head, mouth already full.

"He said he'd picked it up from the *Portalette*, from the GRs. Do you know anything about that?"

"I'm sure Margret knows what she's doing," mumbled Paul.

"That's bullshit," said Donovan. "The Brigade won't stand for the Committee colluding with the GRs."

Chapter 48

GARVIN BOWTER DESTROYED a tranquil evening with the news.

"I knew it! They've drained it, the bastards!"

Margret and Paul were sitting on a bench in the riverside park in Newbridge, watching the river streaming past. The water was covered with the detached wings of flying ants, held by surface tension and coaxed into spirals by the swirling eddies. It was late August, two weeks after the pick-up at the *HubExpress*.

"Drained what, Garvin?" asked Margret.

"The reservoir! It's just gone. Neely's just told me. He says there just acres of mud. All around the club, there's nothing but mud."

"But, it can't just disappear," said Paul. "Can it?"

"I've been noting down the water level here at the dock. Every day, it been lower. Look here, see the numbers: the river dropped another six inches overnight." Bowter held out his clipboard. "I couldn't understand what has been going on. Now we know: they must have opened up the dam. Look, on Monday three inches down, on Tuesday four inches, on Wednesday—"

"Thank you, Garvin. So, first they blow up the clubhouse. Now they drain the reservoir. That seems excessive, even for the GRs," said Margret. It would, she thought, violate the arrangement that Collins had reached with *Madame la Présidente*. If this was true, there needed to be a reset. Having inherited the Committee from Mike, as Chairperson, it would be Margret negotiating with Quebec.

"I have to see," she said finally. "Garvin, does the club still have a couple of mountain bikes? We could ride down the old railway line to Blackwater and look for ourselves."

✦   ✦   ✦

"YOU'RE NOT GOING down there?" asked Paul later that afternoon.

Margret and Paul had stopped on the railway embankment opposite Blackwater Island. The bikes that Garvin had found for them were not in good repair, and it had taken two hours to ride from Newbridge. Some sections of the line were hard-packed with gravel, and fast. In other places, tall weeds had sprouted from the path, and they needed to dismount and push through the vegetation.

From their vantage point on the embankment, they looked down on the roof of the Durkel cabin. Beyond should have been Blackwater Bay. Except it wasn't there. Garvin had been right: a glistening expanse of mud now encircled the island. In the middle distance, they glimpsed the Noire churning a straight course down the middle of what used to be the reservoir.

"Leave the bikes here," said Margret. "We're going down."

✦   ✦   ✦

LATE THAT EVENING, the Margret and Paul arrived back in Newbridge, extremely muddy. They went directly to the washrooms in *les Draveurs* to clean up. It was club night at the hotel. Under the rules of club night, a member chosen by lottery had to prepare the evening meal for everyone. Harvey Kinnear had prepared too much spaghetti to go with his special meatballs.

"Dinner for two," said Kinnear, ladling large piles of pasta onto plastic plates. "So, is it true? Did they drain the reservoir?"

"Yes," said Paul. "Dry as a bone. Well, perhaps not quite." He scratched at the dried mud on his trousers. "We could walk almost all the way around the island."

"Did you find any tools?" asked Garvin Bowter. "The bed of the reservoir beside the catwalk must be littered with them. I was hoping to find a torque wrench that I dropped overboard last summer. It was brand new and—."

"No, we weren't looking for tools, Garvin," said Margret. "We did, however, find the foundations of an old building five hundred metres north of the island. Probably where you almost lost your anchor."

"Ah, there. Well I …" Bowter had bad memories of that occasion. One pleasant afternoon, two summers ago, he had offered to show Philly Delario how to set and pull an anchor. She had seemed pleased with Bowter's suggestion. If things went well, Bowter intended to raise the possibility of Philly crewing for him in the next Sunday race.

Bowter had then spent two hours trying to retrieve that damned anchor. Unfortunately for him, this was all observed from the deck of the clubhouse, where Old Tom took bets as to whether or not he would cut the cable. Philly's comment when they finally returned to the dock was burned in his memory:

"Well, Harbour Master, in future I suggest you stay in the harbour."

She had stalked off to the clubhouse, leaving Bowter with a tangle of mud-covered anchor cable to wash.

"I think Paul and I will eat down by the river," said Margret. "Thank you for the food, Harvey."

Paul followed Margret from the hotel, across the street to the riverside park. They found a bench to sit on by the waterside.

"So, what's your plan after all this is over?" he asked, after finishing the last of his spaghetti. Paul bent over to pick up a twig and throw it into the water. They watched it spin slowly downstream.

"You mean 'over' over?" replied Margret. "It could dribble on for years, tit for tat."

"Yeah, I mean 'over' over."

He heard Margret sigh. The trip downriver to the old club had left her subdued.

"Did you know my great-grandparents had a farm beside the Noire River? Thomas-John Pardle and Maria Markowicz. They did even share a language when they met. It didn't seem to matter." She stopped, staring pensively at the water.

"Yes. You told me before," said Paul.

"My grandmother was also called Margret," continued Margret, as if Paul hadn't spoken. "She wrote a journal. My mother gave it to me."

"And?" prompted Paul.

"She lived in the valley before they flooded it. In a beautiful farm on the best bottom land. 'Be-oo-tiful' she would say, putting on the Irish. She said that's where my great-grandparents became one with a new land. With Canada."

"Is that where we stood today? In the middle of that mud flat? Was that the farmhouse?"

"Yes," said Margret. "And now they've drained the reservoir, I want that land back in the family. I will have it, whatever it takes."

It was quite dark when Phelim Neely found them. They were sitting in silence.

"Pardon me, Ma'am," stuttered Neely, still showing a symptom of his stay in re-education. Neely's face hovered palely over them, like a sick moon.

"Yes, Phelim?" said Margret.

"The *Black and White* is reporting fresh attacks by separatist-terrorists. I thought you would want to know."

"I'm coming."

The three of them walked back to *les Draveurs*. Inside, the bar was busy. Nothing, especially nothing political, could disturb the local talent night. On the stage, Tite and Dooley were pushing out some lively blues.

In the corner was a reserved table. A sign read "Committee business only." The tabletop was covered with open newspapers.

Margret sat down to read. The boys from the Brigade had been busy, it seemed. Over the past fortnight, they had ambushed three delivery vans in the Pontiac. The vans were headed to the new settlements, full of essentials ordered online. Only yesterday, the tires of a ParcelFirst had been shot out on a country road, and its contents removed. It had been carrying disposable diapers, the latest target of panic buying. The headline in the local Pontiac paper read, "It's a Bummer!" In the French press, it was "*Assez, c'est Assez!*"

Margret was furious.

Protest in support of a free Pontiac was supposed to be carefully calibrated. Each initiative was to be discussed between the parties to the deal Mike Collins had negotiated with Colonel Mauricie: controlled incidents, enough to satisfy the wilder boys in the Brigade, not a free-for-all campaign of diaper robbery. The entente that promised a free state within Quebec required a delicate touch. Too much violence would force Papineau to act; too little, and she would do nothing.

"Well, I've had enough. He'll have deserved it, after what he's done," she said.

"Who?" Paul asked.

"Patrick Bloody Donovan, of course."

Chapter 49

COLONEL MAURICIE OF the Intelligence Directorate of the *Garde républicaine* was at her desk on the fifth floor of *le Château* in Quebec City. The view was magnificent: the lower town below, the docks, *le Fleuve* itself disappearing into the grey distance. She was thinking about the intelligence briefing she intended to give *la Mante* later that morning. This nickname for *Madame la Présidente* was one used, with justice, by her executive staff. It passed from ex-staff members to new recruits with the rapid churn. When the egos of Josée-Mathilde's cabinet members began inevitably to swell, she was quick to decapitate. Mauricie ensured that she and *la Mante* had a good working relationship.

Mauricie ran through her bullet-points for the briefing. There was the report on coordinating surveillance with Mauricie's counterparts in the USBAZ, the linguistic vetting of immigrants, and the security provisions for an upcoming international visit.

The far west of the Republic was a problem. *La Mante* would have noticed in the press the surge in terrorist activity. It was unfortunate that Mauricie could no longer blame Brevet. His network of corrupt cronies had kept the lid on the separatists, an unfortunate fact that Josée-Mathilde might well bring up. Perhaps, she thought ruefully, in Brevet's case she had acted too swiftly.

A map occupied most of the wall screen opposite Mauricie's desk. Every GR regional office had a similar screen, synchronized with the one here at headquarters. The map showed a cobweb of lines radiating from headquarters to the regions. The thickness of each line represented the volume of information traffic: that connecting Quebec City to Montreal was thick, like an aorta: the strands reaching to some of the furthest regions were mere spindly capillaries.

The blinking of a regional office icon on the wall map caught her eye. Simultaneously, a call sign appeared on the screen of her scrambler phone; it belonged to the deceased Commander Brevet. Surely she had ordered Agent Rojas to delete that code? On her orders, Rojas had arranged for a team to scrub Brevet's old office and surplus its extravagant furnishings, communications unit included. She sighed: the call sign should have been retired. Mauricie made a mental note to remind her assistant after lunch.

The call display insisted it was Brevet. Mauricie pushed the button for hands-free.

"*Oui*, who is this?"

"Good morning, Colonel Mauricie. My name is Margret Mankie. We have—or rather, had—a mutual friend."

Mauricie mentally went *en garde*. She found her left hand reaching beside her for the Taser in her jacket pocket. "Ridiculous," she thought, bringing her hand back under control.

"*Et notre ami?* Who would that be?"

"Michael Collins."

Tabernac! Brevet's *maudit club de voile*. "*Alors*, what do you want?"

"I have," said Margret, "a certain document in my possession. Mike gave to me to keep safe. It's an agreement between Quebec and the Committee for Free Pontiac. I see you signed as a witness. It might read to some that you are plotting with terrorists."

Merde! Elle l'a trouvé ou?

"I have no idea what you are talking about."

"No? Then perhaps *Madame la Présidente* will remember. She signed it, after all."

"I'm going to blow your shitty little club out of existence!"

"You already did that, remember? And that reminds me, I also have a piece of the missile that killed Commander Brevet."

"Are you suggesting some arrangement?" Mauricie asked after several seconds.

"I like the agreement you had with Mike Collins. Perhaps we could negotiate something similar."

"Collins agreed to control the terrorist groups—your pathetic Pontiac Brigade."

Mauricie was struggling to get ahead of this conversation. Who the hell was Margret Mankie?

"You needn't worry," said Margret. "The Committee directs the Brigade."

"The Committee? Why should I believe you have taken over the leadership from Collins?"

"Simple. Fly a helicopter over Newbridge tomorrow, and I will arrange to have it shot down. Would that convince you?"

"*Merde*, I—"

"In the meantime, I would like your help."

"What kind of help?"

"It's personal," said Margret.

"*Bien.* Since we have developed such a rapport—"

"I want the title to forty acres in the Noire Valley. The government expropriated the land back in the 1920s."

"Do you think I'm a realtor? That's a private matter."

"The land belonged to Dominion Hydro back in the day, and now to PowerBec. That corporation is run by the Republic, so you can pull strings. The land was underwater until they drained the Noire valley. The market value is, I suggest, zero."

"What on Earth do you want it for?"

"That is my piece of Canada. I want it back in the family."

"But why should I do that for you? What do I get in return?"

"You get Pat Donovan's pig shed."

"*Quoi?* His pig shed? Not the so-called Major Donovan responsible for all these recent outrages?"

"Yes. The Brigade's arsenal is hidden in the pig shed on Donovan's farm."

Colonel Mauricie took a deep breath. "What do you have in mind?"

"Something out of the blue and non-attributable, like you arranged for Commander Brevet. Do that, and I can guarantee a nice, manageable level of partisan activity here in the Pontiac."

Mauricie felt she understood this Mankie woman, a certain *rapport*. "Give me the coordinates," she said.

"I'll see what I can do, but it will take time to arrange. It that all? I have a meeting with *Madame la Présidente* in fifteen minutes."

✧　✧　✧

MARGRET BROKE THE connection and sat back. She swivelled her chair towards the front window of *les Draveurs*. From this vantage, she gazed at the curl of the river around the bay, the line of disheveled houseboats beside the bank, the bridge in the distance. Mist rose from the water. It was time, she judged, to regain control of the Brigade. It was a pity about the pigs.

Chapter 50

When visiting Montreal from Quebec City, Colonel Mauricie seldom ventured to the south shore of the St. Lawrence. Why would anyone go there, *pour l'amour de Dieu?* There was the river, the seaway, a six-lane highway, and a hinterland of nondescript suburbs with names like Brossard and Boucherville. Compared with the attractions of *le Vieux Port* in Montreal proper, they had nothing. Except a St-Hub on every street corner, granted.

But here she was, sitting behind Agent Rojas as he drove slowly along the approach to the bridge, up and over the hump across the seaway, and rolled to a stop at the frontier checkpoint. The stars and stripes hung limply above the Quebec flag beside a former pay station, now occupied by Border Adjustment Force. Extremely pissed-off would have been a gentle description of Mauricie's mood, but *la Mante* had been explicit.

"Ah, Cynthia. We need your good services," she'd said. "Co-ordinate with your CIA contact about this meet with the First Lady. Where, when, what to wear, the security arrangements."

"*Entendu, Josée-Mathilde.*"

"And Cynthia, we want the business in West Quebec settled. You know our wishes."

✧ ✧ ✧

The Border Services agent approached Mauricie's car.

"What business in the Border Adjustment Zone, Ma'am?"

she asked. "Any fruit or marijuana?"

Mauricie held out her identification card. The agent took it and disappeared for five minutes.

"Well, what d'ya know? Drive on, Ma'am. Have a nice day."

Mauricie always felt in need of a shower after crossing into the States. Except this wasn't a state, not even a Puerto Rico, but a mere USBAZ—Border Adjustment Zone—one of several that smoothed the edges of Greater America.

In the accord signed by *la Mante* in the weeks following the "adjustment", the USBAZ was described as a free trade zone, an arrangement between two friendly neighbouring nations. That the trade was asymmetric was, well, what one could expect when a bully dictates an agreement's wording. That an occupying military force had to remain in place was a sad necessity, based on the vague threat from other actors, meaning The Rest of Canada.

In effect, the USBAZ was the northern terminus of a railroad for migration from the southern States, Mexico and Central America: for those seeking relief from ever more frequent droughts and extreme heat. It was a made-in-America solution to climate change. The latest stats Mauricie had seen—for executive eyes only—estimated twenty percent of the population was now Spanish speaking. The USBAZ was now practically trilingual, a "Puertobec." There was nothing that Quebec could do about it.

Rojas followed Mauricie's directions deep into the suburbs: five kilometres along a featureless boulevard, left at a giant four-way intersection, another two kilometers beside the dried sticks of gingkos. Planted by some optimist, the trees occupied the grey space between the traffic lanes. Lately, watering had not been a priority for local government.

"*On arrive, Madame,*" said Rojas, pulling to a halt along a desolate stretch of curb. To Mauricie's right spread row after row of a vast parking area: acres of asphalt which served only to emphasize the isolation of the massive building in its midst. This was the *Centre de Congrès*, a mountain of aluminium geometries and planes of dark reflective glass. Completed ten years previously, just before secession, the grandiose project had been a financial disaster. Built to attract A-grade events—boat shows or home improvement extravaganzas, it had, Mauricie knew, failed to attract so much as a dentist convention.

The parking was not entirely empty, however. A short distance apart from the *Centre de Congrès*, circled like some dark wagon train in hostile country, was a cluster of vehicles, field tents, and prefabricated huts. This was the command centre for USBAZ operations, and—as Mauricie well knew—a black ops site. Antennas of different geometries, satellite dishes, and microwave receivers mounted on scaffolding poked and searched skywards like the skeletal frames of carnival amusements. But this was no funfair; the menace was unmistakable.

A dark green army vehicle pulled up close behind them, almost straddling the rear of their car like a giant insect bent on copulation. Brad and his Hummer, thought Mauricie. Laying it on thick. She watched in the side mirror, as he climbed down from the driver's seat and came forward to speak to her.

"Cyn," the US intelligence officer said through the window. "Good of you to drive all the way over. Come with me. I booked a great little place to eat."

Colonel Mauricie leaned forward to speak to Rojas.

"Follow and wait outside. We'll be at the Lucky 8 motel later."

Then she got out and greeted Brad with a *bec* on each cheek.

"*Cherie*, it's been too long," he said.

After Brad had helped Mauricie into the Hummer, he drove past Rojas and continued for a hundred metres, before turning right at a sign welcoming visitors to the *Centre de Congrès*. Rojas followed at a discreet distance. They drove past row after row of empty parking slots, skirted the USBAZ encampment, and headed for an exit on the far side.

They pulled onto a road which was much the same as the one they had just left: long, grey and potholed. This one ran beside a strip mall: mostly blank windows or boarded-up storefronts, its few open businesses indicated by flickering neon signs. Past the mall, Mauricie glimpsed the low profile of a motel standing back from the road. Only a few chinks of light from random rooms suggested occupancy.

"Found this place quite by accident," Brad said after they'd turned yet another corner. He stopped the Hummer in front of a garishly lit building. Mauricie winced after reading the sign: "International cuisine—Chinese and *exotique*." She had chosen their last rendezvous with care—Pierre Romain's in *le Vieux Port* had been pushing for a fifth star. Brad was making a point.

"They have this great buffet," he assured her.

They slid into a side booth with their trays, face to face across the fixed table. Mauricie had a vegetable chow mein; Brad had picked the General Tao's chicken on a steaming heap of rice. The strip lighting was not flattering, she decided. It emphasized the tension lines creasing Brad's forehead. The wrinkles at the corners of his eyes belied the boyish good looks beneath the buzz cut. She supposed it wasn't doing much for her, either. She resisted adjusting her hair.

"So," he began. "This First Lady visit. You should talk to the Secret Service."

"I prefer to speak to the secret, secret service."

"Sure thing, Cyn."

"*Madame la Présidente* prefers to meet with your president. She regrets that the First Lady's taste in clothes makes it impossible to know what to wear. You understand?"

"Sure, a presidential pull-aside, mano a mano, as it were. No, that's not happening."

"*La Mante* was quite insistent that I ask you personally."

"Does she golf? Can she do a round? No. Listen, Cyn. Your Quebec Republic has two things going for it. One: the seaway is a convenient ditch, so we don't have to build any expensive wall. Two: you are a great market garden, much more productive now we've imported Mexican agriculturalists. And here we are, securing your Republic's borders from Canadian countermeasures. For free, mind you. But as the President likes to say, 'The War of 1812 is unfinished business.' So, *Cherie*, don't push your luck."

So far, the meeting was as expected, thought Mauricie, twirling the chow mein with her chopsticks. Brad would deliver on what the First Lady would be wearing. Just to show off. Just to show a little give and take.

"Did you want another drink, Brad?" she asked.

Sliding out of the booth, she walked to where spigots distributed various froths. She felt him watching. She came back with two sodas.

"Another little thing," she said, five minutes later, after snorkeling the dregs of her drink. "You know that job you did for me before? I need a follow-up."

"Jesus, Cyn. Can't you just borrow a tank? Those drones don't come cheap."

Chapter 51

INSPECTOR LABORDE HAD filed his report on the deaths of Commander Brevet and Captain-Agent Pénard. Suzanne, the *légiste*, had not been pleased. He had ignored her conclusion, based on the forensic evidence, that a missile had exploded the club house. But she was only eighty percent sure, after all; it could still have been a simple booby trap. Still, he could have done without Suzanne's parting verdict on his own competency: "*Espèce de con.* Call yourself a detective!"

He knew, however, that the report would be to Colonel Mauricie's satisfaction. The colonel of the *Garde* had swept into town the day after the explosion. She had summoned for interview at the *Portalette* all who had been involved with the Blackwater Club over the past months. Both the GR surveillance team, and the regular police represented by Inspector Laborde had heard her expectations expressed in no mean terms.

Consequently, his report placed the blame squarely on the separatist-terrorists, members of the Blackwater Sailing Club. They had lured the unfortunate commander and his agent onto the island and into the clubhouse. The bomb had been hidden behind the bar or in the crow's nest—forensics was uncertain on this point—and triggered by an incautious step, or by some other means. The perpetrators had fled the scene. They had taken to the hills, but it was only a matter of time before the combined force of police and GRs tracked them down. As an administrative item, Laborde noted that the police had recovered Brevet's boat, which was now safely back on dry land in the secure compound behind the *Portalette*. It turned out that it had been bought by Commander Brevet as an official vessel of the *Garde républicaine*.

Even so, he was surprised, a few days later, to get a call from Colonel Mauricie herself to ask whether he would consider a transfer. It seemed that the *Garde républicaine* needed sound, experienced men such as himself. He recalled her precise words:

"Frankly, Jules—may I call you Jules?—I think you are wasting your talents in the regular police. A vacant position has arisen in our western division. It is quite senior. You can expect a significant increase in salary."

Laborde begged time to think about it. How significant an increase? He had reached the rank of inspector of police, and for most of his career had regarded the GRs with scorn. He considered them amateurs: ignore them if possible, and offer them the minimum of cooperation. Still, it was also true that further promotion in the police seemed unlikely, and he could do with the extra money. After putting down the phone, sitting on the edge of his bed, he stood and went to change into his cycling gear. A quick twenty kilometres up the boulevard to the new settlements and back would clear his head.

By his return, he had concluded, sadly, that it was an offer impossible to refuse. The next day, he phoned Quebec City and asked to speak to the Colonel. He was transferred to a clerk in Human Resources.

"*Bonjour* Commander. We have been expecting your call. *Félicitations*," said the bureaucrat. "Now, there are a few routine questions I need to ask."

An hour later, Laborde—Commander Laborde—discovered he would start in his new position in a week's time.

✧　✧　✧

LABORDE'S FAREWELL PARTY was a subdued affair, downstairs at the brew pub. His sergeant tried hard. He was known for his jokes—the darker kind that kept officers sane after a day mopping up carnage. Laborde assumed the sergeant was trying to cheer him up.

"*Voyons.* There were these three snowmobilers, see: *trois gars* from Ontario heading out across the ice. The ice cracks and the lead snowmobiler crashes through into the river. The second snowmobiler guns the engine and follows the first through the ice. And the third snowmobilers says ..."

Laborde remembered the incident from the previous winter. They had found the snowmobiles in the Noire River: three machines, strung out like beads on the river bed, their drivers having crashed through the ice into ten feet of water, one after the other. Recovered, and hosed clean of sludge, the snowmobiles had looked as-new in their bright colours. The bodies would be another matter, should they ever be found.

"... and the third says, 'Who's got the rental agreement?'"

"Yes, I've heard that one," said Laborde.

The beer flowed freely, but the evening felt forced. The *Garde* transfer was a promotion, but antipathy between the two services ran deep. Nobody said as much, but Laborde knew his ex-colleagues felt betrayed.

He was also nagged by a case gone cold, the inconclusive end to the investigation of the Collins homicide. As Laborde's investigation had progressed, he had found himself unable to reduce his number of suspects. The interviews with the club members had surfaced many motives: from the injured pride of Bowter; ignoring the racing rules (Tasker); failure to pay his bar tab (Kinnear); petty vengeance for sleights (shared by many), and simple jealousy. He was no nearer to finding the culprit. When obliged by his superior to apprise the GR Commander of his progress, Brevet had smiled at Laborde's frustration.

"Well, *Inspecteur*," he had said in a tone that infuriated Laborde, "I understand you have limited resources at your disposal. I would only say that whoever killed Collins did everyone a favour. *Bien entendu*, sometimes failure is a politically expedient."

Now, Brevet himself was a result.

✧   ✧   ✧

THE DAY AFTER his farewell party, Laborde drove to the Blackwater Sailing Club. One last visit; maybe he would find something he had missed. He parked his vehicle. The gate in the chain-link fence surrounding the club compound was wide open and empty of most of the boat trailers. Of the few that remained, their tires were flat, and weeds sprouted from beneath their cradles.

Laborde walked down *chemin* Blackwater towards the entrance of the club. The frame of the club gate was still there, but instead of leading to "our little piece of paradise," as one club member had described it to him, it opened onto a scene of desolation.

An expanse of ash-grey mud separated the island from the mainland shore. A pale, horizontal band like a chalk mark ran along the rocky apron of the island opposite him. Laborde assumed it marked the old water level, which he estimated must have dropped at least five metres. The island itself seemed higher, now the surrounding water had subsided. Burnt and blackened trees ringing the ruined clubhouse reminded Laborde of a volcano recently erupted.

Two derelict boats lay on their sides in the mud, their bottoms bared and green with slime. Their owners must have rescued the others, he supposed.

Laborde checked his notebook. The two boats that he remembered in particular were no longer there: the *Spindrift*, belonging to the man who had found the corpse, and the *Groaning Anne*, the boat sharing the same finger dock. That second boat had belonged to the eccentric Mankie woman with the collection of figurines.

The catwalk had sagged under its own weight as the water dropped. A retaining cable had snapped, and the wooden walkway now lay snaked across the dry bed of the reservoir. Laborde stepped onto the rough planking. Grounded on the mud, the catwalk felt reassuringly solid. He walked along, and stopped beside the finger dock where the *Spindrift* and the *Groaning Anne* had been moored. The dock itself lay on the ground, its back broken over a protruding rock. Beside it was a heap of what looked like broken pottery: a midden, he realized, of rejects. He saw a metallic gleam in the muck. He kneeled and reached down to pull out a long screwdriver. Useful, he thought.

Laborde lowered one foot over the edge of the catwalk opposite the collapsed finger dock. Gingerly, he tested the mud surface. The crust had dried into a quilt of polygons and seemed firm. Trusting that it would carry his weight, he stepped off the catwalk, and walked across the mud to where he had first seen Collins' body. There was nothing to see now, except for a heap of empty mussel shells: the discarded remnants of a meal, he supposed, of an otter or racoon.

He decided to walk to the club island across the dried bed of Blackwater Bay. The island seemed only a short walk across the mud, and he doubted if he would get his feet wet. He almost made it but, only metres away from dry land, he found his route cut by a deep channel. A small stream trickled along the bottom, flowing back underneath the end of the catwalk where the drawbridge lay twisted against the shore.

The mud looked deep and soft. It looked too risky to cross. Instead, Laborde turned north, skirting the edge of the channel.

Perhaps he could walk all the way around the island? He would be following the route taken by the club swimmers when the reservoir had been full, and by Collins himself. One never knew, thought Laborde, maybe he would chance on a clue, perhaps even find the murder weapon.

Keeping the Blackwater Club on his right, Laborde walked halfway around the island. He felt he was traipsing across a grey desert. On this far side of the island, he could hear the river. He scrambled onto a ledge which protruded like a rib from the mud. Here, the going was much easier.

As Laborde followed the ledge, the river noise grew louder. He reached a rocky outcrop on which stood a squat, wooden tower—the so-called lighthouse. He had reached the easternmost point of the island, where the old reservoir had narrowed to a mere half kilometre between the island and the opposite shore. Bowter, on their tour, had told Laborde that there had once been dangerous rapids here called the Eaton Chutes. Now, fifty metres away, Laborde could see the foam and splashing tops of waves, where the Noire River seethed across the ledge on which Laborde was standing. The rushing water tumbled over an edge, disappearing into a mist of spray. The Eaton Chutes reborn, he thought.

Below the rapids, the river broadened into a wide foam-covered pool which prevented Laborde from completing his "offshore" circuit of the island. He retraced his steps along the ledge and stepped back on to the mud. He would walk north to get a better view of the Blackwater Club from upstream: a different perspective might help. Suddenly, not far in front of Laborde, a section of muddy bank slumped into the water to be swallowed by the boiling eddies of the river. Laborde stepped back hurriedly. Walking on, he kept a safe distance away from the unstable edge.

After five minutes, he came across a square outline shrouded by silt. He guessed this was the foundation of a building. Like furniture under dust sheets in a shuttered house, thought Laborde, as he stepped from the hard crust onto the stump of a wall. There was once a farmhouse here, he realized, presumably abandoned when they finished the dam. He looked back towards the Blackwater Club; it was no longer an island, just a rocky hill, and less like a volcano from this side. A green flush showed at the base, where grass was colonizing the newly exposed ground. A pair of black birds were circling the hill.

The morning had been overcast, but now the sun was breaking through. A gleam of sunlight reflected from near the base of the hill caught Laborde's eye. Rocks? A boulder of white quartz, perhaps? Whatever it was, it shone out from the grey background. Laborde was curious. He walked back towards the hill, the river now on his left, keeping clear of patches of mud that had yet to dry. As he approached, he realized that the light reflected from the cluster of white, rectangular slabs lying on the ground. He thought they looked like gravestones.

They were gravestones! He had stumbled onto a private graveyard. Laborde knew they had been common in these country districts—the nearest church being too remote, or of the wrong denomination. Around the stones were footprints pressed into the mud. Two sets, he judged—one small, possibly a woman's, and the other larger. Someone had been tending the graves.

Laborde leaned down to look closely at the nearest slab. The surface was inscribed. He scratched the remaining mud away with the screwdriver he had found by the dock. The writing was easily legible.

"Red, our shepherd," he read. He moved on. "Black Tom," read another.

The last and biggest slab was a rectangle of pale, polished stone. The stone was slightly tilted up the gentle slope. At the head of the stone, the mason had carved a cross decorated with elaborate intertwining spirals. Irish work, Laborde guessed: he had seen similar designs during the Paddy's Day parade he had once attended with colleagues from the Montreal department. The inscription beneath the cross read:

"Pardle, Sean. 1903-1927. Forgive my brother, for he shot Michael Collins."

Inspector Laborde sat down heavily on the mud beside the stone. He had his clue, but for the wrong murder.

Epilogue

THE TWO MEXICAN fruit pickers arrived at the Blackwater Farm to help with the harvest. They had just alighted from the tram which was making its slow way up the old railway line to Newbridge. They waved their papers from the *pole d'emploi* in Hull Centro in front of them like flags.

Margret met them as they walked down the long driveway leading to the farmhouse. She had rebuilt: a prefabricated building placed squarely onto the original foundation.

"*Hola!*" she greeted the new arrivals, and shook hands. She glanced at the proffered permits.

"This way," said Margret. "I've put you above the barn, in a nice self-contained apartment."

In front of the farmhouse, the bright new flag of Free Pontiac streamed from the flag pole that Margret had rescued from the Blackwater Club. A faded Quebec flag hung beneath it, the weathered victim of several winters. Little else had changed politically: promised language rights, education, taxation remained stalled in the consultative stage. Life, however, had returned more or less to normal; ex-brigade members had found seats on local councils.

The old Pardle farm was a viable enterprise. Newly green pasture ran down to the river, and an enclosure held several alpacas. Rows of vines on the upper field were producing well. The main cash crops were tomatoes, fresh greens, and several varieties of potato.

It had taken five years of hard labour. The first two had been plagued by dust storms, before vegetation had spread over the dried bed of the reservoir. Much to Margret's surprise, when the dust had finally settled, Paul was still there. He became indispensable to the running of the farm, and had started the Whitewater Rafting Experience on the Noire. Adventurous youth up from Hull described the rush across the Eaton Chute as "gnarly".

Far above, a drone circled lazily on a thermal, wheeling with the vultures and dreaming of paradise; searching, searching for a target.

If you enjoyed *Blackwater*, try this title by E.K. Wicher:
The Leda: the geological obsession of Dr. Argile

ekwicher.com